Myra Duffy writes botl
best known for her cosy
Cameron – an ordinar
involved in extraordina
Bute provides inspiration because it offers a 'contained' setting and the history and the geography of the island are important in providing a background to the action.

Myra divides her time between Glasgow and the Isle of Bute and has family connections to the island stretching back several generations.

For more information visit
www.myraduffywriter.com

or contact her on duffyma308@googlemail.com,
@duffy_myra (Twitter) or on Facebook.

THE ISLE OF BUTE MYSTERY SERIES

The House at Ettrick Bay
Long-buried secrets lead to murder.

Last Ferry to Bute
Mysterious deaths at a nursing home and a shady antiques dealer.

Last Dance at the Rothesay Pavilion
Past events cast a shadow over the present as the Pavilion is renovated.

Endgame at Port Bannatyne
The world of film-making hides a deadly secret.

Grave Matters at St Blane's
A proposal to build a theme park is the catalyst for violent events.

Death at the Kyles of Bute
The Kyles of Bute Hydro Hotel is again open for business, but someone has murder in mind.

Bad Blood at Rothesay Castle
A party of American tourists is on Bute, but a killer is stalking one of them.

Deadly Secrets at the Standing Stones
A family wedding is not what it appears to be.

The Brydeshill Affair.
A young man is found dead at Brydeshill. But who is he?

When Old Ghosts Meet
Dangerous events are sparked off by a chance sighting on the Edinburgh to Glasgow train. (Prequel to the series).

MYRA DUFFY

FOUL PLAY AT THE HIGH KIRK

Adams and Straiton

Second Edition 2021

British Library C.I.P.
A CIP catalogue record for this title is available from the British Library.

For Isabel

THE ISLE OF BUTE

The Isle of Bute lies off the west coast of Scotland, only two hours from the city of Glasgow. It has been occupied for over five and a half thousand years but rose to prominence in Victorian days when its proximity to Glasgow made it a favoured spot for the wealthy to build summer houses and the not-so-wealthy to enjoy the delights of the seaside in the many rooms available for rent during the holiday season.

The northern part of the island is Highland in appearance, but the southern part is lowland and fertile. Ettrick Bay is on the western side of the island and here the mile curve of sandy beach looks over the tiny island of Inchmarnock to the Sleeping Warrior of Arran.

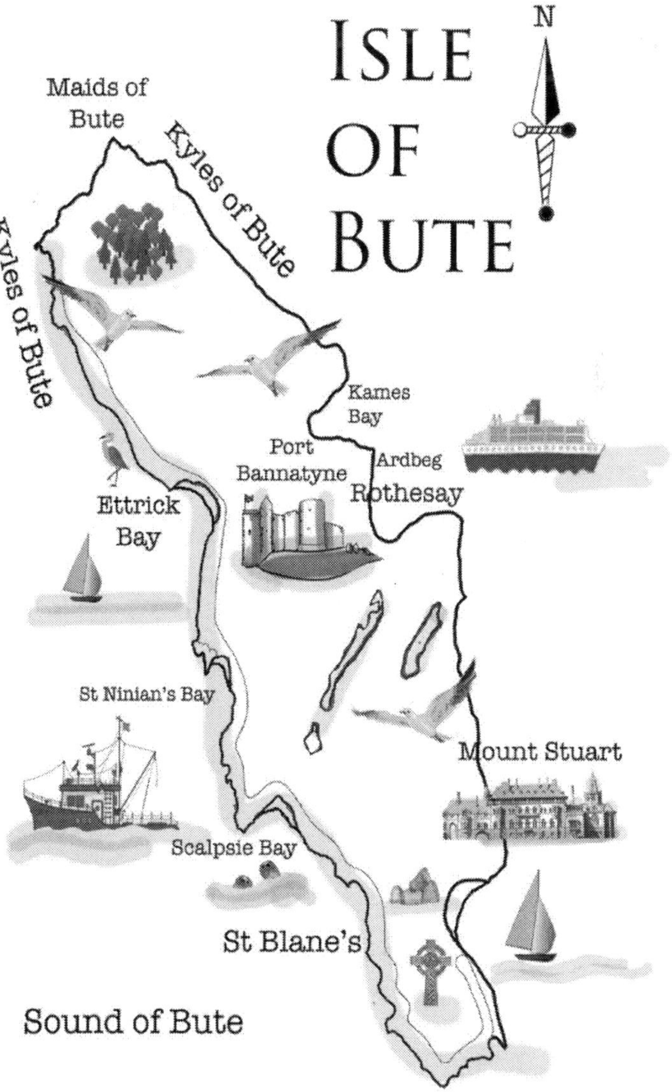

ISLE OF BUTE
N
Maids of Bute
Kyles of Bute
Kyles of Bute
Kames Bay
Port Bannatyne
Ardbeg
Rothesay
Ettrick Bay
St Ninian's Bay
Mount Stuart
Scalpsie Bay
St Blane's
Sound of Bute

PROLOGUE

Cormac McDubh hurried down the steps of the large Victorian building on Sauchiehall Street in Glasgow, muttering to himself. 'Another disaster,' he growled. 'If the performances of Sleeping Beauty are anything like this dress rehearsal, we'll be lucky to have an audience.'

A fine drizzle of November rain had started earlier, and the streetlights reflected in the puddles of water in the potholes in the pavement. Shivering, he turned up his coat collar as he caught up with Felicity Scott, the youngest member of the cast.

'I expect you're enjoying being in your first pantomime. Though it's all very well for you, playing the part of the Queen,' Cormac said, cupping his hand around a match to light up a cigarette from the packet he'd pulled from his pocket. 'You're starting out, have plenty of time to make your mark.' He drew deeply on the cigarette, stopping as he was seized by a spasm of coughing. 'Take advantage of it, that's my advice,' he wheezed. 'It doesn't last.'

As she caught a strong whiff of whisky, Felicity fiddled with the top button of her jacket to hide the look of irritation on her face. 'Oh, come on Cormac. You know that we should all be grateful to be in employment with The Mickle Theatre Company. Think how many actors are out of work. And if this production of Sleeping Beauty goes well, who knows what might happen, what other opportunities there might be.' She shook open her umbrella. 'It's this dreadful weather that's depressing you.'

Cormac turned his head aside to cough, wheezing again as he said, 'If I weren't desperate I wouldn't have considered taking the part of the King. That young upstart Joel Bennett was only chosen for the part of Prince Florizel because he's the star of that absurd TV soap. What's it called again? The Family at something-or-other-House?'

'The Family at Strathloch House,' Felicity said, but Cormac ignored her and continued, 'With my track record, my years of experience, I should've had a better role than this.' He waved his copy of the script around and Felicity instinctively ducked.

'Think how I feel, playing the old Queen at my age, having to disguise how young I am.' But she sounded amused, or even smug, rather than upset.

Cormac went on, as though he hadn't heard her. 'That makeup I've to wear, especially the over-sized moustache. Makes me look like a walrus. And that ridiculous costume. Wilson didn't invest much money in decent props, that's for sure. In the end all I have is a few lines of absurd dialogue.'

Felicity wafted away the haze of cigarette smoke. 'Better not let Wilson hear you saying that. He's so proud of the script he wrote,' she said, staring at him, before adding, 'At Drama School we were taught there's no such thing as a small part. You can make a cameo as memorable as a major role.'

'Oh, really,' Cormac said, making a face.

Felicity tried to control her exasperation. No matter how he tried to disguise it, Cormac's once dark hair was showing noticeable signs of grey. In her opinion he was ideally suited for the part of the ageing King. What did he expect at his time of life? Yes, he'd once had top billing in many major productions, but that was then... and this was now.

She hoped he didn't remember she was the understudy for Esme Forbes, who was playing Princess Beauty. That would have been the final straw for Cormac. Not that she wished any ill to befall Esme, but she couldn't help fantasising. There might be an evening when Esme developed a cold or a sore throat. One opportunity to show what she could do, that was all she needed. And with the Company booked to give performances on several of the West coast islands it would be a demanding tour, especially at this time of year.

She allowed her mind to drift, only vaguely paying attention to Cormac babbling on about Shakespeare. Yes, she and Esme were much the same height and size so there would be no problem about the costume, and she had the advantage of her blonde hair being her natural colour. Almost.

'I have to go,' she said, coming back to what Cormac was saying.

'...and to think we have to tour the country performing in draughty church halls and dilapidated community centres. It's ridiculous.'

'Oh, I don't know. I think travelling to the islands might be fun. And I'm sure we'll be made welcome. Everyone loves a panto.'

'Only because we're not good enough to secure a booking for one of the theatres in the city.'

'Oh, come on,' Felicity protested. 'We're a small company. Joel Bennett is the only big name we have. We're lucky he agreed to sign up. This might be the break of a lifetime.' At least for us younger members of the cast, she added silently.

'And as for that woman who's making all the

arrangements…'

Felicity frowned. 'You mean Valeria?'

'Yes, Valeria.'

'Oh, don't be so down, Cormac. We should be grateful to be in work for such a long run. You know that.'

Cormac looked at the front page of the script. 'Where are we going first?'

'The Isle of Bute,' Felicity said. 'We start there with four days of performances in early December before moving on to Arran.' She shook her head. 'Wouldn't it be better to put that script away before it becomes soaking wet?'

'Bute? I've never been there.' Cormac made no move but continued to gaze at the script.

Felicity smiled. 'I used to go to the island on holiday with my mum and dad when I was little. My brother and I loved it. I'm looking forward to being there just before Christmas. I've always wanted to visit Mount Stuart House. Though I suspect it might be closed during the winter months. And thank goodness we're performing in the High Kirk Hall. I checked it out on the internet. It looks modern and Wilson says the pop-up stage is perfect. No draughty church hall for us!'

Cormac sighed. 'Suppose so.' No point in saying to Felicity that travel to the islands in winter wasn't as easy as in summer. Felicity and one or two of the others weren't too bad, but Joel Bennett incensed him. Thought because he'd landed a part in that TV series that he was a real actor. He needed taken down a peg or two. Cormac chuckled. He might be the person to do exactly that.

'Goodbye, see you tomorrow for the start of the tour. Remember Wilson said we've to meet at

Wemyss Bay at 9.30 for the 10.05 ferry to Bute.'

Before Cormac could reply, Felicity moved away. She was pleased about the part she'd landed. To have the role of the Queen when she was not long out of Drama school was a triumph. And to be working with Joel – goodness knew where that might lead. And not only for her career prospects.

As she walked along Sauchiehall Street away from the makeshift rehearsal rooms the pantomime Director, Wilson Wright, had rented she couldn't resist a daydream again where Esme had to call off. 'Can't go on with this cold,' she'd say. 'You'll have to take over tonight.' And Felicity would find herself playing opposite the fanciable Joel.

Cormac watched her quicken her pace, unable to let go of the bitterness gnawing at him. It was fine for Felicity. She had years in front of her. To think he'd come to this, he who'd once trod the boards at the most important theatres in Scotland, had top billing. It was bad enough to have to lower himself to playing in a pantomime. But to be reduced to playing an aged King with hardly any lines in a script written by Wilson, an amateur who thought he could write the script as well as direct the show. It was too much to bear. That and the humiliation of working for a two-bit company, having to trek around the Scottish islands in the depths of winter.

It was more than likely the venues Wilson had managed to book would be packed (if they were lucky) with rowdy kids and adults only there because they believed it was something they should do at Christmas. They probably didn't have much in the way of entertainment on the islands. And he didn't want to think about the accommodation. He'd been in some rundown hotels in his long career.

There had to be something better than this at his time of life. But he couldn't think what it might be. Meanwhile he had to return to his flat in Woodlands Drive and pack for the trip to Bute. Brushing off the drops of rain from his jacket, he threw his cigarette down, grinding it underfoot before trudging off slowly into the darkening afternoon, pondering the unfairness of life.

ONE

The radio was turned up to maximum volume, but the noise was still unbearable. The din didn't seem to bother my husband, Simon, but then he was the one making it.

Bang, bang, bang went the hammer.

'Are you sure you should be doing this?' I shouted, watching him balance precariously at the top of a long ladder.

'Perfectly. I wish you wouldn't fuss.' He paused from his attack on the false ceiling in the living room. Dust covered everything, including Simon.

I moved to one side in case he dropped the hammer he was wielding, thinking, I'll certainly be fussing if you have an accident and have to be taken off the island to the mainland in the air ambulance. But now wasn't the time to have an argument.

Following the end of Simon's contract in Washington he'd decided to take early retirement and we'd been unsure about where to settle down. 'If I do choose to go back to work, I can easily source another contract in Britain. And I'll be able to find work nearer where we eventually decide to live,' he said, 'but it's time to bow out…at least from full-time employment.'

I'd mixed feelings about this. After so many years and several busy careers, how would he take to retirement? And would he expect me to retire also? Though, to be fair, with my work as a writer location didn't matter and taking on fewer commissions might suit me.

Encouraged by my friend Tara, who lived on the island, we'd found a property on Bute. 'Why don't you buy a house on the island while you make up your mind? You know it well and have often said how much you enjoy being here,' Tara had suggested. 'That way you can have a holiday home no matter where you finally decide to live.'

She didn't realise this was the problem. Simon favoured moving back to London, while my preference was for Glasgow. Not least because of the cost of properties in London, though it would have the advantage of being near my daughter Maura and her family who had settled in Kent.

We were living in a tiny flat in Glasgow I'd been renting while Simon wound up his project in Washington, so when Tara emailed me with details of a property on the island she thought we'd like, we decided we'd come over to view it. Even if it wasn't what we were looking for, we'd enjoy a day out on Bute.

In the end there was no choice – as soon as we saw the cottage with the name Cladach etched on the brass plaque adorning the old wooden gate, we fell in love with it. The cottage was half-way along the Shore Road leading to Port Bannatyne and described as "compact" in the estate agent blurb, with a tiny porch, quirky rooms, a small frontage and a miniscule back garden. But the view overlooking the bay, glinting steel grey in the autumn light, sold it to us at once.

True, the interior left much to be desired, having apparently last been decorated in the 1950s. That didn't worry us. We loved it immediately. With no property to dispose of in the city and the flat there nearing the end of its lease, the deal was quickly concluded.

Perhaps we should have paid more attention to the Home Report and not been tempted by seeing the cottage on a warm autumn day. If we had, we might have noticed the smell of damp that greeted us as soon as we opened the front door on the day we took possession. Not to mention the bowed wall to the side of the property. And that was only the beginning.

Much to my surprise, Simon was demonstrating an eagerness for DIY. And while it was true this small cottage needed loving attention, I harboured doubts about Simon's ability, if not his enthusiasm. He'd shown no inclination for undertaking work in any of the houses we'd lived in before. But then I told myself he'd had a busy career, latterly in America, which rather curtailed any ambitions in that direction.

The DIY zeal was partly sparked by one of the many things we'd discovered since moving. All the tradesmen on the island were extremely busy. And the prospect of a long delay in starting the renovation wasn't acceptable to someone used to immediate action. Though I should have protested when Simon said, 'I'll begin with that false ceiling in the living room. It makes the room feel small and cramped.'

What could possibly go wrong, I reasoned, and once finished and snug, we'd have a comfortable base from which to begin our quest for a permanent home on the mainland.

The cottage had lain empty for some time and once we'd installed some of our furniture, we realised how small the rooms were. In the past it had possibly belonged to one of the workmen who had plied their trade of boatbuilding at Port Bannatyne, a tradition continued at the boatyard and the Marina at the far end of the village.

Fortunately, although the main living area and the bedrooms were small, a larger than expected kitchen diner downstairs (thanks to an extension) was a benefit. But this limited space was the reason why most of our belongings were in storage in Glasgow.

'I'm going into Rothesay,' I said, turning the volume on the radio down to a more acceptable level to make myself heard. 'It might be a good idea to stop working while I'm out. It's too dangerous to be up that ladder on your own. I won't be long. I'll be back before dark.' With the days in December being so short, this gave me a window of a couple of hours. Time enough to buy essentials and chat with anyone I might meet in town. I hadn't been on the island for some time and there was sure to be lots of gossip to catch up on.

'I'll finish this bit,' he said, turning back to his task, acknowledging my departure with no more than a grunt. I shook my head. All I could do was warn him.

A thin film of frost lingered on the pavements where the low winter sun hadn't reached, and I picked my way cautiously over to the car parked at the edge of the pavement. The cottage had been built long before there was any need for a driveway, though we might consider one at some point. But right now it was way down the list of priorities.

We'd agreed to use our cars less now we were on an island where everything was within easy reach and there was a good bus service. We'd sell one of them soon, but on a day like today I was glad of my own transport.

As I drove through Ardbeg towards Rothesay I felt my spirits lift. Garlands of fairy lights had been switched on early, sparkling pin points of light strung out between the streetlights along the seafront, brightening the gloomy afternoon.

As I approached the ferry terminal, the MV Bute was leaving, churning a deep furrow of foam as it swung around out of the harbour to gather speed and head for Wemyss Bay. In the centre of town a large Christmas tree, suitably festive, stood guard over Guildford Square. Much of the time I'd spent on Bute in previous years had been in summer or Spring and the opportunity to once more wander around the main shopping area, Montague Street, at this time of year, added to the pleasure of being back.

'Mrs Cameron! Great to see you. I'd heard you'd returned to Bute,' a voice beside me said.

I turned from admiring the well-lit display of toys and Christmas gifts in the windows of the Bute Tool Company to reply to Mrs Underwood, who owned the Chateau Holiday Flats in Duncan Street. 'Are you here for a break…' she smiled mischievously, '…or are you here on the trail of another mystery?'

'How are you?' I hadn't seen her since my contract at the Kyles of Bute Hotel a few years previously, but I remembered her as being helpful in the crisis we'd had there. She was something of a chatterbox and it was several minutes before I could edge away, conscious I hadn't yet been to the Co-op.

I waved goodbye and watched her scurry off to talk to someone further up the street. This was one of the reasons shopping took so long on the island.

In the window of Bute Treasure Trove, a souvenir shop near the supermarket, a large poster advertising The Mickle Theatre Company's pantomime Sleeping Beauty was prominently displayed. I stopped to look at it. A pantomime…that was interesting.

THE MICKLE THEATRE COMPANY
PRESENTS

SLEEPING BEAUTY

Starring

★ **JOEL BENNETT** as **Prince Florizel**

★ **Esme Forbes** as **Princess Beauty**

- **Phil Aitken** as **Dame Nelly**
- **Neville Kenworthy** as **Muddles**
- **Binita Grove** as **the Fairy Godmother**
- **Rhoda Hunter** as **Somnia**
- **Lucian Lange** as **Rudolph**

with

Felicity Scott as The Queen

Cormac McDhub as The King

Written and directed by Wilson Wright

I hadn't been to a pantomime for years, not since the children were small. As I stood reading the poster, the shop door opened and a tall, sturdy woman came bustling out, the wealth of bracelets on her arms jangling as she thrust a leaflet into my hands.

'It promises to be a great show,' she said. 'They plan to travel from island to island, though they're usually based in Glasgow. We're lucky they've decided to include Bute.'

'I thought the Bute Players put on a pantomime every Christmas.'

She shook her head. 'Not this year, sadly. They had a full programme this autumn and have decided to give their usual pantomime a miss for one season. There were a lot of disappointed people until we heard The Mickle Theatre Company was coming over. I mean, it wouldn't be Christmas without a pantomime…'

'Thanks,' I said, slipping the leaflet into my bag.

'It's sure to be popular,' she called after me, 'Joel Bennett is the star of the show so if you want tickets I suggest you buy them soon.'

'Joel Bennett?'

'You know, that actor who stars in the TV soap The House at Strathloch,' she said.

I smiled. Although I didn't watch the programme it would be difficult not to have heard of Joel Bennett.

Shopping completed, I hurried back to where I'd parked the car in Stuart Street outside the Bute Museum, suddenly noticing there were posters for the pantomime everywhere. There was one in the display box at the Museum, several on the doors of the Moat Community Centre and more on the windows of the Rothesay Library.

Shopping safely stowed in the boot, I sat in my car

for a few minutes, watching the seagulls wheeling above the ruins of the 13th Century Rothesay Castle. Part of the castle was obscured by scaffolding and polythene covers flapping in the breeze, hiding its unusual circular shape. Winter was probably a good time to do repairs while the castle was closed to tourists.

Casting a last lingering look at the castle, I shivered before starting up and driving back to Port Bannatyne. As I pulled up outside the cottage, the living room was in darkness and I felt a surge of fear. Oh, no. Had Simon had an accident? I shouldn't have left him on his own.

'Simon, Simon,' I called as I fumbled with the key to unlock the front door, dreading what I might find. But as I hurried down the hallway there was a smell of freshly-brewed coffee and I pushed open the kitchen door to find him sitting nursing a large mug, the local paper spread out on the table.

'There's coffee in the pot,' he said as I reached over and picked a couple of bits of plaster out of his hair, taking a deep breath, hoping he wouldn't notice how alarmed I'd been.

'I'm going for a shower,' he said glumly. 'I'm not sure I should have started on this work.'

Refraining from the inevitable comment, I sat down at the table, pulling the leaflet advertising the pantomime from my bag.

'I picked this up when I was in town,' I said, placing it in front of him.

He frowned. 'A pantomime? It was fine when the kids were young, but why would I want to go to one now?' He gazed at the leaflet for a few seconds.

'It might be fun and…' I began, but he interrupted with, 'Wait a minute. Wilson Wright is the director? I wonder if it's the same person?'

'You know him?'

Simon peered at the small, rather blurred, photo. 'It looks like the person I know. Or rather knew. He was one of my students when I was in further education.'

'You didn't teach drama.' He must be mistaken.

He shook his head. 'No matter what they were studying, the students had to do a short course in Management. It was part of broadening the curriculum at the time. Another educational fad.' He smiled. 'Well, well. His was a great group. They were all mature students and I sometimes joined them for a pint on Fridays in the local pub. I wonder how he ended up with The Mickle Theatre Company.'

'Let's go along to the pantomime. I can easily get tickets, but I've been told it will be popular, so we'll have to book soon. They're scheduled to be here for four days next week. The Bute Theatre Company isn't putting on a pantomime this year and this is sure to attract a large audience.'

Simon continued to look thoughtful as he stared at the flyer. 'Wilson Wright? That is curious…that he should end up here on Bute. Yes, I think you're right. It might be interesting.' He handed me the leaflet. 'I can't recall which course he was on, but it may well have been drama.'

Not that it mattered. It would be an evening out, away from the mess, and put us in the mood for Christmas.

TWO

The Mickle Theatre Company arrived on Bute to great excitement. There was a two page spread in the local paper and interviews on Bute Island Radio. The van, bearing the company name and a purple and gold triangular logo, was difficult to miss. There was a mix of curiosity and fascination from the islanders, trying to spot the actors in town. Or rather attempting to spot Joel Bennett. Little groups of teenage girls gathered at possible locations – the Discovery Centre, Harry Haws, Helmi's – chattering excitedly. A persistent cluster congregated at the entrance to the High Kirk Hall, where the pantomime was to be staged. Being chased away by the caretaker didn't dampen their enthusiasm. They regrouped the minute he was back inside.

'I've tickets for the first night on Thursday,' I said to Simon, waving them triumphantly as I squeezed past the living room furniture crammed into the hallway to join him in the kitchen.

After his initial interest in demolishing the false ceiling, Simon had abandoned the task. 'I'll have to find someone to help,' he said.

A friend on the island had promised to speak to one of the local builders but so far no one had appeared, and the room sat unused. There was a fine layer of dust everywhere, despite our best efforts to clear up and where there had once been an unsightly ceiling, there was now an unsightly ceiling with a gaping hole.

'You said you know the Director?'

'Wilson Wright? Yes, he was one of my students.'

'I thought it might be fun if you contacted him. We could ask the cast to autograph a programme. Especially as Joel Bennett is the star of the pantomime.'

Simon raised his eyebrows and grinned. 'I didn't know you were a fan,' he said.

'No, but I think Deborah is.'

'Isn't she rather old to be a fan of Joel Bennett?'

'You're probably right. But it would be a good opportunity.'

He paused, looking thoughtful. 'Yes, it might be a good idea to meet with Wilson, have a pint and hear what he's been doing.'

This sounded promising and not wanting to lose the opportunity, I said, 'There's a phone number on the leaflet. We might be able to go backstage after the performance.'

'Okay, if you're keen. I'll call him and see what he suggests. But,' lifting a warning finger, 'don't be too hopeful. Thursday is the first night – they may want to go back to their digs as soon as possible after the end of the performance.'

That was true, but I was sure Simon could manage to persuade Wilson. I'd never been behind the scenes at a theatre production. It would be good to see the famous Joel Bennett in real life, find out what the fuss was about.

True to his word, a little later Simon made the call to Wilson, putting on the speakerphone for my benefit.

'Great to hear from you, Mr Cameron. I don't keep up with the old crowd – we've all gone our separate ways. So it would be good to catch up.'

'Yes, a lot has happened since we last met,' Simon laughed. 'Quite a change to be in charge of a theatre company.'

'It's something I've always wanted to do – have my own company. It's been my dream for many years and I'm determined to succeed.' He smiled. 'You'll enjoy seeing how a pantomime works, I'm sure. Oh, and by the way, it's quite a mouthful so we usually call it The Mickle.'

So, when Thursday arrived, I was looking forward to the performance, but was also increasingly eager to go backstage after the show.

Being in good time, we easily found a parking place at the Rothesay Leisure Centre and set off for the short walk up to the High Kirk Hall.

'I didn't realise we'd have to go through a graveyard to reach the Hall,' I said as we approached.

Simon pointed to the blue directional notice on the post on the opposite side of the road. 'The small building over there is all that remains of St Mary's Chapel, the Chancel,' he said. 'The building in front of us is the High Kirk: the Hall beside the High Kirk is where the pantomime is being staged.'

On either side of the path leading to the Hall, many of the gravestones were ancient, some toppled over, others with only fragments of inscriptions remaining to indicate who lay beneath.

'The Hall is modern,' Simon grinned. 'No ghosts there.'

We joined the queue and inside were guided to a flight of stairs at the end of a corridor housing what looked like a series of offices, with a kitchen at the far end.

If the theatre was a temporary structure it was

exceptionally well done. Although we'd arrived early, it was crowded, every seat taken and there was an atmosphere of expectation, a buzz of excitement as we settled down. I spied a small crowd of teenage girls in the front row, giggling and chatting loudly. Fans of Joel Bennett, no doubt. Glancing around, I recognised several people from my previous trips to the island and as the lights dimmed I sat back to enjoy the show, feeling quite at home.

'The programme says Wilson was responsible for writing the script,' I whispered. 'I thought Sleeping Beauty was a standard pantomime.'

'Don't think so,' Simon said. 'The story is the same, but from what I know there are lots of versions. I guess this one will have a Scottish flavour.'

He was right. This Sleeping Beauty panto more than lived up to expectations and Wilson had cleverly incorporated jokes with references to Bute. If he didn't know the island he must have spent time in research. The running time was much longer than I remembered from previous visits to pantomimes when the children were young, but the audience seemed not to notice, clearly enjoying every moment.

While there was the usual throng of parents and grandparents with noisy small children, the groups of teenage girls in the audience made their presence felt by screaming every time Joel Bennett appeared on stage. I sensed he accepted this as no more than his due and played to their adulation at every opportunity.

I wasn't sure he was making the same effort to keep to the script and once or twice I caught a look of surprise on the faces of other cast members. Either he was improvising or had forgotten his lines. Unless he was deliberately upstaging them. I didn't think that would go down well.

'Are we to go backstage straightaway?' I said to Simon as at the end of the performance the Walkdown, with its spectacular costumes, finished and the final curtain came down to thunderous applause.

He shook his head. 'No, Wilson said to wait here, and he'd come and fetch us.'

I settled back, watching the excited crowds bustle out. Several of the teenage girls were whispering together in the corner. It was likely they were plotting to ambush Joel, but had little hope of success, judging by the steely-eyed usher guarding the stage exit.

Time wore on and the last of the audience drifted away, leaving us alone in the theatre. Simon couldn't contain his impatience, tapping his fingers on the armrest of his seat. Twice he said, 'Let's go. Wilson isn't coming – he's probably forgotten.'

'Let's wait a little longer. It'll take some time for everyone to wind down after a performance.' I didn't want to give up the opportunity to see backstage.

The caretaker came in, starting to put off the lights, then stopping when he saw us.

'The performance is over,' he said abruptly. 'You'll have to go.'

'Yes, we're waiting for the Director, Wilson Wright. We're supposed to be meeting him after the show,' Simon said, adopting the authoritative tone he'd probably once used with his students.

'No one told me,' the caretaker grumbled. 'I have to put these lights off and check this part of the building is clear before I go upstairs to the actors' dressing rooms.' He stood still, his finger poised over the light switch, ready to plunge the auditorium into darkness.

Simon stood up and nodded to me. 'Let's try going

backstage, Alison. Something must have delayed Wilson.'

'Or else you're right and he's forgotten.'

'Mmm. Let's go anyway.'

I walked with Simon out of the theatre, to go around to the door giving access to back stage. As he lifted his hand to knock, I pointed to the notice:

PRIVATE. NO ENTRY EXCEPT TO AUTHORISED PERSONS,

but he continued knocking.

Suddenly there was a burst of noise, excited shouts, and then a loud scream.

We stopped. 'What was that?' Simon said.

'No idea. Perhaps the actors are celebrating?'

'Doesn't sound like a celebration,' he replied, frowning.

The door burst open, and a wild-eyed man rushed out, coming to a halt as he saw us.

'It's Wilson,' Simon muttered to me.

This tall, skinny individual with owlish spectacles, his thick dark brown hair dishevelled, had only a slight resemblance to his publicity photo, but I shouldn't have been surprised. Even my limited experience with actors has shown their publicity photos don't always bear much similarity to how they look in real life.

'Sorry,' Simon said. 'It's me, Simon Cameron. We were supposed to meet you after the show.' Then as he saw the look on Wilson's face, he added, 'But it appears it's not convenient.'

Wilson stared at me, then looked over to Simon. 'Mr Cameron. Gosh. Yes.' He ran his fingers through his bushy hair, making it stand on end. 'It's terrible. I've no idea how this could have happened.'

One thing about Simon: he's good in a crisis. He

grasped Wilson's arm. 'What's wrong? Can we help?'

Wilson gulped. 'What? I can't understand it. What was she doing there?'

'Take a deep breath,' Simon said.

Wilson gasped, taking a couple of breaths before saying, 'This is terrible. It's Valeria Dixon, our …administrator…our manager…she's…'

He stopped.

'Has she had an accident. Do we have to call an ambulance?' Simon said.

Wilson gulped again. 'Yes. No, no, not an ambulance. Yes, maybe. Trouble is, I think she's dead.'

Simon didn't reply but pulled out his phone to dial the emergency number and I followed Wilson as he turned and scurried to the stage, turning on one of the side lights to illuminate the area.

A body lay at the foot of a stairway on the far side.

'Where do these stairs lead?' I said, averting my eyes.

'What? Oh, these lead to the corridor where we have the actors' dressing rooms. They're a temporary structure only used for the appearance of the Wicked Fairy. Let's her make a spectacular entrance. The performance was over, everyone had left…'

He appeared rooted to the spot. 'She must have fallen down the stairs.'

He looked bewildered, wringing his hands. 'What was she doing? There was no reason for her to be here.'

So much for an enjoyable night out.

THREE

Once he knew the ambulance was on its way, Simon quickly assumed command, edging Wilson away from where Valeria lay on her back, a scatter of papers around her. There was no mistaking what had happened by the way she was lying, her awkward position at the foot of the flight of stairs.

By now we'd been joined by other members of the cast and the actors crowded around in a babble of noise, shocked and confused.

Simon was doing his best to calm Wilson. He steered the distraught Director by the elbow towards the backstage area, checking his phone as he did so.

'I've phoned for an ambulance,' he said.

Of the small group clustered around the body, several were still in costume, Princess Beauty cowering in the arms of Prince Florizel. Ah, this was Esme Forbes and the famous Joel Bennett. Even under his heavy stage make-up I could see why his good looks would make him appeal to teenage girls. He'd taken off his wig to reveal hair so blond it was almost white. I was struck by finely chiselled features, and he had the lithe figure of someone who worked out regularly. Perhaps Esme wasn't too upset to have this opportunity to be close to him, then I scolded myself for such an unkind thought.

The man playing the part of the Dame, Dame Nelly, appeared from the wings and moved forward to take charge. Like the other members of the cast, it appeared he'd been in the process of taking off his stage costume when the accident happened. He was still wearing the Dame's large, hooped yellow skirt, with no more than a vest on top, showing the tattoos covering his arms from wrist to shoulder. I snuck a look at the programme I'd kept tightly clutched in my hand, ready to have it autographed. No chance of that now.

I glanced at the cast list. This must be Phil Aitken and in the hubbub around him, he appeared to be the most capable of taking command.

'Stand back,' he ordered, physically pushing several of the actors aside and moving closer to where the body lay.

Simon said, 'Has anyone phoned the police?'

'What?' Wilson appeared to have come out of his daze.

'They have to be informed when there's a death such as this,' Simon said.

A young woman, still in make-up but clad in jeans and a jumper, frowned at him. 'And you are?' Ah, this must be Felicity Scott who'd played the part of the Queen, judging by the crown she was carrying.

Simon ignored this question, nodding to Phil's reply, 'Yes, they're on their way. I suggest everyone goes back to the dressing rooms and waits there.' He stepped deftly out of his voluminous yellow skirt and threw it quickly over the prone body of Valeria, giving her some dignity.

A couple of the actors began to move off slowly, whispering, but the others appeared reluctant to leave.

Wilson suddenly seemed to collect himself and shuffled forward, glaring at Phil as though resenting this attempt to take charge. 'It might be better if you left,' he said to us, a tremor in his voice. 'The police will be here shortly and there's nothing you can do to help.' Turning around, he addressed Joel, Esme and Felicity who were lingering behind the rest of the cast, 'Phil's suggestion is right. Go and wait in the dressing rooms.'

Felicity stopped to cast a glance back at poor Valeria, but Joel grabbed her by the elbow. 'Come on. We're better off out of here.'

Having had far too many dealings with the Rothesay Police over my years of visiting Bute, the last thing I wanted was to be at the scene of this accident when they arrived.

'We should leave,' I said to Simon, tapping him on the arm. 'There's nothing we can do.'

Rhoda Hunter, still in full costume as the Wicked Fairy, Somnia, remained standing beside Wilson, seemingly reluctant to move from the scene.

'That order includes you,' Phil said, giving her a nudge.

But as Simon and I turned to leave a man came bumbling along the corridor, a cigarette dangling from his lips, to stop abruptly as he saw the body of Valeria.

'What's going on here,' he wheezed. 'I heard all the commotion.'

'It's Valeria,' sobbed Felicity. 'She's had an accident, Cormac.'

Ah, this was Cormac McDubh. I remembered him in his heyday when he'd been a famous actor, even starring in a couple of minor films. He was still in full costume, but given he wasn't tall, he cut a much less imposing figure than Joel. He'd certainly changed from the last time I'd seen him in a performance of Murder in Four Days at the King's Theatre in Glasgow.

‘What do you mean, “had an accident”?’ His eyes glittered as he gazed around, waiting for a reply.

Wilson stepped forward. ‘It looks as if she fell down the stairs. I’ve no idea what she was doing in this part of the theatre.’ He repeated, ‘There was no reason for her to be here. What’s more all the lights were out.’ He gestured to the flight of stairs out of sight of the audience.

‘What!’ Cormac made to bend down, presumably to lift the garish yellow skirt covering on Valeria’s body, but Wilson laid a restraining arm on Cormac’s shoulder.

‘Leave it,’ he said firmly. ‘The police are on their way. I’m asking everyone to go back to the dressing rooms and wait there for the police to arrive. And put out that cigarette, Cormac. You know you can’t smoke here.’

The remaining members of the cast began to move away quietly, Joel still with his arm protectively around Esme. Felicity followed on, but the look on her face as Joel leaned in to say a few words to Esme made me think she also was smitten by this young star.

Cormac whirled around. ‘Where is everyone else?’ he said.

‘Rhoda was in a bad way. She and Valeria were friendly and as for the others, they wanted no part of it. I think they might have been in shock.’

‘Who discovered the body,’ Simon asked, ignoring my attempts to urge him yet again to leave.

Wilson turned as Cormac shook off the arm that had been restraining him. ‘It was Joel,’ he said. ‘As I came along the corridor to go down to the auditorium to collect Simon and Alison, there he was, standing over the body.’

Cormac raised his eyebrows. 'Suspicious then. Even if Valeria was here for some inexplicable reason, why would she suddenly miss her footing and trip?'

'Don't be stupid,' Wilson said. 'There could have been any number of reasons for Joel making the discovery…none of them sinister. You know she wasn't directly involved with the cast. And it's much more likely it was an unfortunate accident.'

Poor Valeria. To be so easily dismissed

'We should go.' I said to Simon yet again, this time tugging at his sleeve. With the police due any minute, I'd no desire to linger a moment longer.

This time he nodded in agreement, and followed me out, as Wilson said, 'I'll give you a call, Simon. We're due to leave on Tuesday for Arran.' He stared unhappily at the shrouded body. 'Though goodness knows what will happen now.'

A narrow escape. We came out of the building in time to see an ambulance and a police car draw up outside. Fortunately they didn't notice us as they hurried into the building, and we walked quickly away from the Hall and down the High Street to pick up our car.

'What a terrible thing to happen,' I said as we drove off. I didn't dare mention our escape might be temporary. The police would want to interview us at some point.

We made our way through a silent Ardbeg. At this time of night everywhere was shuttered and dark, but the lights from Christmas trees in the windows of the houses shone out as we drove past, making a cheerful sight. But all I could think of was Valeria lying at the foot of the stairs in the theatre.

As we came into Port Bannatyne, I suddenly realised I was still clutching the programme for

Sleeping Beauty and before sliding it into my handbag, I'd a quick look at the cast list, trying to remember what Wilson had said about those actors who hadn't been at the scene of the crime. I counted up. There were nine members of the cast in total but as I pondered what had happened, I realised there was something odd. Most of the cast had appeared at some point.

Why had it taken so long for Cormac to come on the scene? With so much noise, surely he must have heard. I remembered Wilson's puzzled expression – what had Valeria been doing in that part of the theatre.

Stop this, stop it at once I told myself. This was nothing to do with me. There were more than enough problems to deal with at home. There was no need to become involved in this accident. What was more, Wilson was Simon's acquaintance, not mine. Let the police sort out what had happened to Valeria. And determined this time to stick to my decision, I sighed with relief as we drew up outside the cottage.

FOUR

My decision not to be involved didn't last long. Valeria's death niggled away at me. Wilson was adamant there was no reason for her to be anywhere near the stairs at the side of the stage. Their only purpose was to facilitate a grand entrance for the Wicked Fairy.

Simon refused to discuss the problem. 'Leave it to the police,' he said next morning, a hint of concern in his voice when I broached the subject. It appeared he'd abandoned the idea of arranging another meeting with Wilson any time soon.

But events have the habit of catching up with you.

It came about because of Simon's suggestion as we sat over coffee in the kitchen. 'Let's go to the Black Bull for lunch. The forecast for today isn't good and if it doesn't clear up a walk is out of the question.'

I stood up, pushing back my chair to move to the window and pull aside the kitchen curtain. The rain was torrential, the small garden a sea of mud, the last of the autumn flowers wilting and bedraggled. "Isn't good," was an understatement. He was right. A trip into Rothesay would give us a break from the chaos of the unfinished DIY so I said, 'Sounds fine.' While the kitchen was large and cosy with the advantage of a range cooker (though of ancient vintage), this room was also on the list for renovation. The units were of dark wood chipboard, the room painted a deep blue and the overall effect on a wet December day was as dark and depressing as the view outside.

We parked in town, outside the Bute Museum, and walked quickly down to The Black Bull, now contending with a gusty wind as well as the persistent rain. The pub was busy as we came in through the front door, remembering to duck as we did so. There was a fug of dampness, of clothes gradually drying out in the warmth overlaid with a welcome smell of food. The main lounge was full, and we squeezed through the close-set tables to the back room, opting for a table in the far corner.

'This should avoid the worst of the draughts,' Simon said.

But the table we'd chosen wasn't as wind-proof as we'd hoped. As we scanned the menu the back door opened, bringing with it a gust of cold air.

'Why, hello,' a voice said. It was Wilson. He towered over us, shedding little droplets of water as I wriggled back in my seat to avoid getting wet.

'Mind if I join you?' he said and without waiting for a reply, pulled over a chair from an adjoining table to squash in beside us.

The waitress came over to take our order, but Wilson shook his head when asked what he wanted to eat. 'A pint of Special is fine, thanks,' he said.

I'd an idea The Black Bull wasn't the first hostelry he'd visited that day and he took a long gulp of his pint as soon as it was set before him.

The waitress left promising, 'Your food order won't be long.'

There was an awkward silence, broken by Simon saying, 'Escaping for an hour or two?' at which Wilson looking increasingly gloomy before replying.

'Something like that. The police are everywhere, asking questions, examining everything.' He paused.

'What's worse. They won't confirm Valeria's death was an accident. Something to do with the angle of her body. There will be an inquest because of the circumstances. But what else could it be but an accident and…'He didn't finish the sentence.

There was another silence before I said, 'That's no more than you'd expect surely? The police must examine the scene, make certain nothing's missed. After all, it was a sudden death.'

Wilson stared at me. 'You appear to know a lot about it, Alison.'

Simon jumped in before I could reply. 'Alison seems to have a nose for trouble on her trips to the island,' he muttered. 'Thank goodness this is nothing to do with us this time.'

Fortunately Wilson was only half-listening, his mind clearly on the immediate problems of The Mickle and what Valeria's death would mean for the remainder of the tour. For a small organisation, operating as I guessed on a tight budget, something like this could spell disaster.

'I don't understand it,' Wilson said, putting his pint down on the table with a bang, spilling some in the process. He paused to mop up the liquid with one of the cork beer mats. 'It must have been an accident. She was one of the quietest members of the team. Mouse-like in fact. Her death has left us with a problem.'

'Was she well-liked?' I couldn't resist asking, though the look on Simon's face showed he was keen to change the subject.

Wilson frowned, as though considering the question. 'Well-liked? I don't think any of us knew her well enough to have an opinion. She was one of those people who was just there, working away in the background, but no one knew much about her. She was recommended by Phil when we set up. He'd worked with Valeria before. We needed someone who could handle the bookings and the travel arrangements, leaving me free to concentrate on the production. You can imagine how difficult it is to find staff in a small company. We can't afford to pay much. Most people, including actors, only come to a company like ours for the experience, then they're off to work that pays better.'

Or are at the end of a career, like Cormac, I thought, but aloud I said, 'And what will happen now? Will the tour be able to go ahead as planned?' I waved my arm to emphasise my question, almost upending the tray with the plates of food the waitress was bringing to the table.

'Oops, careful,' she said, setting them down before us as I muttered an apology.

Wilson drained his glass and wiping the froth from his upper lip said, 'We were lucky to be able to rent the Hall, though some of the cast have to share the dressing rooms.'

He stared morosely into his empty glass. 'The police say we can go ahead if we leave details of the other venues, but I'm not sure we've the heart to do it.'

Simon tried to sound encouraging. 'I'm sure you won't want to disappoint your audiences. Lots of people will be looking forward to it.'

'I expect so.' Wilson sat up straight. 'Yes, you're right of course. This has been an ambition of mine for so long. I'm not going to give up.'

There was a steely note in his words. 'We're fully booked for the remaining performances on Bute. It would be more difficult to cancel than to go ahead. And more costly. And we've bookings for the performances on the other islands. We'd have to return all the ticket money.'

No wonder he was miserable. Poor Wilson.

Simon and I made a start on our meal, though it was uncomfortable with Wilson sitting there in silence, sunk in gloom. I hoped he would leave soon. Perhaps I could encourage him. 'I'm sure you and Simon will want to meet later,' I said, trying to sound upbeat. 'And Arran's the next stop on your tour?'

'We're due to leave for Arran next week. We're supposed to be performing there from Friday on. After that weekend we should be touring Mull, Islay and Colonsay before heading back to Glasgow. That lets us have Christmas Day with our families – those of us who have families, that is.'

It was a hard life, I thought, being part of a small theatre company and I admired their dedication.

Wilson stood up somewhat unsteadily, lifting his empty glass. 'I must go back, see what's happening. There's so much to do and it's going to be difficult without Valeria. She was so well organised, kept everything slick. I didn't have to worry about any of the details.'

He put his glass down on the table with a thump. 'I don't suppose you know anyone local who's a good organiser? Someone who could fill in until we find a proper replacement. It would only be for Bute – there's a couple of people in Glasgow I can call on, but they won't be able to join us immediately, probably until we reach Arran. It's not a big job and Valeria had everything set up. It's only a matter of double-checking the schedules for the other venues. I don't have time.'

'Sorry,' I began, 'I don't know anyone ...,' as Simon said with a laugh, 'The only person I know who's used to organising is Alison, but that's not much help.'

As I saw the gleam in Wilson's eyes and a smile cross his face, I could at that moment cheerfully have murdered my husband.

FIVE

Once back at the cottage I could contain myself no longer. 'What on earth were you thinking?' I said to Simon. I'd preserved a stony silence during the car journey back, but now I felt ready to explode.

He had the grace to look sheepish. 'Sorry,' he said. 'I wasn't thinking. I didn't mean to involve you.'

That was all very well but given the predicament the theatre company was now in, it was hard not to agree to help. After some toing and froing in discussion with Wilson, I'd finally relented. 'I'm not sure how much I can do,' I said. 'I know nothing about the world of theatre. And my experience is in writing, not in this kind of organising.'

My closest involvement with the world of drama had been as an assistant scriptwriter on A Man Alone, a film made on Bute about the life of James Hamilton who'd owned Kames Castle. But that had been a while back. And I still shuddered when I recalled how I'd been persuaded to take on a small part when one of the cast had dropped out.

Wilson had seized on Simon's suggestion at once. 'All you have to do is check the arrangements Valeria made for the rest of the tour. I left it to her, and I don't have time to go through her files. For the different venues she sorted out the ferry times, the digs, the contacts we need at each place.'

This sounded less and less appealing. As someone who leaves her tax return till the last minute, much to the despair of my accountant, I wasn't convinced I was the right person to take on this task. But Wilson was desperate, and it would be sad to see a small company like this fail. I persuaded myself this was like any other research task I'd undertaken. And if Valeria was as prepared as he said, it would be no more than a matter of double-checking everything and reporting back to Wilson.

'As long as I don't have to do more than that,' I said, a firm note in my voice in case he had other work in mind.

'No, no,' Wilson said, leaning forward eagerly. 'Once you have everything in an order I can understand, it will let me get on with the serious business of making sure the pantomime is as good as possible. We need this to be a success and I have to make more tweaks to the script.'

What could I do after that plea for help? But it didn't make me any less annoyed with Simon and I retreated to the bedroom to lose myself in my latest book.

A little while later Simon put his head around the door. 'Thought you might like a cuppa,' he said coming over and setting a large mug of tea and a cake on the bedside table.

What could I do but laugh at the expression on his face and peace was restored. If this task was as simple as Wilson had suggested, it would only be for a few days before the company travelled to Arran and the replacement for Valeria arrived. And with luck Wilson's contact in Glasgow might arrive sooner than expected.

And now that I'd had the opportunity to think about it, I was rather looking forward to my new project. It would be interesting to see behind the scenes at the theatre, especially such a traditional form of entertainment as a pantomime.

As I came downstairs, Simon held up his mobile, saying, 'That was Wilson. He wondered if you could pop along later this afternoon, make a start on Valeria's records, do a first check.'

There wasn't much of the afternoon left, but I appreciated the urgency of the situation. The sooner I started the sooner I'd be finished.

'Fine,' I said. 'Probably a good idea to begin right away.' I stopped. 'Assuming they can leave Bute for the rest of the tour as planned. Much of that will depend on what the police find.'

Simon frowned. 'It shouldn't be a problem. What else could Valeria's death be but an accident.' He stopped. 'You don't think there's anything suspicious about it, surely?'

I smiled at the expression on his face. 'No, I'm sure she tripped on the stairs.'

'Good. Do you want me to come with you to the Hall?'

'I don't know how long it will take me to check out Valeria's information,' I said. 'My plan is to go through everything quickly and pass the information to Wilson, but I've no idea how long I'll be.'

And leaving him staring at the ceiling in the living room – or what remained of it – I set off.

Fingers crossed he'd be able to use his contacts to find a professional to make good the work he'd started. If not, it would mean spending Christmas Day sitting in the depressing kitchen, a prospect I didn't relish.

SIX

The Hall was busy as I came in through the side door, the actors' entrance, to be greeted by a strong whiff of synthetic lavender. The cleaners had been busy. Notwithstanding the disruption of Valeria's death, mundane tasks had to carry on.

The area where Valeria had been found was screened off by police tape. If it was out of use for the performances Wilson would have to reblock several important scenes.

Finding Wilson was my first concern, and I stopped an actress I recognised. Out of make-up and the elaborate costume of Somnia, the Wicked Fairy, she looked almost waif-like. I racked my brains for her name – ah, yes this was Rhoda Hunter.

'Hi,' I said, 'I'm looking for Wilson. Any idea where he might be?'

Rhoda frowned. 'Are you the police?'

'No, my name's Alison Cameron. Wilson asked me to check the arrangements Valeria made for the rest of the tour. I'm helping till he can find someone to replace her,' I added hastily. I didn't want her to have the wrong idea.

She looked puzzled then smiled. 'Of course. You were here when the accident happened. I thought I recognised you. Wilson did mention you'd agreed to help. Just as well as none of us would have a clue where to begin.' She sighed. 'Though I'm not sure why Wilson employed Valeria, to be honest. She had...' She stopped abruptly before continuing, 'Wilson's in the theatre with some of the cast, going over a couple of changes to the script. Follow me.'

She scurried up the main stairs as I trailed behind her, trying to keep up. As we reached the theatre, I could hear raised voices. Whoever it was sounded angry. Probably part of the script, I thought, a notion quickly dispelled as we entered.

Wilson was standing at the front of the stage engaged in an argument with Cormac, hands on hips, his face suffused with anger.

Rhoda and I stopped at the back of the hall, watching the scene being played out in front of us. Rhoda put her finger to her lips.

'You've already cut enough of my lines,' Cormac was yelling, brandishing a sheaf of papers like a weapon. 'At this rate I'll have none left.'

'We have to cut the performance time,' Wilson replied. 'You knew that this might happen, that the first performance was a way of judging the running time.'

'Well, cut someone else's part then.' Cormac turned as though prepared to storm off, then caught sight of a shadowy figure in the wings.

'Cut some of **his** lines, why don't you?' he said, pointing as the young man playing Rudolph came out onto the stage.

Wilson sighed. 'Don't be unreasonable, Cormac. Lucian's part is important for moving the plot forward. As the Prince's best friend and confidant a lot of the action can be condensed into a few lines as they chat.'

'What plot? What is there to condense?' Cormac was becoming increasingly red-faced. 'At the Princess Beauty's christening Somnia casts a spell, the princess pricks her finger, falls asleep and a hundred years later is awakened by a kiss from a handsome prince. Everyone knows the story.'

Wilson shook his head. 'I have to do it this way. I hoped you'd be understanding,' he said, fidgeting with embarrassment.

Phil moved forward. 'Wilson's right. We have to pull together more than ever now.'

'Fine for someone with the part of the Dame,' Cormac snorted. 'Though I suppose there's a good reason why you need to earn as much money as possible.'

Phil frowned and appeared to be about to reply but Joel, who'd been standing in the background, moved towards Cormac, saying, 'Face it. You were lucky to get a part. You might have been a popular actor at one time, but everyone has a shelf life.' The smirk on his face as he said this only served to enrage Cormac further.

'We'll see about that,' he said, storming down the steps leading to the auditorium. Wilson stepped forward.

'Let him go,' Joel said, laying a restraining hand on Wilson's arm. 'His lines are so few that if he does decide to leave us, he won't be missed. Someone else can double up for his part.'

'That's not the point,' Wilson muttered. 'He knew the score when he signed the contract. Why can't he be more understanding.' He was clearly finding it difficult to keep control of the cast.

Joel shrugged. 'He has an inflated idea of his worth.' He paused. 'Mind you, he was a big star at one time. It must be awful for him.' He didn't sound the least bit sorry. And the way he said it suggested he'd no anticipation such a fate would befall him.

‘Better catch Wilson now,’ Rhoda whispered to me, urging me forward.

I was becoming less happy about being involved with this company. There were so many problems, so many egos. But I was committed.

Wilson said, shading his eyes against the glare from the stage lights, ‘Is that you Esme? You should be up here. Beauty is in the next scene.’

As though on cue Esme appeared from the wings, walking slowly.

‘Did you call, Wilson?’ she said, sauntering on to the stage with a book in her hand.

‘Where’s your script?’ said Wilson, whirling around to face her. ‘I’m not paying you to spend your time reading.’

But Esme was having none of it. ‘Don’t think you can bully me the way you do the others,’ she said tartly.

‘Of course, of course,’ mumbled Wilson, taking a step back.

Possibly aware there was about to be another row, Rhoda hurried down the aisle towards the stage, pulling me with her.

‘All is well,’ she said. ‘Alison has turned up. You can concentrate on the production now, Wilson.’

‘Thank goodness,’ Wilson said. ‘In the nick of time.’ He gestured to the group of actors on stage. ‘Take fifteen while I show Alison to Valeria’s office.’

He jumped down from the stage rather than using the stairs and started off at a rapid pace through one of the side doors, leaving me to hurry after him.

‘Is it always like this?’ I whispered as Rhoda came up beside me.

‘Pretty much,’ she said, with a shrug. ‘Don’t worry. When you get a lot of strong personalities together this is the result. And Wilson isn't good at sorting it out.'

I caught up with him in the corridor where the offices were located. He flung open the nearest door and motioned me inside. 'It's not much,' he said, 'but then you don't need a lot of space to do the admin. Valeria had everything pretty much sorted.'

The accommodation Valeria had occupied wasn't so much a room as a broom cupboard. Boxes had been hastily piled up against one wall to allow a small desk and a chair to be crammed in. A large cardboard box labelled The Mickle Theatre Company sat perilously on another chair next to the desk.

'Everything you need is in that box,' Wilson said from the doorway because there was no way more than one person could fit in this tiny space. Perhaps because it was so small, there was no sign of a computer.

'Don't worry,' he said, as though guessing my thoughts. 'Valeria was rather old-fashioned. She didn't trust the technology. Always insisted on having a paper copy of everything. My office is a couple of doors along if you need help.'

Wilson's final words as he left, 'Better get back. I'll let you get on with it,' didn't inspire me with confidence.

I squeezed into the space between the desk and the chair and sat down, gazing around me. Wilson had left the door open but even so the room felt claustrophobic. The only natural light came from a small window, heavily barred, set high up on the wall behind me. It looked as if it hadn't been opened in a long time.

There was no clue to Valeria's system. An old coffee mug containing an array of pens and pencils and a notepad with a few scribbles on it were the only evidence that this was being used as an office. Swivelling around to lift the lid on the cardboard box, I peered inside. Perhaps the information would be here. Ah, good. There were several folders, the top one labelled The Mickle Theatre Company tour: Isle of Bute.

I began to sort through them, taking my time to make sure I didn't miss anything. The first folder contained receipts for the ferry and for several other items of expenditure, including a booking and a deposit for The Four Winds Hotel. Putting that to one side, thankful that one of the venues had been dealt with, I lifted the second folder. To my surprise there was nothing inside this one except a list of venues and dates, not the tickets and accommodation bookings I'd have expected.

Valeria must have had a separate file for each island on the tour, I thought, but a quick look through the other folders in the box was equally unenlightening. Each one was carefully identified by a large label, indicating the name of the island and the dates of performances, but most had no more than a single summary sheet and the last one at the bottom of the pile, described as Expenses, was empty.

What was going on? Wilson had given me to understand that Valeria had been the lynchpin of the organisation, had a system in place which allowed everything to run smoothly, leaving him to deal with the important task of managing the production. Where were the tickets, the ferry receipts, the deposit receipts for accommodation?

I sat back as best I could, given the confines of the space. This was odd. I must be missing something, I thought, taking my time to go through the box again.

But it was no better on a second search. Perhaps Wilson was wrong, and she'd transferred the information to a folder in the desk drawers. But this was of no help. The drawers were empty except for a pile of crumpled sweet wrappers. Valeria had clearly had a sweet tooth.

I thought about Valeria's death and latest news that the police were refusing to confirm it had been an accident. Were they suspicious?

Why was I spending time speculating? Pulling myself back to the task in hand, I started again, but another hunt revealed there was nowhere else in this tiny office Valeria could have kept information about the arrangements for the tour. And Wilson had been sure everything was in the box next to the desk. Had someone been in and tampered with the files? It seemed the only way to explain the lack of information.

I gazed around the room, hoping a solution would somehow present itself. There was a wastepaper bin in the far corner, but the contents I shook out onto the desk revealed no more than a couple of pink pieces of paper with some scribbled numbers on them.

Despite Wilson's assertion that Valeria preferred hard copy surely she would have worked on a computer and only run off what was necessary. Any copies in the box would be no more than that – copies. Everything would be stored on the computer. Time to have another word with Wilson. And track down Valeria's computer.

SEVEN

Frustrated by the lack of documentation, I couldn't proceed until I'd spoken to Wilson. I stepped out of Valeria's office into a deserted hallway. Wilson wasn't in his office, and I stood for a moment, listening, but there was no sound except the faint murmur of voices from upstairs. The actors must be in the theatre, rehearsing the changes to the script for the evening's performance. But a quick glance in showed Wilson wasn't with them, and I decided to try the corridor where the dressing rooms were.

As I reached the top of the stairs a door at the far end opened and Cormac came bustling out. He stopped when he saw me, leaning forward aggressively.

'What are you doing here?' he said. 'Members of the public are barred from this area.' Out of his guise as the King, and close up, he looked every year of his age, his face lined and with the flush of the heavy drinker. A smell of stale cigarette smoke hung about him, and little drifts of ash had settled on the front of his jumper.

'I'm here to help with sorting out the details of the tour,' I replied frostily. 'I'm looking for Wilson.'

For a second he looked non-plussed. 'Oh. Sorry. Yes, of course. He'll be on stage. That's where I'm going.'

'I looked there,' I said.

'He'll have used the back stairs,' Cormac said. He

appeared sorry for his earlier lack of grace, saying, 'Follow me.'

In silence I trotted along behind him to the theatre. I wasn't in the mood to make conversation, being too busy thinking what I'd say to Wilson. There was no easy way to tell him that the arrangements for the tour he thought Valeria had put in place were not, as he'd suggested, in the large box on her desk. The only possibility was that the police had taken her computer and, contrary to Wilson's belief, she hadn't downloaded everything.

There was a buzz of activity on stage: the cast were in the middle of the scene where the Wicked Fairy, Somnia, lays a curse on the infant Princess Beauty because she hasn't been invited to the christening, a scene which involved most of the actors except Prince Florizel and his faithful friend Rudolph. Lucian was standing in the wings, holding his script but of Joel there was no sign.

I didn't want to interrupt Wilson, who appeared flustered and anxious as he directed the actors, so I crept down to take a seat in the auditorium and watch the proceedings on stage.

But Cormac was in trouble.

'Where have you been?' Wilson gestured Cormac into position. 'We've been waiting for you to finish blocking this scene.' He leaned towards the actor, sniffed, then frowned. 'This is one of the scenes where you do have some lines to say. I'd have thought you'd be eager to be here on time.'

Cormac mumbled a reply I couldn't hear as he slouched over to stand behind the cradle supposedly holding the infant Princess Beauty.

This rehearsal went slowly and there were several interruptions where one or other of the actors appeared uncertain about their lines. What's more, Cormac missed several of his blockings on stage and then fluffed an important cue.

'You have to come down centre stage when Rhoda appears,' Wilson said, a note of frustration in his voice.

Rhoda rolled her eyes. 'Thank goodness there will be a Prompt for the performance,' I heard her say and I suspected she wanted to be overheard as she continued, 'The King has been having a pre-prandial or two, I guess.'

Cormac ignored Wilson's anger. 'It's a lot easier when you have a proper part,' he snarled.

A commotion at the side of the stage brought the rehearsal to a halt and Joel appeared dressed in the costume of Prince Florizel, though I noticed he wasn't made up. There was a sulky look on his face. 'I don't understand why I can't be in this scene,' he said.

Though I knew little about him, I could see that even when he wasn't involved in the action, he made sure the rest of the cast were aware of his seething resentment.

'Because,' Wilson said patiently, 'it would make nonsense of the story. How could the Prince be at the christening of Princess Beauty?'

Joel wasn't satisfied. 'It's only a story. My being at the christening is no more ridiculous than the Prince kissing a hundred-year-old woman.'

Wilson shook his head, then said, 'Why are you in costume? This is only a rehearsal. And you're not due on stage until later.'

Rhoda coughed to disguise a titter. The annoying Joel being taken down a peg or two pleased the other members of the cast.

Joel showed no sign of being intimidated. 'I'm about to be interviewed by one of the Nationals,' he said, 'and I considered it appropriate to be dressed as the part I'm playing. I'd have thought you'd be grateful for the publicity.'

'Why have you arranged an interview? All such requests have to come through me,' Wilson said through gritted teeth, 'and…'

Joel didn't wait for the rest of Wilson's reply, stomping off muttering, 'It's me the audience want to see. This production would be nothing without me,' as Wilson called after him, 'You may well have to be in this scene after all. We might have to ask everyone to double up as courtiers if the stage looks too bare…' But if Joel heard, he gave no sign.

Wilson grunted, turning his attention to Benita who was tugging at his sleeve.

'I don't know why you have to keep changing the script,' Benita said. 'It confuses everyone.'

Wilson could scarcely conceal his anger as he moved to stand close beside Benita. 'I haven't done much cutting of your role,' he said. 'As the Fairy Godmother you've one of the biggest parts in the pantomime.'

Benita stood her ground. 'Yes, I appreciate that,' she said. 'But we're a team and everyone's part is important.'

There was a murmur of agreement from the other actors, and I had to concur with her, though there was no way I'd comment. A glance at my watch showed it wouldn't be long till the next performance. Why was Wilson messing about with the script at the last minute?

There was no opportunity to talk to him now. The stage had to be set up, the actors costumed and made up. That took time in normal circumstances, but with a pantomime where there were so many elaborate costumes, this took longer than usual.

Deciding a better plan would be to lock up Valeria's office and tackle Wilson in the morning, I slipped out through the side exit without a word. There was no point in waiting here.

EIGHT

The more I saw of Wilson, the more ineffectual I judged him to be. Simon's management course hadn't made much impression on him.

Even if Valeria had made most of the bookings online, there would be receipts or other items in the box. I had to find a way of checking out her computer.

With my mind on the puzzle of Valeria's arrangements for the tour, at first it didn't register when I drew up on the road outside the cottage behind a van labelled Handy House Repairs.

Simon was in the hallway in conversation with a tall, burly man I didn't recognise. He had the ruddy appearance of someone who worked outdoors, his sparse hair standing up in little tufts, his ample belly straining over the too-tight belt of his faded jeans.

'This is Benny,' Simon said. 'He's come to give us an estimate for the work in the living room.'

Benny nodded, then said sorrowfully, twisting his calloused hands, 'Right mess you've got there, Mrs Cameron. Terrible that the previous owners would have left the room in such a state. You don't want to go tampering with these things if you don't know about them. It's not safe. Still, there's no accounting for people, is there?'

Trying to stifle my laughter, I couldn't help but notice Simon was avoiding my gaze.

'And,' Benny said, 'while we're at it, I'd advise you

to get rid of that old panelling on the walls. It's a fire hazard apart from anything else. It'll be a simple matter to strip the lot and put on a new coat of plaster.'

'This wasn't something we'd considered,' Simon said. 'But it seems a good idea to have everything done at the same time.'

Benny pulled a baseball cap from his pocket and rammed it on his head back to front, saying, 'I'll send that estimate through and you can let me know. I've had a cancellation next week, so I can fit you in then. I'd sue those people you bought the place from. I can give you the number of a local lawyer if you need it.'

And with a nod he walked past me and out to his van, muttering to himself.

Before I could speak, Simon raised a hand. 'Don't ask. I decided this morning that if we're to be living here for a while the sooner we get the place into order the better. I ran into Max in The Golfers Bar a couple of nights ago and he gave me Benny's number. I decided I'd follow it up, but I didn't think it would come to anything. Just a bit of luck that Benny could help.'

'What was that story about the previous owners?'

Simon gave a nervous laugh. 'Benny assumed that we'd inherited the problem from the previous owners, and I didn't disabuse him of the idea.'

No point in reminding him, even in jest, he'd caused the mess. I was glad the room would soon be habitable. 'Thank goodness. Unless the cost is prohibitive, I suggest we go ahead while Benny's available, given the difficulties of finding a tradesman.'

'Even better, Benny's brother is a painter and will do that part of the work. Hopefully by the end of next week the room should be ready. Benny seems confident that he can do it in the timescale, with the room being so small.' There was a note of relief in Simon's voice.

I sighed. 'It will be good to relax in the evenings in a comfortable room.'

Changing the subject, Simon said, 'How did you get on at the theatre company?'

'Let's go through to the kitchen and have a cup of tea while I tell you.'

Simon was as surprised as I was about the story of Valeria's box. 'You're right. She must have everything on the computer. Unless she had the receipts, and someone has taken them. But who would be interested in doing that?' he said.

'No idea. And as there's no record of anything other than the arrangements for Bute, I've no way of knowing. I'm pinning my hopes on the information being in her computer. Wilson seemed to think she liked to keep a hard copy of everything, but he may well be wrong.'

'And what did Wilson say when you told him about the problem?'

'I didn't have the chance to ask him,' I admitted. 'He was busy trying to sort out the script.'

Simon looked puzzled. 'But the show is already underway. They've given the first performance. Why would he be doing that, messing with the script?'

'No idea. But I think one of the reasons might be that he considers the running time too long and is cutting some of the lines. I'll speak to him tomorrow, but I'm not looking forward to it.'

Just then my mobile rang. It took me a few minutes to find it in the depths of my handbag by which time the call had gone to voicemail. It was Rhoda.

‘I wonder what that was about,’ I said, checking my voicemail, but she’d only left the briefest of messages. Ringing her back proved unsuccessful but I did leave a response to let her know I’d picked up her call. Probably she’d switched off while getting ready for the evening’s performance.

‘How did she get my number?’ I said.

‘Probably from Wilson,’ Simon said.

But I couldn’t imagine why she would phone me. Something else that would have to wait till the next morning.

NINE

I managed to catch up with Wilson by going along to the Hall early the next morning, but Rhoda wasn't around.

The weather had turned again, and an easterly wind had sprung up. I popped into the Co-op in Guildford Square to buy a newspaper and a coffee from the machine.

'Cold, isn't it?' I said as I handed over my money to the girl at the checkout.

'Might snow,' she said, glancing out of the window. 'People think because there are palm trees on Bute that it's a Mediterranean climate, but they're Cabbage Palm trees, native to New Zealand, quite a different variety.'

Something else I'd learned, and I set off for the Hall contemplating the prospect of a white Christmas.

Wilson was sitting in the front row of the auditorium, absorbed in going through the script with a red pen and I coughed loudly to attract his attention.

'Mmm,' he said as I tried to explain what I'd found, or rather not found, in the box in Valeria's office. 'I don't understand that. There should have been some receipts at least.'

'Yes, that's what I expected,' I said. 'I know you said she liked hard copy, but almost everything is booked online these days. Strange that there's no computer in her office. Surely she had a PC or a laptop?'

'Yes.' He looked as if he was expecting me to ask another question. When I remained silent, he said, 'The police took it.'

'Really?' Even stranger. 'Why would the police do that?' This was what I'd expected but I wanted to find out if there was a particular reason for doing so.

'To make sure, I expect. A sudden death… you know…' His voice became a whisper. 'They wanted to check her online activity.'

'You mean the police don't think her death was an accident?'

He crossed his arms. 'I'm sure it's no more than a precaution. They have to go through all her contacts. But it's not relevant. As I told you, she always liked a hard copy. We had some disagreements about that, but I suppose it was her way of keeping track of all the payments for each venue. Those must be somewhere.' He stood up, flexing his back. 'I'll have to get on, Alison. I'm sure if you have another look, you'll find the information is somewhere in the office, if not in the box.'

'I'll check again, but I've looked everywhere in her office,' I said, doubting a second search would reveal any more than the first one. Then it occurred to me. Perhaps there was a reason why he was so distracted. 'How was last night?' I asked.

He looked down at the script, avoiding my gaze. 'Okay, I guess. But there are still a few glitches to sort out. I might have to reconsider Cormac's part as the King. He's made such a fuss I'm not looking forward to telling him. But I don't know where else I can cut. The King is the least important part in the pantomime.'

He seemed to recollect himself and sighed. 'I'll work on it this morning, but there's not much time.

There's a matinee this afternoon. I might have to leave things today. We've a few days spare before we perform on Arran.' He frowned. 'Anyway, that's my problem. What were you saying, Alison?'

Again I went over what had happened when I investigated Valeria's box and searched the room. This time he registered what I said, though he was as much annoyed as mystified.

I could tell Wilson's mind was still on the problems of the pantomime script and my dilemma was an unwelcome intrusion.

'Can't you sort it out?' he said, biting his thumb nail. 'I've enough to be going on with here.'

'I don't see how. There's nothing to go on. I've looked everywhere.'

'But everything was paid for through the theatre expenses account. It should all have been perfectly straightforward,' he said at last.

'And did Valeria deal with that?' He must know something of how the arrangements were made.

'Yes, she was the person in charge of the expenses account. She and Phil were the signatories.' He stopped. 'Damn…that's something else I'll have to sort out.' He sighed. 'I'd nothing to do with that part of the business. My job is busy enough without becoming involved in other people's responsibilities.' He sounded defensive and suddenly I felt sorry for him.

Action was needed and soon. 'The best thing is to check the bank account, see what was paid out and when.' Without that information there was nothing we could do.

'Okay.' Wilson scratched his head.

'You can access the online account, can't you?'

Was this another problem?

‘I’m not sure. Valeria had the password.’ He looked embarrassed. ‘I did know it at one time…’ He coughed.

‘Well, Phil will know it if he was the other signatory.’

Wilson frowned. ‘I’ll ask him, but I’m not certain. As far as I know all he did was sign cheques where necessary and there aren’t many of those nowadays. Most payments were done through the BACS system. We left all that to Valeria.’

That seemed ridiculous. ‘You mean she was the only person who knew how to access the account?’

‘I’m sure she’ll have kept the password somewhere safe,’ he said. ‘Perhaps in her diary. I’ll have to contact the police and explain the problem. They’ve taken everything.’

‘I’ll leave that with you,’ I said. ‘As long as you can give me the bank statements, I can tie up what she spent money on. I’m assuming the main account is in the black?’

‘Of course.’ Wilson looked affronted at this suggestion. ‘We had a start-up grant this year. That’s why I can’t understand what’s going on. She must have another box with all the information.’ He looked more cheerful. ‘Yes, that’s it.’

As I’d searched the tiny room twice over, I wasn’t convinced. I said, ‘Let me know when you’ve checked the expenses account and downloaded copies of the bank statements.’ Then as he stood up to leave, I said, ‘Do you have a detailed copy of the itinerary? It would be helpful to have a look at that in the meantime. The one in the box was scrappy.’

Before he could reply, there was the sound of a commotion at the back of the auditorium and Joel came rushing down, waving his script.

‘What’s this all about?’ he shouted, his face suffused with rage. ‘Why are you cutting my lines?’

Wilson took a step back. ‘I had… it was…’ he stuttered but Joel was in no mood to let him finish.

Eyes bulging, Joel moved closer. ‘I’m the star of this show. I’ve taken a huge drop in salary to be here. I did it as a favour to you.’

Wilson took a deep breath, seeming to assert himself. ‘It’s only a couple of lines, Joel. I’ve had to cut most people. That seemed the fairest way to do it. The first night overran and even with cuts it was still too long. We can’t do that.’

Joel looked far from satisfied with this response. ‘You should have sorted that out before we started. This is hopeless, Wilson. Why I ever agreed to become involved in this amateur production I’ve no idea.’

All credit to the Director. He stood his ground in the light of Joel’s anger, though I could see him clench his hands behind his back. ‘You have to understand everything here is being done on a tight budget. You always knew there would have to be changes.’

‘Just make sure there are no more cuts to my part,’ Joel said, stomping off up the aisle and slamming the door behind him.

We sat in silence for a minute before Wilson said with a nervous laugh, ‘He always did have a bit of a temper.’

I made no comment. I’d enough to do without becoming involved in Wilson’s spat with the cast. If it were true that he was continuing to cut most parts, Joel wouldn’t be the last person to question his decision.

‘Returning to the subject of Valeria’s box,’ I said, trying to distract him from the problem with Joel, ‘I can't do anything till you check with the bank. Meantime if I could have a copy of the full itinerary?'

He looked blank, then said, 'Oh, of course. Come along and I'll give you that now.' He stood up awkwardly, grimacing as he did. 'Sorry, wrenched my ankle. I tripped the other day.'

If he expected me to feel sorry for him, he was wrong. 'Let's get that itinerary,' I said.

I followed him to the room he used as his office, the first one in the corridor at the main entrance.

I've seen many rooms in a state of disorder in my time, but this was the worst ever. Considering this was a temporary office and that the company would be moving on in a few days, I marvelled that Wilson could create so much chaos in a short time. It was a much bigger room than mine, or rather Valeria's, with the luxury of a filing cabinet, a proper office chair and desk and a comfy seat beside a low table. Everywhere was strewn with papers, books and newspapers.

The top drawer of the filing cabinet lay half open, and several empty coffee cups sat on the low table beside a box containing what looked like clumps of hair. Then I chuckled. Of course, these were some of the wigs used in the production. A second box held a variety of objects which didn't look as if they'd be used in this production: several swords, a couple of guns, an embossed shield, and a toy monkey.

'Sorry about the mess,' Wilson said, tossing his jacket over the back of the chair and rolling up his sleeves as he sat down at his desk. Pushing aside a pile of scripts, he said, 'I don't have time to keep the place clear.' He gestured to the box. 'And as though there's not enough to do, some of the cast are complaining about the wigs being uncomfortable. As if I can find replacements at this late stage.'

It was little wonder everything was in such a mess if this was the way he organised his private space.

He opened the top drawer of the desk and scrabbled around for a bit before pulling out a pile of papers. 'Ah, here it is,' he said, waving one of the sheets triumphantly. 'I knew I had a copy.'

He passed it over to me before opening up his laptop and logging on, frowning in concentration.

'I thought you didn't have the password?' I said.

Wilson's face grew red. 'I did have it at one time, but as Valeria dealt with all that, I'm not sure I can remember it.'

He bent over the computer, gnawing at his bottom lip as I glanced at the itinerary he'd given me. It told me little more than the couple of papers I'd found in Valeria's box.

Although I couldn't see what he was doing, I guessed he was trying several passwords. This might take a while, if not forever. I lifted the pile of newspapers from the seat beside the low table and put them on the floor, noticing the top one had an article circled in red. I glanced at it as Wilson became increasingly frustrated with his attempts to access the bank account, muttering to himself from time to time.

The article was a review of The Mickle's last performance – a play written by Wilson called A Fine Inheritance. It would appear this critic from a well-known Scottish newspaper had been less than enthralled with the production. The script was described as "thin and poorly plotted," while the only member of the cast to receive favourable comments was Rhoda Hunter. Ah, that explained the move to pantomime and the inclusion of Joel Bennett. A chance to retrieve the fortunes of the company.

Aware suddenly that Wilson was on his feet, I dropped the paper beside the others. ‘Did you manage to access the account?’

‘No, I bloody well didn’t,’ he said. ‘I’ll have to find Phil and hope he’s remembered the password.’ My question had clearly irked him, revealed how little he took to do with the day-to-day workings of the company.

What could I say? If Phil didn’t remember the password, I didn’t see how we could understand how Valeria’s system worked...if it did. Then I had an idea. ‘I could check with CalMac about the bookings. They’ll have a record and if I explain the situation they might be willing to help. How would Valeria have booked the accommodation? Would she have used the Tourist Board site, Visit Scotland?’

‘No idea,’ Wilson said, ‘but it’s worth a try. If all else fails I’ll have to make a trip to the mainland to talk to the bank.’

‘Don’t worry, I’ll make a start on finding out about the ferries.’

‘Yes, I have to prepare for this afternoon’s performance. No doubt there will be more complaints from other members of the cast once the word spreads about the cuts. I’d hoped to get to them beforehand. Now Joel will have stirred everyone up.’

I couldn’t help with that, and I shrugged as I left him to go back to the office and start on the search, reflecting on how stupid a system it was that allowed only one person in the company to have access to a bank account. Or at least that only one person knew the password.

TEN

Following my discussion with Wilson, I spent the rest of the morning on the phone, trying to locate the details of the ferry trips to the other islands and find out what accommodation had been booked on each of them.

Shirley at the CalMac head office did her best to be helpful. You didn't have to book the ferry to Bute and the receipts for the ferry crossing were in the box. With Arran and the other islands I drew a blank. There was no information to tell me when Valeria had booked, and I had to make a guess from the list of venues and the dates the company would be performing.

'Let me check what we have,' Shirley said.

I waited patiently, listening to the click of the computer mouse and the rustle of paper until finally, 'I'm sorry,' she said, 'I've checked everything twice and there's no record of ferry bookings for The Mickle to any of the islands you mentioned. I've looked as far as the end of January, but there's nothing.'

Thanking her, I rang off and sat staring at the itinerary Wilson had provided. Perhaps Valeria had wrongly assumed that being winter there was no need to book in advance? Yet that was an odd assumption. Bute was one of the few islands where booking wasn't necessary. And if she'd decided to wait until arriving on Bute before booking the next stage of the trip, that was unwise. Lots of people would be travelling to visit family and friends at Christmas and New Year, and this was the busiest time of winter.

Having failed to find information about the ferry crossings, I turned my attention to the issue of the accommodation. As the theatre company was on a tight budget, whatever Valeria had booked was likely to be at the cheaper end of what was available. The actors and Wilson were staying in The Four Winds Hotel on Bute, offering a basic level of comfort, and I guessed Valeria would have opted for similar lodgings on the other islands.

Not that this hotel pleased everyone. 'You expect a hot breakfast at this time of year,' I'd heard Joel complain to Wilson. 'Fruit juice, cereal and cold milk doesn't cut it.' But then Joel complained a lot… about everything.

I checked the Visit Bute website to find out what the charges were for The Four Winds. That would give me a start to compare what might be available at much the same price on the other islands. I decided to begin with Arran, as that was the next venue after Bute, but to my surprise there weren't as many possibilities as I'd expected.

It was a laborious process. First of all, I tried the Arran Arts and Theatre Trust to make a list of places the company might stage the pantomime. From their website, I guessed the Brodick Town Hall would be first choice and then I had to try possible places, mostly Bed and Breakfast, where the cast might stay. I was sure Wilson would want everyone to be near the theatre, so I concentrated my search round West Mayish and Manse Road.

Then I had to rank them in order. The cast would

want if possible to be accommodated together and some of the establishments were little more than family-owned homes where a couple of rooms were let out. Others were closed over the winter months. Finally I was left with a list of three possibilities: The Angler's Rest, Tign-na-bru and Home from Home.

I started with Home from Home. The owner was pleasant but quickly assured me she'd had no contact with anyone from The Mickle. My phone call to Tign-na-bru was equally fruitless. The owners were listed as a Mr and Mrs MacDonald but when I phoned there was a surprise. The hotel might have a Gaelic name but the accent of the person I spoke to was Eastern European.

'Not easy to understand,' he said. 'Repeat, please.'

I went through the details once more, pausing from time to time to make sure he understood. It was a complicated story.

'It cannot be they would book here,' he said. 'My wife is not here to help you. We have just bought the property. It closed now for making it better before the summertime. If you call back later she will explain.'

I thanked him and looked at the last one on my list – The Angler's Rest. If this didn't work out, I'd have to start again with those in the next price range up. What had been a part-time job to help Wilson over a difficult period was turning into a full-time task.

With a heavy feeling I dialled the number and waited. The phone rang and rang and I was about to replace the receiver when it was picked up at the other end and a breathless voice said, 'Yes, yes.' Then as though recollecting there was a formula, the voice added, 'The Angler's Rest here. How can I help?'

Mindful of my last phone call, I spoke slowly and

carefully by which time the owner of the voice seemed to be less breathless.

'So sorry,' she said. 'I was out in the garage, and I thought my husband would pick up. I'm Kay Norrison.'

There was a pause before she said, 'I don't recognise the name, but let me check the bookings register. We are fully booked for the Christmas season and I'm sure I'd remember if there was a large group here.'

I heard her put the receiver down and her footsteps echo as she scurried off.

A few minutes later she returned, saying, 'There's no one of that name booked in next week. Let me look back. But reservations are taken by myself or my husband.' Another pause as I heard the click of the computer mouse.

'Mmm. That's strange. There was a provisional booking made, but it was never followed up. A woman called Valeria Dixon called us in late October enquiring about rooms. We keep details of all enquiries – at a slack time we can email out with a special offer. It works well and we've had several…'

I cut in, 'Do you remember what Valeria asked?'

'Yes, I do. She wanted detailed information – what each room cost, how many the hotel could take, what the menus were like, what additional costs there might be. I was sure she intended to make a block booking, but nothing came of it. I did warn her that she would have to confirm in good time, because not everywhere on the island stays open at this time of year and we can be busy.'

'And that was the last you heard from her?'

'I did try contacting her when there was no booking confirmation by the beginning of November. We're a small business and while such a large group would have taken all the rooms in the hotel, we couldn't afford to hold them longer. I phoned her a couple of times, but it went straight to voicemail.'

There was nothing else Kay could tell me, and I thanked her and rang off. Here was indeed a mystery. Arran was the next stop on the tour. If Valeria hadn't booked the ferry tickets or the accommodation, this would be discovered as soon as the Bute run was over. How did she intend to deal with that?

My guess must be correct: her plan was to leave it till the last minute and book immediately before leaving Bute. But that wouldn't have worked. There would be no guarantee that there would be ferry availability and from what Kay Norrison said, accommodation on Arran would be scarce at this time of year.

There was nothing else for it. I'd have to wait until Wilson had either obtained the password from Phil or the information from the bank account before exploring the ferries and accommodation on the other islands. After drawing a blank with Arran, there was little chance I'd have success with the other islands.

What had Valeria been up to? She must have known the situation would be discovered quickly as soon as the Bute tour was over. I could think of no explanation for her behaviour. Unless, as The Mickle was such a small company, there were money problems. What had started out as a simple task was becoming more complicated.

ELEVEN

Amid the concerns about the travel arrangements I'd forgotten the phone call from Rhoda. On the way back from buying a sandwich for lunch, I bumped into her in the entrance hall. At first I couldn't think what she meant when she said, 'Ah, Alison. I've been trying to catch up with you.'

She glanced around, moved nearer and said in a low voice, 'Valeria had problems.'

When I didn't respond, she said with a note of triumph in her voice, 'I know what she was up to.' She stopped and stood looking at me, a wry smile on her face.

Torn between curiosity and a desire not to be involved in gossip, curiosity won. 'And that was…?' I said.

'There was something strange going on with her and Phil. They were always together, whispering. And the day before she died I caught her having an argument with him. You know how tiny that office she was using is. She never closed the door. We'd all been dismissed for the day after Wilson had spent hours reblocking a couple of the scenes, but I'd forgotten my scarf and as I passed the office to go back to my dressing room, I heard them going at it hammer and tongs. I think it was something to do with Wilson.' She laughed, then changed it to a cough as she saw the look on my face. Why was Rhoda telling me?

‘I guess Wilson has fallen out with most members of the company,’ I said, wondering how she expected me to respond. ‘I’m sure the way he keeps changing the script doesn’t go down well. Perhaps that was the cause of the disagreement?’

‘Yes, I know there have been lots of issues about alterations to the script, but this sounded different. Surely if it was about that, they’d be arguing with Wilson, not each other.’

‘And did you hear what it was about?’

‘I couldn’t hear much,’ she said slowly, then more quickly, ‘It was something to do with Phil being angry with Valeria for something she’d done. But I couldn’t catch the details. It must have been about the arrangements for the tour.’

‘And do you think it was serious?’

She shrugged, ‘Anything is…’

Just then, there was the sound of footsteps on the stairs and Joel came bounding down. He stopped when he saw us.

‘A little break for a gossip, ladies?’ he said. Then to Rhoda. ‘You’re wanted in the theatre. Wilson has decided he’s not happy with the roll out of the changes to the script. He frowned. ‘Though I told him what to do with his script if he tried to cut my lines again. Good luck, Rhoda.’

Rhoda made a face. ‘I was on my way into town to buy the local paper, see if there was anything about the company in it.’ She sighed. ‘A decent review perhaps.’

‘Later, later. Wilson must be obeyed,’ Joel said, smirking.

Muttering to herself, Rhoda turned to go back upstairs, leaving me to follow her slowly, pondering what she’d said. So there had been an argument and it sounded (if what Rhoda told me was true) as if Phil had had concerns previously about the arrangements for the tour. Was it true? Or was Rhoda exaggerating? After all, she'd admitted she'd only heard part of the conversation.

This rehearsal couldn't have taken long, and Wilson appeared sooner than expected. The news wasn't good. I was sitting in Valeria's office (I refused to own it by calling it mine), eating my sandwich when he came rushing in, clutching a folder.

'I can't understand it,' he said, shaking his head and setting his mop of hair bouncing. 'There must be some mistake.'

After my recent investigations of the CalMac ferries and the hotels on Arran, I suspected what the answer might be.

'I've managed to get access and it would appear,' he said, 'there is almost no money in the expenses account.'

'Is it a separate account then?'

'What?' Wilson looked as if he hadn't understood the question. Then he frowned. 'Oh, yes. We decided that would be a good way to do it. Separate the money for expenses so that Valeria could go ahead and book everything with Phil as a co-signatory, though from what he's said all he ever did was sign the occasional cheque. The main account is different and has to have the signatures of two of the three authorised persons.'

'And who were they?'

'Me, Valeria and Phil.'

'Isn't that unusual? Phil is just a member of the cast, surely?'

'Yes, but that hasn't stopped him interfering.'

'And how much was in the expenses account?'

‘Thirty-five thousand was what we allocated. I thought it was rather a lot, but Valeria persuaded me it would be easier that way and as most of the money was in the main account…’ His voice trailed off. Seemingly recollecting himself, he looked around as if for somewhere to sit and being unsuccessful, perched on the end of the desk while pulling out a sheaf of papers from the folder he carried.

‘Look at this,’ he said. ‘Valeria made regular withdrawals over the past year. So where is the money if it wasn’t spent on travel and accommodation?’

‘If it was a grant, surely you had to make regular financial returns?’

Wilson shook his head. ‘Yes, but I dealt with that. Valeria only had access to the money for expenses. It was a great help that there was a loan from Sir Donald McDilgenson. You’ll have heard of him.’

‘Nooo…’I ventured.

‘He was always interested in the theatre, backed a lot of productions. I met him several times when I was a young actor, and he took a shine to me. To be honest I was astonished when he agreed to put in money to help fund The Mickle.’

‘I can understand that,’ I said, ‘but was it only for the pantomime?’

‘Yes,’ Wilson said gloomily. ‘And this business is a headache. Oh, Sir Donald was generous, but he’ll want to see a return for his money. The idea was that he would fund us for the tour expenses but receive twenty-five per cent of the profits until the money was repaid.’

‘But the pantomime isn’t the first play you’ve staged?’ I thought about the review I’d seen lying on top of the pile of papers.

Wilson avoided looking at me directly as he said, 'No, we started off with A Fine Inheritance – but it wasn't successful.' He looked even more dejected if that was possible. 'In fact it was a flop. That's why we decided to put on a pantomime. A much better opportunity to make a profit.'

There had been a full house for the first performance of Sleeping Beauty, but even if that continued in the remaining venues, the costs of a travelling pantomime would be much greater than one staged in a single location. Better not to add to Wilson's distress by pointing this out. I concentrated on the bank statements he'd thrust before me.

Yes, there it was in detail – regular withdrawals from the expenses account, starting within a month of the account being set up.

'And you're sure Valeria made every one of these withdrawals?' I said.

'Yes, she'd set up a separate password. Although he tried every combination possible, Phil couldn't remember it. Then it came to me. We'd been talking about it one day and I'd scribbled it down on the back of an old theatre programme.'

This seemed foolish but then from what I'd learned I shouldn't have been surprised. We were always being warned about keeping passwords secure, but Wilson had demonstrated how disorganised he was.

Uncertain about what Wilson expected me to say, I made some conciliatory noises. But there was no way around it. The expenses bank account was almost empty and there was nothing to show what the money had been spent on.

It was looking more and more as if Valeria's death hadn't been an accident.

TWELVE

Wilson refused to believe Valeria had been stealing from the company. The difficulty was there was no way of accessing Valeria's own bank account while the police investigation was underway and I could tell this worried him.

He seemed to know little about her. 'I'm sure she mentioned a sister somewhere,' he said when I asked. He kept biting his lip and he'd good reason to worry – it was incredibly reckless to entrust the expense account to one person, even if the company was small.

'You must know something about her background if you hired her,' I said.

'She was recommended by Phil,' he muttered. 'He said she was someone he'd known for a long time, had lots of admin experience. He'd worked with her on several productions.'

'You'll have to talk to Phil, tell him what you've found out,' I said. 'From what you've said, he knew her well. And Phil has to take some responsibility for this. Valeria shouldn't have been allowed to be the only person dealing with this account. That seems unwise.'

Reluctant as he appeared, Wilson had to agree but, 'Not immediately,' he said, avoiding looking at me. 'I'll wait until tonight's performance is over. This one is by special invitation only. The audience will mostly be adults so we should be able to have a better idea of the running time.' Without constant interruptions from Joel Bennett's fans, I thought.

My plan was to go home. There was nothing I could do at the theatre meantime. Once the money situation was clearer, I might be able to sort out the arrangements for the remainder of the tour. Then again if there was no money, there was no possibility of booking the ferries and the accommodation.

The weather, though cold, was now bright and sunny with clear blue skies. Ideal for a brisk walk, especially as it had been some time since Simon and I had been on Bute together on holiday. Now with a place of our own there were opportunities to walk those island routes we'd promised ourselves on previous trips. If the weather permitted.

As I left, Wilson caught me by the elbow. 'You'll be here for the performance tonight, Alison, won't you?'

'I hadn't planned to,' I said, wondering what Simon's response would be if I were to disappear off to the Hall yet again. Still, he was the person who'd been responsible for my involvement, and I did feel sorry for Wilson, now trying to keep the show together on his own.

'Okay,' I said, 'but I won't stay for the whole performance. I'll try to persuade Simon to come with me and then we'll go on somewhere to eat. We can leave at the interval.'

Wilson seemed happy with this arrangement. 'It'll give you a better understanding of how the company works.'

'And tomorrow we'll discuss the ferry and the accommodation for Arran,' I added. 'Once you've spoken to the police about Valeria's bank account.'

'Yes, yes, fine.' With his mind on other matters, my

suspicion was he'd pushed the issue of the bank account to the bottom of his list.

As it happened, Simon understood the problem perfectly. 'They'll be leaving Bute later this week,' he said, 'and after that it won't be your responsibility, no matter what.'

We arrived early, squeezing into a couple of spare seats at the back Wilson had reserved for us. I was rather excited to see the pantomime again, find out if the script changes Wilson had made had improved the show.

We settled back as the lights went down, the loud chatter around us fading to a whisper and then silence except for the rustle of sweet papers and sounds of excitement from a group of girls in the front row, in expectation of Joel's appearance.

I'd a strong suspicion they were the same teenagers we'd seen on the first night, that they might be here for every performance and given what Wilson had said about an invited audience, I wondered how they'd managed to sneak in.

Immediately it was clear that Wilson's decision to shorten some of the scenes was working well. Although Muddles still introduced the pantomime as in the original script, we were soon into the scene at the castle and the christening of Princess Beauty. This was one of the most lavish sets in the performance and whatever economies had been made elsewhere, money had been spent here in recreating the court of the King and the Queen with a vivid backdrop and elaborate furnishings. The thrones the King and the Queen sat on were highly ornate and gilded, decorated with fairy lights to make them sparkle in the tiny spotlights strategically placed around the stage.

There was a gasp from the audience when the main lights came up and the full scene was revealed: below the King and the Queen on their thrones the courtiers' colourful robes covered in sequins caught the light whenever one of them moved. Wilson's insistence on exact blocking had paid off.

All the actors had more than one role in this production, and I spied Joel Bennett costumed as one of the courtiers. From the look on his face I guessed he wasn't happy about having to appear in a scene where he wasn't the star. The fans in the audience spotted him though, and there was a satisfied smirk on his face as they made their devotion felt, much to the annoyance of a group of elderly women in the row behind them. On several occasions Joel made a move to upstage whoever was speaking. A way to make himself even more unpopular with the other members of the cast.

Phil as Dame Nelly was in the most spectacular costume of all, and I marvelled how he could so easily move about the stage given the enormous hooped skirt and extravagant wig he was wearing.

'I'm not sure Wilson will be happy with this,' I whispered to Simon. 'With Joel scene stealing.'

'Not much he can do about it,' Simon muttered. 'And I guess,' he added, confirming my suspicions, 'that those fans were here last time.'

Even so. I turned back to what was happening on stage. The Fairy Godmother was proclaiming her many gifts for the infant Beauty with much waving of her magic wand and sprinkling of glitter everywhere.

As she finished, bowing to the King with elaborate ceremony, we waited for the evil fairy Somnia to appear and put a spell on Beauty. No matter how well you knew the story, how often you'd seen the pantomime, there was still a thrill of anticipation at what might happen next.

But firstly Cormac, unrecognisable in his costume as The King, stepped down from his throne and came forward. 'Time to toast Princess Beauty,' he said. 'And wish my daughter long life and happiness.'

Joel went over to a side table and picked up a tray with several silver goblets before coming over, bowing low, and presenting it to Cormac with a great flourish. Even in the simplest of roles, Joel couldn't help trying to steal the scene.

'We must salute our lovely daughter,' Cormac said. There was a moment's hesitation as he appeared to be undecided which goblet to choose, then picking up one in the middle he lifted it high into the air. 'Come, everyone, drink to the health of Beauty. Wish her a long and happy life.'

The remaining members of the cast jostled forward to pick up a goblet as instructed. It looked as if this part of the scene hadn't been blocked well and two of the actors bumped into each other, spilling their drinks.

Cormac lifted his goblet high again before tossing off his drink in one swift movement. Then, as the courtiers were milling around, offering their gifts to the baby, he staggered suddenly, clutching at the table for support.

A few moments later he seemed to recover and began to speak, 'We come…' he paused and staggered again. 'We are here…'

At that moment, there was a clap of thunder and Rhoda, the evil fairy Somnia, arrived from the side of the stage in a cloud of thick smoke. Whoever was creating the smoke was a little too enthusiastic. It became increasingly difficult to see the stage and several members of the cast started to cough loudly.

No one in the audience seemed to notice – perhaps they thought so much smoke for Rhoda's dramatic entrance was part of the performance.

They did notice what happened next, however.

As she came striding across the stage, swishing her black cloak in an exaggerated manner, the King began to lurch towards the front of the stage, before stumbling and clutching at his throat. With a loud thud he fell at Rhoda's feet.

THIRTEEN

A brief pause, a moment of complete silence before the audience realised Cormac's action wasn't part of the play. The smoke was only slowly dispersing, and it was difficult to make out what was happening on stage.

Wilson came rushing in from the wings. 'Give him air, give him air,' he shouted, and then the chaos was revealed.

What on earth had happened? Cormac had seemed perfectly fine delivering his lines earlier. If anything he'd been over passionate, waving his hands around as he spoke in a booming voice, possibly remembering his heyday as a Shakespearean actor.

Several members of the audience stood up, uncertain what to do next, and the noise level rose as the full impact of the events unfolding in front of them became clear.

Amid the increasing hubbub Wilson stepped out, flapping his hands and shouting, 'Get the bloody curtain down,' and after a few seconds it came down with a thump, cutting off our view, though we continued to hear the commotion.

'Perhaps I should go and…' I began to say, getting to my feet, but Simon pulled me back. 'Don't get involved. This is nothing to do with you.'

I sat down. He was right. The suddenness of Cormac's collapse could only have one explanation.

He hadn't fainted… his lack of any movement could only mean he'd had a heart attack. I thought back to the times I'd seen him – never without a cigarette dangling from his lips, a faint whiff of the whisky he favoured lingering about him.

'How old do you think Cormac is?' I whispered.

'What? What has that to do with anything, Alison.' Simon sounded bemused by my question.

At that moment the curtains parted, and an agitated Wilson strode onto the apron stage, wringing his hands.

'Ladies and Gentlemen,' he said, his voice choked, 'I'm sorry to announce that Cormac McDubh is ill. We're waiting for the ambulance and I'm afraid that means the performance will have to be cancelled. I hope you'll understand. The stewards will direct you out. Please follow their instructions and leave as quickly as possible.'

As he spoke several stewards appeared in the aisles beside us and began ushering us out, row by row. People left in silence, apart from a few mutterings, still stunned by what they'd witnessed.

'What's going on?' an elderly woman in front of us whispered to her companion. 'Did he faint?'

'Probably forgot his lines and created a distraction,' her friend said. Someone not impressed with the performance.

'Won't be a minute. Wait for me in the car,' I said as we came out into the foyer. Before Simon could stop me I ran to the back of the stage. I had to find out what was happening.

Most of the cast had disappeared and the stage was clear except for Cormac, lying where he'd fallen, covered with a rug from the stage set. Joel picked up the goblet Cormac been drinking from and placed it back on a nearby table as Wilson and Phil stood guard over the body.

'What are you doing here, Alison?' Wilson muttered as I approached. His glasses were perched on the end of his nose, and he kept pushing them up.

'Is there anything I can do to help?'

'Why would you think that?' Phil said. He'd taken off his wig and his heavily made-up face and bright costume gave him an incongruous air.

'We've sent everyone back to wait in their dressing rooms meantime,' Wilson said.

'But the ambulance is on its way,' I said, wondering why little effort was being made to help Cormac. But then he did look remarkably still.

Wilson said, 'There's nothing to be done, Alison. He's dead.'

Phil glared at him, no doubt cross Wilson had told me. On the other hand I could have worked this out for myself. Even so it was a shock.

'It must have been a massive heart attack,' I said. 'Not surprising, given his lifestyle.'

Wilson gave me a look I could only describe as shifty. 'That's probably what it was,' he said, but he didn't sound convinced. 'We'll have to wait for the police.'

About to say, 'The police?' I then remembered that as this was again a sudden death by law the police had to be called.

'Where's that bloody ambulance?' Joel came storming in.

'I thought I said everyone was to wait in their dressing rooms,' Wilson shouted.

'That's all fine for you…'

But Joel didn't get the chance to finish as there was noise from the auditorium and the ambulance men came rushing through and onto the stage, closely followed by a couple of police officers.

'Best if I leave,' I muttered, trying to sidle into the wings before they could see me.

Wilson didn't try to stop me. He was too busy explaining what had happened.

Suddenly I noticed Joel was right behind me as I hurried along the corridor to leave by the side door. 'He's no loss to the company, that Cormac,' he muttered.

'Why do you say that?' This was a callous comment to make at any time, but especially now.

'What?' Joel suddenly became aware I was there. 'Oh, he's…was…always complaining. Thought he should have had a bigger part. Rudolph perhaps, or even Prince Florizel.' This idea seemed to amuse him, and he chuckled loudly. 'He was well past his best – lucky to get a part at all. Wilson had to threaten him once or twice with being sacked if he didn't quit drinking.'

'He was a well-known actor in his day,' I said. I'd no reason to defend him as I scarcely knew him, but there was something about Joel that annoyed me.

'That was then. We'd even caught him having the odd sly drink on stage when he thought no one could see him. Anyway,' Joel said, pushing open the door where his name was prominently displayed, 'I'd better wait here as commanded. Wouldn't want to upset Wilson.' The way he spoke it sounded as if that would be the last thing to trouble him.

My first thought was that he'd already displeased Wilson on many occasions, but all I said was, 'Goodbye. Sorry this has happened.' I didn't add that Cormac's death so soon after Valeria's accident might well mean discontinuing the rest of the tour.

There was no point in lingering in the theatre. Simon and I were sure to be questioned by the police along with the rest of the audience, but right now all I wanted to do was go home and forget The Mickle and its problems.

That was easier said than done. Simon was waiting in the car, drumming his fingers on the steering wheel.

'What's going on?' he said as I climbed into the passenger seat.

'I'm not sure, but it looks as if Cormac might have had a massive heart attack. Wilson seems to think it's not a surprise, given his lifestyle.'

Simon grunted and started up the car but as we drove away and back to Port Bannatyne, I couldn't forget that scene on the stage. Surely there could be no other explanation for what had happened. Cormac's death had to be the result of a coronary. He had all the classic signs of someone with this waiting to happen: he was overweight, he smoked incessantly and, according to rumour, in his later years he'd started to drink more and more heavily. I thought about what Joel had said about Cormac even drinking on stage.

There was something niggling at me, somewhere in the recesses of my memory, but I couldn't for the life of me think what it was. I closed my eyes, trying to picture the scene of Princess Beauty's christening, remembering Joel stepping forward to offer Cormac the goblet to toast the Princess. Was it possible the goblet hadn't contained the usual stage prop of watered-down blackcurrant juice, but alcohol. It was no secret that he and Joel didn't get on. Joel might have thought substituting whisky for blackcurrant juice was a good joke.

Then I remembered Cormac's hesitation in selecting a drink. Could he have tampered with the tray, unable to perform without the help of alcohol?

The more I thought about it, the more I became convinced this hadn't been a heart attack. He'd have had some warning like severe chest pain. Though it was possible Cormac had been suffering but kept quiet, worried he might lose his part in the pantomime.

There was another possibility. But it was one I preferred not to dwell on.

FOURTEEN

When we arrived back at the cottage there was a message on the landline answering machine from Benny.

'You'll be glad to hear we can start on Monday, Mr Cameron,' he said after clearing his throat several times. 'And the painting can be done as well. The whole job will take about a week.'

Suddenly this didn't seem such a simple plan. Basic as the cottage was, having workmen in such a small space would be difficult, especially at this time of year.

'How will we manage to live here while the work is going on?' I said.

Simon scratched his head. 'I suppose we could move upstairs. And the kitchen is fine. It's only for a week.'

'He said "about a week" which could mean anything.' I'd more experience than Simon of workmen and I knew how much could go wrong in their timescale. I thought about the dust that would be generated with the false ceiling and the wall panelling coming down. It had been bad enough with the area Simon had tackled.

'What do you suggest?' Simon said as I followed him through to the kitchen. 'I suppose we could go over to the mainland. Do you think Deborah would be able to have us to stay for the week?'

'Unlikely.' Though my younger daughter had finally bought a property in Glasgow, it was a tiny flat, and not suitable for three adults. 'Besides,' I added, 'don't you think it would be a good idea to stay on the island? In case there are any questions? Any problems?'

'I suppose so,' Simon said, sounding glum. He took a couple of mugs from the cupboard and switched on the kettle.

'We could book in somewhere.' The last thing I wanted was to be at the cottage while the work was going on.

'Where do you suggest?' Simon sounded hesitant. 'Are you thinking it would be better to postpone the work till the better weather?'

'No,' I said. 'You know how busy the trades on the island are. And as soon as Spring approaches, Benny will be inundated with work. He's fitting us in because he has a cancellation.'

'Mmm.' Simon didn't sound convinced, and I hurried on, 'I'll make some enquiries about hotels. Not everywhere is open at this time of year, but there must be a few places available. We only need one room.'

Leaving him making a pot of coffee, I went upstairs to make the calls from my mobile. Finding accommodation might be difficult, remembering my experience with hotels on Arran. Only one way to find out.

The first few calls I made weren't promising. One hotel was closed, the second was full for the holiday season and there was no reply at the third.

I sat back, sighing. It looked as if I'd have to wait till the morning and go along to the Tourist Office at the Discovery Centre. Now that we'd started we had to find a way of having the work done. I'd no intention of cancelling Benny, determined to have a proper Christmas celebration in our new home.

Where else might be open and have rooms to rent? I'd only scored three off a list of twenty. Then I had an idea. The cast were staying at The Four Winds, and I was sure Rhoda had suggested the hotel wasn't full. Yes, that was it. 'The owner said she was glad to have us booked in as otherwise the hotel would be almost empty in the run-up to Christmas and New Year,' Rhoda had said.

Was The Four Winds a possibility? There was one problem. I wasn't sure how Simon would feel about staying in the same hotel as the cast of The Mickle, but it was only for a short time, I told myself. It was surely worthwhile putting up with a week in the same hotel as the actors. We didn't have to socialise with them. The alternative was to carry on going through the list of hotels, with no guarantee there would be vacancies.

I scrolled down to The Four Winds phone number, hoping that there would be at least one room spare. Then I had to persuade Simon this was the best option.

FIFTEEN

The phone was answered on the second ring, Gladys Jaxman identified herself as the owner of The Four Winds Hotel and she sounded delighted to take my call.

'Yes, we have a large double room left,' she said. 'We've been so lucky to have the cast of the pantomime staying here. We only decided to open at the last minute because it seemed silly not to take the opportunity when, what was that woman's name again...? Oh, yes, Valeria. When she phoned and wanted so many of the rooms. We were about to have the whole place refurbished, costly as it is, as we usually close at this time of year, but we've postponed that for...'

'Yes,' I said, 'that sounds fine,' but Gladys was clearly eager to chat and I had to spend several minutes saying, 'Yes,' and 'Sounds excellent.'

'How long will you want the room for?' she said when she eventually stopped to draw breath.

'A week should be fine,' I said, crossing my fingers we'd have no need for a longer stay and we agreed a time for us to check in.

As expected Simon wasn't so delighted when I told him about the arrangement. He was sitting in the kitchen reading the newspaper as I came in.

'You've booked us into the same hotel as the pantomime cast?' he said, sounding incredulous as he pulled his glasses down to peer at me. ‘I’m not sure I want to spend that amount of time in their company.’

‘It won’t be more than a few days,’ I said. ‘They head off to their next venue on Arran soon.’ If arrangements can be made after the sudden death of Cormac, I thought, but I didn’t mention this to Simon.

‘I suppose it will be all right,’ he said grudgingly. ‘What’s the hotel like?’

‘It’ll be fine for a week,’ I said trying to sound positive. I ignored the voice in my head reminding me of Joel’s comments about the food. ‘We were lucky to get booked in. Many of them close for the winter. And think how worthwhile it will be to get the cottage renovation finished and the place snug for the new year. Better than having to do it yourself.’

This thought cheered him considerably (probably recalling his last attempt at DIY). ‘Yes, you’re right, Alison,’ he said and went back to reading his newspaper.

In the meantime there was plenty to do. Anticipating the painter wouldn’t require much time, given the size of the living room, we’d added in painting the hallway to his list of tasks and we set to, clearing as much as possible and covering everything in the bedrooms with old sheets to avoid the worst of the dust.

It was late at night when we finished and realised we hadn’t stopped to eat.

‘I’ll go into Rothesay and buy fish and chips,’ Simon said.

That sounded an excellent idea – I was far too tired to think about cooking and most of the restaurants would by now be closed.

I heard Simon phone his order ahead and then the front door slammed as I pottered around the kitchen, putting plates in the oven to warm and setting the table. I sat down in one of the easy chairs we'd moved temporarily into the kitchen and, tired out, began to nod off.

A while later I heard the front door open and I jerked awake, disorientated for a moment. As Simon came through bearing a brown paper parcel I glanced at the kitchen clock. 'Was there a queue?' I said, lifting the plates from the oven, considering he'd been away for some time.

'No,' he said opening the box and popping a chip into his mouth as he put the fish and chips on to the plates. The vinegary aroma made me realise how hungry I was.

'Ouch, that's hot,' he added, sucking his finger. 'Sit down and I'll tell you.'

There were a few minutes silence as we began to eat, then he said, 'The girl in the café seemed to know who I was and that you were working with the theatre company. She began to talk about the "tragedies" that had befallen them. To be honest I was only half paying attention until she said, "That Wilson Wright is a bit of a character." My ears pricked up when she said that.'

'Did she explain?'

'All she said was that he'd been working all around the country before he started up The Mickle.'

'And what would be wrong with that?'

'Apparently he hawked the idea around all sorts of people. He got nowhere until finally Sir Donald McDilgenson agreed to fund the tour expenses.'

'But I thought he had a business grant…' I began to say then changed tack. 'Given that prolonged conversation it wasn't surprising it took so long to collect the fish and chips.' I pushed back my plate, saying, ‘That was delicious, but I couldn’t manage another mouthful. They do serve large portions.’

‘And that’s not all,’ Simon said, waving his fork in the air, ‘There’s a suspicion that Cormac’s death was no heart attack. He was deliberately poisoned by whatever was in the goblet.’

I wondered where that story had come from. Despite my suspicions I’d not said a word to anyone. And it wasn’t likely the police would have provided information about Cormac’s death. But someone had been putting the rumour about. If it was a rumour.

SIXTEEN

After a restless night, the result of eating a large portion of fish and chips so late, I rose early while Simon was still sound asleep. The kitchen was chilly, and I switched on the portable heater. That was yet another item on the list. The cottage lacked a proper heating system, making it fine as a house for summer, but less suitable in winter.

After pulling back the curtain, I sat at the kitchen table, my hands clasped around my mug of coffee and gazed out. The sun had begun to rise in a fiery red sky, casting a rosy glow over the frosty back garden, making the grass sparkle. Here and there a brave sparrow strutted about, pecking at the hard ground, looking for food. It would be some time yet before the swallows and the house martins made the perilous journey from North Africa to Bute for the summer months.

As I rinsed out my mug at the sink, Simon came through, rumpled with sleep.

'You're up early,' he said, yawning.

'I have to go over to the Hall,' I said. 'There's so much to sort out.'

'Do you think that's wise? Surely they won't want you around while the death of Cormac is under investigation.'

'I promised I'd do the admin,' I said. 'It's only for another couple of days.' Though as Wilson had shown no signs of engaging a replacement for Valeria, I wondered how he was planning to organise the remainder of the tour. 'And I'll pop into The Four Winds Hotel and check on the arrangements for our booking.'

'Mmm. Well, stay away from trouble,' he said, but he'd opened his tablet and his mind was on the morning's online news.

Was he reading my mind? I did have a feeling of responsibility for the task I'd taken on, but I was also curious about what the girl in the cafe had said to Simon the previous evening. Was it possible my suspicions were correct, and Cormac had been murdered? How quickly a story travels around the island, but someone must have had a good reason for believing the death was no heart attack.

Half an hour later – because I decided a second cup of coffee was needed – I made my way to the Hall. The frost I'd seen on the back garden lingered on the shaded parts of the pavements, unusual here so near the sea, but a warning it would remain cold all day.

Wilson was in his office, but of the other members of the cast there was no sign. This might be a good opportunity to have that postponed discussion about his plans without fear of interruption.

He was absorbed in a document on his desk and looked up, startled as I knocked and put my head around the door. He swiftly pushed the document to the bottom of the pile, a guilty look on his face.

Pretending I hadn't noticed, I began by saying, 'Any luck with a replacement for Valeria?'

'What?' A puzzled look crossed his face. 'Oh, no.' Then sounding as if he felt the need to justify himself, he added, 'I haven't had time to think about that.'

'Will you still be able to go over to Arran as

planned? If so, I can organise the ferry and the accommodation, but you'll have to sort out the payment.' It would be something to do meantime, as there was no evidence he'd made progress with the problem of the bank accounts.

'The police have said we can go but have to be prepared to be called back for questioning. We can't afford to cancel Arran. Next to Bute it's our biggest venue.'

'That's fine. I'll start at once.'

'Yes, that would be great, Alison. You have the itinerary. If we could begin with Arran it would be one place ticked off the list. Don't worry about the payment. Once the trip is arranged I'll confirm.'

'I can't promise anything,' I said. 'There are few hotels open and those that are may well be full. You might have to settle for booking into several, rather than having the entire cast in one place.'

'Fine, fine,' he said eagerly, 'whatever you think.' I noticed his glasses were askew, appeared not to fit properly.

'Any word about Cormac?' I couldn't resist asking.

Wilson had turned back to perusal of the document on his desk. 'What? Oh, yes, Cormac.' Then a frown crossed his face. 'What have you heard?'

This was tricky. I didn't want to repeat what Simon had been told, what I also suspected, spread gossip, but I was interested to hear what Wilson thought.

'The police are dealing with it,' he muttered, avoiding my gaze.

'Why, is there something suspicious about it? It was likely he'd had a heart attack. Not improbable, given his lifestyle,' I said.

'A sudden death has to be investigated,' he said. He looked up and stared at me. 'You should know that,

Alison.'

Oh, dear, someone had been telling him about my previous visits to the island. Wilson was still talking. 'Why are you so concerned?'

'No reason.' I shrugged. 'As I'm now working with the company, I wondered how the actors might cope with two deaths in such a short space of time.'

'We'll know soon enough,' Wilson said. 'I'm sure Valeria's death was an accident and, as you said, Cormac had the kind of lifestyle that made a heart attack almost inevitable. That's what the inquest will find.' He sounded positive

Feeling I was being fobbed off, I said, 'I did hear that there might have been something suspicious about Cormac's death. Something to do with the goblet he drank from in the christening scene.'

Wilson sprang to his feet. 'Where did you hear that? There's no proof he was poisoned. Someone is trying to spread malicious rumours.' His face was bright red, suffused with anger and I took a step back, holding up my hands.

I hadn't mentioned poison, but his reaction confirmed my suspicions. 'It's okay. I know how distressing this must be for you, for everyone, and I suppose the quicker the causes of the deaths are determined, the better.'

He didn't reply, but sat down again, staring at the papers on his desk.

'I'll make a start on those bookings,' I said, attempting to inject a light note into my voice and starting to leave the room.

'Hold on a minute,' he said.

I stopped, waiting for him to continue, wondering what he would have to say.

'It's not easy running a company like this,' he said,

'trying to do it all on a shoestring with a motley collection of actors, some like Cormac who were well past their prime or youngsters like Felicity who need to be nursed along.'

'But you managed to sign up Joel Bennett.'

Wilson gave a hollow laugh. 'Yes, I did. But there was a reason he agreed. Viewing figures for that soap opera he stars in have been dropping in recent months and his agent persuaded him doing this pantomime would give him greater exposure, maybe help him move on to other productions in case the TV company pulls the plug on The House at Strathloch.'

Ah, that in part explained Joel's surly attitude.

'How will you manage without Cormac? Will one of the other actors double up?' Joel might be glad of the opportunity to be on stage more, though I didn't see him in the role of the old King somehow.

Wilson was dismissive of my concern. 'No, that's not a problem, thankfully. We'll go with the Queen on her own. That will cut the production time, something I've been trying to achieve without much success.' He frowned. 'It will mean having another word bash and the actors won't like that, but it has to be done.'

Seeing the baffled look on my face he gave the ghost of a smile. 'It's a way of getting the actors to concentrate on picking up the cues. We do a very quick read through without any of the moves.'

Now that he was in a mood to talk, it seemed there was no stopping him, but I wanted to bring him back to the topic of Cormac's death. 'I guess Cormac's lifestyle made him likely to have a heart attack. And he seemed very unhappy.'

Wilson looked at me, as though trying to decide what he should say next.

'You might be right, Alison.' He hesitated. 'But the police removed all the goblets from the set. Everything hinges on the post mortem.'

'And if it turns out Cormac's death wasn't because of his unhealthy lifestyle, that can only mean one thing,' I said, watching for his reaction.

I didn't elaborate, and I didn't remind him it was Joel who'd offered Cormac the goblet.

SEVENTEEN

A fleeting idea that Joel might have had something to do with Cormac's death was quickly dismissed as fanciful. What possible reason could Joel have had for killing Cormac? The elderly actor was no threat to the young star.

And as though he regretted telling me about the police removing the goblets, Wilson said briskly, 'I'd be glad if you could sort out that Arran business today, Alison. We're running short of time. Meanwhile there are a few problems with the props.'

He stood up abruptly and strode off, leaving me gazing thoughtfully after him. There were so many complications in this company, that was for sure. There was more for Wilson to worry about than the two deaths. The missing money was going to cause more problems.

Best to head back to Valeria's office and make another attempt to sort out the ferry and the accommodation. I'd a feeling I'd have to keep badgering Wilson about a replacement for Valeria. To date there was no sign he'd made the slightest effort to find someone.

But before I left, I couldn't resist having a peek at the papers on Wilson's desk, in the hope I might find a clue there. I might be wrong but I couldn't shake off this feeling that Wilson wasn't being entirely honest with me.

Aware he might return at any minute, I rifled through the bundle of papers, trying to find the one he'd tried to hide.

Most of the pile seemed to be regular correspondence: flyers for other productions, newspaper clippings, bills and, at the bottom, an invoice from The Sauchiehall Rooms in Glasgow with a Final Reminder PAY NOW in large red letters across it.

At the sound of footsteps outside I pushed the invoice back to the bottom of the pile, dislodging several papers as I did so. Too late to pick them up. I'd have to make a hasty retreat.

But it wasn't Wilson returning, it was Joel and he stopped, a look of surprise on his face as he saw me.

'What are you doing here? Where's Wilson?' he said. Out of costume, casually dressed in jeans and a sweatshirt, he looked every inch the heartthrob he was.

'I was having a chat with Wilson about the Arran trip, about what I might book for…'I began to gabble.

'I don't see any sign of Wilson,' he said, looking around the room in an exaggerated manner. He narrowed his eyes, waiting for my reply.

'I know – he left a minute ago. I'm on my way to Valeria's office.' I could feel my face going red and I tried to disguise my confusion by turning away, hoping he wouldn't notice the papers lying scattered on the floor.

Unfortunately he did. 'What's this?' he said, bending down to retrieve them.

'No idea. Some stuff belonging to Wilson,' I muttered as I reached the door.

Joel dropped the papers onto the desk. 'He's so messy, it's a wonder how he gets anything done.'

‘I think he said he was going over to the theatre, had one or two things to check out.’

Before Joel could reply, I hurried out and along to Valeria’s office, flopping into the chair with a sigh of relief.

I stared at the information for Arran in front of me. Being a Sunday in winter, the Tourist Office would be closed, so I’d have to rely on the website to augment my sketchy list of hotels on the island.

It was hard to concentrate. I kept thinking about that Final Reminder on Wilson’s desk. He’d given me to believe he knew nothing about the missing money, that he didn’t deal with the expenses, but if so why did he have that invoice? And if I did manage to sort out the accommodation, was there enough money in the main theatre account to cover it? It appeared The Mickle was in greater financial difficulties than Wilson was willing to admit. But he must know the situation of the company was perilous, no matter how he tried to hide it.

EIGHTEEN

In the end the plans for Arran came to nothing. One of those quirks of fate.

Having promised to help, I spent a couple of hours searching websites to find accommodation on Arran at a reasonable price. Some of the hotels, the ones still open at this time of year, had vacancies, but not enough free rooms for everyone in the cast to be together in the same hotel. In the end I decided to book any rooms available – the allocation of these I'd leave to Wilson. I suspected there would be a few unhappy people.

There were also problems with the ferries. The timetable at this time of year was limited though after some juggling I managed to book, but over three ferries. One of the main issues was the large van with a huge amount of equipment and even with that sorted out, I'd a feeling there would be complaints about the arrangements.

By late afternoon, having worked right through lunchtime, I'd managed to find accommodation for everyone except Wilson and Phil. Not that it was ideal – it looked as if most of the actors would have to share a double room, and in one case there would be three of them in a family room. The logistics of this would take some working out. And I wasn't sure how happy Joel would be about sharing with someone, given his well-publicised insistence on his star status.

I'd heard he'd made such a great fuss about having his own dressing room, Wilson had in the end given way.

Feeling rather pleased with my efforts I stood up, wriggling my shoulders to ease the stiffness from most of the day spent hunched over the computer Wilson had managed to find for me, before walking along to his office clutching the printout I'd run off. Now Wilson had to sort out who went where …and pay the costs.

He was deep in conversation with Phil, and they seemed to be having a disagreement judging by the look of anger on Wilson's face.

'I've told you before, it's not possible.' He thumped the table, then stopped as he saw me at the open door.

'I can come back later,' I said, unwilling to be a witness to a row.

'No, no, come on in,' Wilson said. 'Phil is leaving…right now.'

Without a word Phil turned on his heel and almost ran out of the room.

'Ignore him. It's partly his fault we're in this mess. He should have kept a closer eye on Valeria. He recommended her,' Wilson said, shaking his head and forestalling any questions I might have. 'How did you get on with the bookings?'

'I've managed to sort it out,' I said, feeling rather smug. Then I thought I'd better warn him about the complications. 'The accommodation isn't ideal. At least everyone has a bed.'

Briefly I explained what I'd done and though he raised his eyebrows at the suggestion that most members of the cast would have to share, he seemed relieved that the performances on Arran could go ahead.

'Most of the accommodation is reasonably priced,' I said. 'One of the hotels is rather expensive – but it was the only one left on my list. You might have to spend a bit more on that one. I wanted to ask you before I confirmed with them.'

'Anything, Alison,' Wilson sighed. 'I'm happy we can continue with the tour.'

'Now all you have to do is pay,' I said. 'The sooner you do that the better.' I put the list on the desk in front of him. 'I'm off to buy some lunch. I haven't stopped since I came in.'

If I expected a word of thanks, I was mistaken.

As I reached the doorway, I hesitated. 'Are you sure the police are happy with you leaving the island?'

'What?' He sounded cross. 'Oh, yes, I told you. Though we have to give them details of the rest of the tour.'

Injecting a firm note into my voice, lest he thought I might continue helping, I said, 'The replacement for Valeria will sort everything else out.'

Wilson merely grunted and pulling the sheet of information towards him, lifted the phone to make a start on paying the deposits. I made my escape. I'd done the best I could – it was Wilson's responsibility now.

I came out of the Hall into a biting wind. I pulled up the hood of my jacket, shivering as I walked down the path to my car. The blue skies of earlier had given way to lowering clouds scudding across the sky, and as I reached the town the waters of Rothesay Bay were being whipped into a frenzy of foam, crashing on the shore and up over the prom, catching a few walkers unaware.

This didn't bode well for the trip to Arran.

As I drove back to the cottage, the rain began in

earnest and even on full speed the windscreen wipers could scarcely cope. Deep puddles peppered the road in places, and the last of the autumn leaves danced madly in front of me. I drove slowly past the bus depot where the water running in torrents down the steep slope created a hazard for the unwary.

I was glad to reach the cottage, saying to Simon as I came in, 'That's a bad storm on the way.'

He looked up from the newspaper he had spread out over the kitchen table. 'Yes, and it's set to get worse. The ferries are already on Amber alert.'

'But it might blow over?'

He shook his head. 'Not according to the weather forecast. Looks like it might be this way for the next few days at the earliest.'

I could feel a surge of frustration. 'But that means The Mickle will be trapped here on Bute. Not able to get over to Arran.' After all my hard work, I thought.

'Yes, you're right. But you know how unpredictable the weather can be at this time of year. The forccast might change.'

He turned back to reading his newspaper while I went over to switch on the kettle, gazing out of the kitchen window at the gathering storm. Already in the small garden the skeletal trees at the back had lost some of their thinner branches and one of the ornamental pots had fallen over, spilling its contents of earth on to the paved area outside the kitchen door.

I shuddered a little, hoping the weather forecasters were wrong and that the storm would soon blow over. For several reasons. And the most important one was what Simon would say when he realised we might be trapped in The Four Winds Hotel with the cast of The Mickle for longer than we'd thought.

NINETEEN

The storm raged through the night, the cottage creaking and groaning under the force of the strengthening winds. About two o'clock I wakened and lay listening to the howling in the old chimneys. It had seemed a good idea to buy a quaint cottage in Port Bannatyne, but now I wasn't so sure. Summer would be fine, but at this time of the year the comforts the cottage lacked were all too apparent.

The soughing of the wind didn't seem to disturb Simon, but once awake, I couldn't get back to sleep. The business of Cormac's death kept going through my mind and I rewound that scene on stage as though it was a film.

Why had Cormac chosen that particular goblet? I remembered again Cormac's hesitation when Joel approached with the tray. I'd have to discuss this with Wilson next time I went to the Hall.

Then, of course, lots of other questions crept in. Was Valeria's death really an accident? And was it true she'd been stealing money from the expenses account? If so, what was she doing with it?

I remembered Rhoda's story about overhearing the quarrel between Phil and Valeria. Was he involved somehow? But then Wilson said Phil had recommended her. It was a muddle.

Eventually, realising I was wide awake and trying to sleep was futile, I slipped out of bed and lifting my dressing gown from the hook on the door, crept downstairs.

The kitchen clock said 7.30 a.m. and it was still dark. The storm continued to rage, the rain hammering against the windows, making the panes of glass rattle in an alarming way. I switched on the overhead light, blinking in the harsh glare as I filled the kettle, then put on the radio in time to catch the weather forecast. The storm was headline news, rampaging across Scotland, with road and rail services disrupted and warnings to drivers not to travel unless strictly necessary. That didn't bode well, and I checked the CalMac App on my phone to find, as I expected, all ferry services were suspended till further notice. The interruption to the Rothesay to Weymss Bay ferry didn't surprise me, but if the wee ferry from Rhubodach to Colintraive was also off, the weather must be bad indeed. We were stranded.

I'd been caught in a storm like this once before on Bute and it had lasted most of the week. My first thought was what were the cast of the theatre company going to do now? The Arran trip would have to be cancelled or postponed, which would mean rearranging the other venues.

A murky grey dawn began streaking the sky in spite of the relentless rain. If I left soon I'd be able to speak to Wilson on his own. He was usually the first to arrive.

I skipped breakfast – I could pick up something at the Electric Bakery later. My visit would be short. Benny planned to start the work on the cottage in the afternoon and Simon and I had to pack for the week at The Four Winds.

Leaving Simon still sound asleep, I tiptoed out of the cottage.

The rain slackened off as I drove towards Rothesay, but I decided to take the High Road rather than the shore road. A sensible choice. The wind continued to strengthen and buffet my small car and I was glad to reach my destination.

As expected, Wilson was already in his office when I arrived at the Hall, staring despondently at the computer screen in front of him, nursing a large mug of coffee.

'Morning, Alison,' he said, looking up as I came in, but his expression didn't change.

'Thought I'd come over and find out what the situation was with your plans to travel to Arran,' I said.

Wilson put his head in his hands and groaned. 'Can anything else go wrong?' He pointed to his computer screen. 'The weather forecast says this will continue for another three days. There's no possibility of leaving the island before then.'

I bit my lip, trying to think of something reassuring to say, but nothing came to mind. Wilson was right – we were at the mercy of the weather.

'I can organise the cancellation if that helps.'

'I'd be grateful for that, Alison,' he said. 'Though it means we'll lose money.'

'In the circumstances you might be able to postpone rather than cancel the trip to Arran. But,' I hesitated, 'this will throw your schedule out.'

'I know, I know. I'll have to decide about the other venues, possibly cancel one of them. But that means takings will be down.'

'Let's get Arran sorted first,' I said. One thing at a time. 'I'll make a start,' I said, edging out of the door. 'Do you intend to cancel the performance tonight?'

He gave a hollow laugh. 'No, we'll go ahead and

hope people who've booked will be keen enough to see the show to come out in this weather.'

I left him staring at the computer screen and hurried along the corridor. I'd no intention of staying at the Hall longer than was necessary to cancel the arrangements for Arran. He was so despondent I abandoned my idea of quizzing him about the circumstances of Cormac's death.

As I reached Valeria's office, Rhoda came out of the kitchen at the far end of the corridor.

She stopped suddenly as she saw me, a furtive look on her face. 'I was looking for Phil,' she said.

'With the ferries being off, perhaps he's still at the hotel.'

'Of course, of course,' she said, striking her forehead. 'I should have remembered. I'll try again later,' she said as she scurried away.

I stood staring after her. Was she really looking for Phil?

Not my problem. I had to cancel the Arran trip and then go home to pack for The Four Winds Hotel.

The hotel! Oh, no. I'd have to find a way to tell Simon. The actors would be staying on Bute for longer than expected.

TWENTY

All arrangements for Arran cancelled, or rather delayed, I said goodbye to Wilson and drove through the rain and the wind to reach the cottage. Fortunately the Arran hotels I'd booked had been most understanding, especially as it was only a postponement.

Simon had already packed – a small suitcase.

'Is that all you're taking?' I said, thinking of the extra-large case I planned to take.

'Of course. What else would I need? We can always come back if there's anything we've forgotten.'

Unsure about how easy it would be to gain access to the cottage once the work started, I was certain Simon would regret his decision, but I made no comment and we loaded up the car in time to see Benny's van come careering round the corner, belching smoke from the exhaust.

He screeched to a halt beside us and wound down the window. 'Ready to go, then?'

As he stepped out, Simon handed him a key. 'I've left a note of where we're staying, and our telephone numbers are on the kitchen table. If there's a problem give us a call.'

Even in those few minutes the rain had soaked them.

Benny nodded and pulled off his cap to stuff it in his pocket. 'Don't worry. I've done loads of jobs like this,' he said. At least I think that's what he said as his words drifted off into the wind.

Simon looked doubtful and as though about to speak again, but I tugged at his sleeve and we got into the car, struggling to close the doors against the sudden gusts.

With a final, 'Remember to call if there's a problem,' Simon started up the engine, but I don't think Benny heard, or if he did, he ignored it.

There had been no opportunity to update Simon about the trip to Arran and as we drove through the buffeting wind, I tried to think of a way of telling him we'd be in the company of The Mickle cast longer than first anticipated. Best to let him concentrate on the driving.

The Four Winds Hotel was situated on the far side of Rothesay, near Craigmore. Once a grand house had stood on the site, but that had been demolished many years before and in its place stood a sixties style building in the kind of design so popular back then – that is, square and bland with no redeeming features.

The sixties style of architecture was confirmed when we went inside. An attempt had been made to brighten up the interior lobby by the addition of a large Christmas tree and lots of tinsel, but it couldn't disguise the fact the owner was right – the building was badly in need of a facelift.

Our room was basic, but the bed looked comfortable enough and given the day I'd had so far, it looked tempting. It didn't take long to unpack, and Simon said, 'Let's go out to eat now.'

'Sounds good to me,' I said, and we agreed we'd go back into Rothesay.

As we came into the lobby to hand in our key to the bored receptionist, a familiar figure came walking in, shaking off the rain clinging to his coat. It was

Wilson. He stopped, a look of surprise on his face.

'Why Alison, Simon. Good to see you. What are you doing here?'

'We're staying here for a week while some work is done on the cottage. It seemed a good idea to be away from the disruption,' I said, hoping Wilson wouldn't launch into the story of having to postpone the Arran trip before I'd had the opportunity to tell Simon.

But Wilson's next words made me regret my decision not to tell him earlier. 'Yes,' he said, looking glum, 'we're stuck here until this storm blows over.'

The expression on Simon's face changed and he said, 'You're staying on here?'

'Yes,' Wilson said. 'It was lucky the hotel has no one else booked in. And the Hall is free – the Country Capers festival that was planned has also had to be cancelled because the singers can't get here from the mainland.' He sighed. 'It's been such a lot of work to rearrange everything.' Then, looking directly at me, 'Thank goodness you were able to help with the reorganisation, Alison.'

More than help, I thought. But I said nothing, merely smiled weakly, avoiding looking at Simon.

'Best get on,' Wilson said, beginning to move away. 'I intend to keep the rehearsals going, fine tune the script…'

'What will you do now Cormac is…dead?' Simon interrupted.

Wilson scratched his head. 'It's amazing how everyone wants to have a say. Rhoda suggested I could ask one of the others to double up, but Joel wasn't happy with that.' He gave an embarrassed laugh. 'Joel keeps wanting me to expand his part.'

And no doubt that would lead to more complaints from the other members of the cast, I thought.

‘No,’ Wilson went on, ‘I’ll stick to my original plan, and I’ll drop the King altogether. He’s not essential, not really, and the Queen can do that bit about toasting the Princess.’ He brightened. ‘And I could add to some of the other parts… a line or two. That would help…and please Joel. Yes, that’s the best idea.’

It appeared Joel was proving difficult once again.

‘Oh, Mr Wright,’ the receptionist called over to Wilson. ‘There’s a message here for you from Mr Bennett.’

‘What’s he up to now?’ Wilson opened the note she handed him.

‘Bad news?’ I said.

Wilson shook his head. ‘No. He’s taken Benita over to Strathloch House. She’s been pestering him since we arrived on the island.’ He laughed. ‘Perhaps she thinks she’ll get a part in the Soap. I’ll have to go. I’ve phone calls to make.’

Simon stood looking after Wilson who was hurrying over to the lift. ‘Glad Cormac’s death has solved some of the problems about the script,’ Simon sniffed. ‘Honestly, what are they like, these theatre people.’

He turned to me. ‘Why didn’t you tell me the actors would be here for the rest of the week?’

‘Why, what difference does it make? I didn’t have time to fill you in on the details of postponing the Arran trip. You might have guessed they’d have to stay on here.’

‘I suppose so,’ he muttered. ‘I didn’t make the connection.’

Trying to sound optimistic, I said, ‘Don’t let’s worry about it. You heard what Wilson said. If he’s making more changes to the script the cast will be fully occupied with that. They'll be spending most of their time at the theatre. Let's go and eat.'

I linked my arm through his as we left the hotel, but I could tell Simon wasn't persuaded.

On the other hand, there was no way he'd want to cancel Benny now. And if he did, I'd remind him about his ill-fated attempts at DIY.

TWENTY-ONE

The storm continued the next morning, then appeared to slacken off about lunchtime, only to come roaring back as daylight faded.

We'd decided on an early breakfast, hoping to avoid meeting the cast of Sleeping Beauty in the dining room, but now the day stretched ahead of us with little to do.

'We have our wet-weather gear with us,' I said, as we left after a meal of cereal with cold milk and toast. Joel was right – a hot breakfast would have been more welcome. 'We agreed we'd use a car as little as possible on the island. We could wrap up and go into Rothesay. It'll be fine once we're out.'

'I suppose so,' Simon said, but he sounded less than enthusiastic.

In the end we agreed a walk in the rain was more attractive than staying in the hotel and we set off to walk from Craigmore into Rothesay. By the time we reached the edge of the town the shops were beginning to open, and we made our first stop at Helmi's for coffee and, in my case, cake, though Simon resisted the tempting display in the glass chiller cabinets. Fortunately it was too early for the café to be busy, and the only other customer was an elderly man, engrossed in his newspaper.

As we sat, gradually drying off in the fuzzy warmth, Simon's phone rang. He looked at the screen and frowned. 'It's Benny,' he said.

Oh, no, I thought. Surely something hasn't gone wrong already.

Able only to hear one side of the conversation, I edged closer, hoping to pick up what Benny was saying, trying to control my unease.

'Is there a problem?' I whispered. Visions of the roof joists above the false ceiling being rotten sprang to mind. We should have known the age of the cottage would mean problems.

Simon ended the phone call and sat frowning for a minute. 'Benny wants us to go over to the cottage. He says he's something to show us.'

'What is it?' This was intriguing, but it didn't sound alarming.

Simon continued to frown. 'He wouldn't tell me. Says it's better we see for ourselves.' Then, noticing the expression on my face, he smiled. 'Don't worry – it's nothing to do with the renovation. It's something he's discovered.'

I stood up. 'Let's go now,' I said but Simon shook his head. 'He's gone over to the timber yard to collect supplies he needs to continue the work. He'll be back this afternoon. We can find out then.'

How was I to contain my curiosity till the afternoon? All kinds of scenarios flashed through my mind, none of them good. It was still only eleven o'clock and how were we to pass the intervening hours?

But Simon didn't seem concerned. 'Don't fret about it, Alison. I'm sure it's nothing of importance. I think Benny's the kind of person who fusses about everything. I suspect he likes a bit of drama.'

'Let's walk up to the Hall,' I said. 'I left my cardigan in Valeria's office. I may as well collect it now.'

Simon said, 'That will mean a longer trek back and there's no sign of the storm lessening any time soon.'

But he agreed he didn't have a better suggestion and the option of returning to the hotel didn't appeal.

'We can take the bus from Guildford Square to the Port and then back to Craigmore,' I said.

The rain had stopped but the wind had gained strength. The boats tied up in Rothesay Harbour swayed dangerously, the sound of the rigging bells like the screeching of a crowd of banshees.

I put my hands in my pockets – despite my thermal gloves they were chilled.

We were glad to turn up towards the comfort of the Hall. The caretaker was sitting at the far end of the foyer, reading The Racing Post, as we came in.

'Any good tips?' Simon asked as the caretaker sprang to his feet, a guilty expression on his face.

'Can I help you?' he said.

'It's fine – I've come to collect my cardigan. I left it last time I was here,' I said as we walked towards the offices, leaving a trail of drops of water.

The caretaker grinned and flourished his copy of the paper. 'That Phil Aitken is the one you want to ask if you need a tip for the horses. He seems to know all the runners and riders.'

'I'll bear that in mind,' Simon said but I knew he was merely being polite.

Simon stood at the door of Valeria's office while I squeezed in to lift my cardigan from the back of the chair.

There was a noise outside an office further along the corridor and one of the voices sounded like Joel's. He was angry, berating someone, but I'd no idea who the other person was, nor could I make out what was being said.

'Let's get out of here,' I said. 'We don't want involved in disputes among the actors. There's enough going on already with the deaths of Valeria and Cormac.'

We turned to make our way back down to the entrance, when suddenly a figure appeared from the far end of the corridor. It was Rhoda Hunter. It was clear she'd been crying, and she stopped when she saw us.

'What are you doing here?' she said, wiping her eyes.

'Came to collect my cardigan. I forgot it yesterday and might well need an extra layer in this cold weather. You know how chilly…'

Aware I was babbling I stopped as Simon said, 'Are you okay?'

Rhoda made a face. 'As okay as anyone can be in this theatre company.' She made to push past us, saying, 'I'm going back to the hotel to speak to Wilson. Joel won't get away with this.'

Ah, so I was right. It was Joel who'd been talking to Rhoda. 'Away with what?' The words were out before I'd time to stop myself.

She stared at me, as though uncertain as to what she should say.

'Come along, Alison. This is none of our business.' Simon tugged at my arm.

But now she'd stopped crying, Rhoda seemed in a mood to talk. 'That Joel,' she said. 'He thinks because he has a starring role in that stupid soap opera he's in charge of everything.'

She bit her bottom lip, looking more and more angry. 'I'm going to tell Wilson about his accusations.'

'What were the accusations?' Simon tugged at my arm again, but there was no way I was leaving now without finding out what Joel had said.

'Only that I was responsible for Cormac's death.'

'Why on earth would he think that?'

She scowled at me, as though trying to decide how much she should tell me, before bursting out, 'Haven't you heard? It's been confirmed. It was no heart attack that caused his death. He was poisoned. It was my job to fill up the goblets for the christening scene. But it wasn't me who put the poison in one of them. Why would I do that?'

Why indeed? Rhoda seemed close to tears again. 'And how would I know which one would be given to Cormac? They all looked the same – any one of the cast could have been given the goblet with the poison.'

Ah, but wasn't the suspicion that one of the goblets contained alcohol and we all knew how partial Cormac was to that. He must have tampered with one of the goblets after Rhoda had filled them. That was why he'd hesitated when Joel presented him with the tray of drinks.

'Why is it up to you to organise the drinks?' I asked.

'What? Oh, we've all had to take on extra jobs since Valeria died. There's a large bottle of diluted blackcurrant juice in the fridge. That's what I used.'

'And when did you fill the goblets?'

If she thought my interest surprising, Rhoda gave no sign. Perhaps she was still too shocked about Cormac's death.

'Before I went to change into my costume and do my make-up. Wilson would go mad if I spilled blackcurrant juice on my outfit, so I did it well in advance. There were complaints that the juice was warm because it had been sitting out for a while, but too bad.'

'The drinks were sitting out on the table for some time, then?' An opportunity for Cormac to substitute whisky for the blackcurrant juice.

'Yes, yes, of course.' Her frown made me suspect I was accusing her of being negligent and I quickly added, 'Yes, it would be hot under the stage lights.'

So anyone could have tampered with the goblet, put poison in it. But how could the killer be sure Cormac would be offered that one? Unless it was someone who knew Cormac well and understood his habit of having a drink on stage. And knew what he'd done in substituting whisky for the blackcurrant juice.

TWENTY-TWO

There was no time to mull over this news about Cormac's death. Simon was anxious to go back to the cottage to find out what Benny had to report.

'I'm sure it will be something simple,' I said. 'If there's a major issue with the renovation, he would surely have said so.'

'Whatever it is, I hope it isn't something that will cost a lot of money,' Simon said glumly. 'It will be my fault – ugly as it was we could have lived with that false ceiling and the panelling for a while.'

'We'll find out soon enough,' I said, and we drove the rest of the way in silence.

As we parked outside the cottage we could hear sounds of hammering and banging. 'Whatever the problem is, it hasn't halted the work,' I said.

Simon merely shrugged and we pushed open the front door with some trepidation.

'Hello,' Simon shouted.

There was a clatter from the living room and Benny appeared, wiping his hands on his overalls.

'How are you getting on?' Simon said, as I tried to peer past him into the living room, then wished I hadn't.

'Aye, well, the job itself is fine. We'll be finished within the week as promised. It's more what we've found…'. His voice trailed off. 'Come and see.'

We followed him into the living room, picking our

way tentatively through the debris of the false ceiling. Most of the wall panels were carefully stacked up in the corner, but small pieces lay all over the floor.

'I'll tidy that up later,' Benny said with a grunt and nodded to the young lad working on the panelling over by the window. 'It was Gus here who noticed it, hidden behind the panelling where the fireplace would originally have been. That made a good place to conceal it.'

My heart began to thump. What could Benny have found? Thoughts that it might be a skeleton immediately sprang to mind. That would mean calling the police. Luckily I was wrong.

Benny bent down and pulled a dusty cloth bundle from the box of tools in the centre of the room.

'I thought you'd want to see this at once. Gave us quite a start, didn't it Gus?'

Gus gave a gap-toothed smile and nodded. He was a young man of few words, which was fine. Benny could talk enough for both of them.

'What is it?' I said as Benny handed the bundle to Simon. 'See for yourself,' he said.

Simon took the bundle gingerly. As he began to unwrap it, little clouds of dust rose into the air, making me sneeze.

'Aye, it's been there a long time,' Benny said, wrinkling his nose. 'You can smell it.'

He was right. The bundle had a musty smell of something long-forgotten.

Simon pulled aside the cloth to reveal something wrapped in a sheet of ancient newspaper. As he started to unwrap it, little pieces of the brittle newspaper crumbled off and fell to the floor, leaving what appeared to be a chunk of stone.

I picked up a fragment. 'It says 1891,' I said in

astonishment, but Simon was too busy examining the object hidden in the newspaper to reply.

'What's this?' he said, weighing the stone in his hand. We exchanged a glance. Surely Benny hadn't summoned us over to see a lump of stone.

'Lay it on this – you'll be able to see better.' Benny pulled his workhorse over and Simon placed the opened package onto it, again taking care with the remains of the newspaper and the cloth wrapping.

'Gosh,' he said. 'Look at this, Alison.'

Now that it was in the light we were able to see what at first had seemed to be nothing more than a lump of stone, was an elaborate carving. Closer inspection revealed the outline of the figure of a medieval knight in armour, complete with sword, though some of the detail had worn away.

'You found this behind the panelling,' I said. 'How did it come to be here?'

'Not a clue,' Benny shrugged. 'Maybe left there by the previous owner? Though why anyone would hide a lump of old stone is hard to imagine. Was about to chuck it, wasn't we, Gus, when I thought, better…'

Simon interrupted Benny's rambling story. 'You did the right thing by calling us. I'm no expert, but I think this is more than "a lump of old stone". It looks ancient.'

Benny made a face, then said, 'Why hide it away if it's got value? What's the point of that?'

'Simon's right,' I said, tracing the outline of the figure on the stone with my finger.

Benny looked more interested. 'Did right by calling you, then. Might be worth something after all. You see all sorts of old stuff on that programme – what's it called? The one where people bring along their junk, hoping they'll be told it's worth a fortune.' He laughed. 'Though I don't think this will be in that league.'

'There's only one way to find out. We'll have to find someone to advise us. Then we might be able to track down the owner.' Best to know more about this find before we became too excited.

'Mmm,' Simon said, carefully wrapping the stone carving up again. 'Can you put this in your bag, Alison? The Bute Museum might be able to suggest someone who could help.'

While I agreed this was the best action to take, I was reluctant to have the inside of my bag covered in dust and going through to the kitchen I rummaged in one of the drawers for a plastic bag to wrap the bundle.

In the kitchen I paused for a minute, looking out over the garden, trying to make sense of this find. Whether or not it was of value, who had decided to hide this statue behind the panelling…and why?

'Better to keep what the statue was wrapped in,' Simon said as I returned with the plastic bag.

Together we slowly slid the stone carving and its wrappings into the plastic bag. Benny might be right. This might be of no value whatsoever. On the other hand, it was difficult to imagine why it would be so well hidden if it was of no significance. And it would give us a purpose for the next couple of days while we investigated.

'I'm going to collect an extra pair of gloves from the bedroom,' I said and left Simon and Benny deep in conversation.

Perhaps Benny was beginning to regret calling us about this strange object he'd found.

TWENTY-THREE

When I came back into the room, Benny was giving Simon a detailed account of how the stone statue had been found.

'…and then Gus said, "There's something stuck in the old fireplace." Didn't you?'

Gus nodded, but made no comment, shuffling his feet, his face bright red as though embarrassed at being the centre of attention.

However it had been found, Benny's discovery left us with a problem. The easiest thing to do would be to hand this into the police, explain how we'd come to find it, but I was curious about why it had been hidden…and who might have done so. Besides on closer inspection it didn't look to be of much value.

Simon wasn't convinced by my suggestion that we try to find the owner. 'As this was a solicitor's sale, Alison, and the cottage had lain empty for years, how would we know where to begin to find the owner?'

'Even so.' I shrugged. 'How much effort can the police put into finding the original owner? They're busy enough at the minute with the problems of the deaths at The Mickle. We could at least try.'

Benny stepped forward as we stood looking at each other, uncertain how to proceed.

'There'll be someone on the island who remembers who owned this place,' Benny said.

We turned to stare at him. Absorbed in the problem

of the statue, we'd almost forgotten he was there.

As we didn't reply, he went on, 'You could try Old Phinn up on Castle Street. He's lived in the Port all his life. He may be over ninety, but he's still sharp as a tack. He knows everyone here. And his father lived till he was almost a hundred. If anyone can tell you about this, it will be Old Phinn.'

'I don't think we can go knocking on his door and asking questions about people in the village,' Simon said doubtfully.

I'd have no such misgivings and at Benny's next words, 'I wouldn't worry about that. He lives on his own and doesn't get out much. He'll be glad to have a bit of company,' I could see Simon was wavering.

'Let's do as Benny suggests,' I said, anxious not to lose the advantage. 'We'd be helping an old man who might be lonely.'

'Mmm. Okay, but even if he has information, remembers who might have hidden it, I still want to go to the police with it.'

'Yes, but I'm sure they would be pleased to have information rather than starting from scratch. If Phinn can't help, we'll do as you first suggested and go to the Bute Museum. The police have so much else to do,' I reminded him, 'with the deaths at the theatre company.'

This plan of action, if it could be called that, seemed enough for Simon to say grudgingly, 'Fine, but I want to do this sooner rather than later.'

'He's partial to a drop of whisky,' Benny said, interrupting out discussion. 'You'll be extra welcome if you bring that.'

'We'll pop into town and pick up a bottle,' I said, 'and then go straight up to Castle Street.'

'I'll have to get back to work if I'm to finish the job

before the end of the week,' Benny said, shuffling his feet to imply we'd been delaying him.

He called over to Gus, 'Let's crack on with the panelling on that far wall.'

Simon didn't appear as convinced as I'd hoped by Benny's suggestion. 'I think going to the museum first would be better.'

'Yes, but they might take ages to have an expert look at it – there would be no harm in going to see this old man that Benny mentioned. And we can take a bottle of whisky,' I said in an attempt to persuade him.

'Suppose so.'

'And if that doesn't help, we'll go to the museum.' Later, I added silently. Aloud I said, 'Besides we'll be doing a good deed, visiting a lonely old man. And,' my trump card, 'what else is there to do on a day like this. I don't fancy going back to sit in the hotel.'

That decided it as far as Simon was concerned. The cast of Sleeping Beauty might be in the Hall rehearsing yet again a new version of the pantomime Wilson had created. On the other hand they might be lounging about in the only sitting room in the hotel. Better not to take the chance.

We left Benny and Gus to continue with the work of stripping the panelling in the living room and after a trip to Rothesay to purchase the bottle of whisky, we parked the car near the quay and walked slowly up Stuart Street to Castle Street, stopping only to check the address Benny had given us.

Sounds of laughter and music were coming from the Port Bannatyne Hall – and from the thumping noises it could only be a local Keep Fit class. Something I should join, I thought guiltily, then promised myself I'd do that in the new year. One resolution I might manage to keep.

Phinn's flat was on the second floor of a newer block half-way along the street. Each flat had a little balcony, scarcely big enough to squeeze in a small table and a couple of chairs, though several residents had opted instead for a profusion of flowers and shrubs. On a sunny day in summer the flats here would have an almost continental air – sadly this was not the case today and the greenery looked sparse and dismal, straggling over the wrought iron as though trying to escape.

'What shall we say?' I asked Simon as we climbed to the second floor. 'How shall we start?'

Simon shrugged. 'We could say Benny suggested that as we're now living in the Port, he thought it a good idea that we contact one of the oldest residents, find out a little about the village.'

This was a good suggestion to start the conversation, and I took a deep breath as Simon lifted the dull brass knocker to rap loudly on the door.

There was no reply. 'Try again,' I whispered, though why I was whispering I'd no idea.

Simon knocked again, more loudly this time, and we stood waiting, at last hearing the sound of someone fumbling with the door latch.

'Did you forget your key again?' Confronting us, was a tiny man, his gnarled hands leaning heavily on a zimmer, his wispy hair giving him a gnome-like appearance.

He peered at us over thick spectacles. 'Who are you?' he wheezed. He might be old, he might be tiny, but he sounded fierce.

Simon thrust forward the bottle of whisky, but that seemed only to confuse him even more.

'I don't buy stuff from strangers,' he said, preparing

to close the door.

This was tricky. If he shut us out now, we might not have a second chance.

'Benny suggested we call,' I said in a loud voice. 'We're new to the Port and we're hoping to meet up with a few of the …' I stopped myself from saying, '…old …' changing it to 'well-known residents…' in the nick of time.

He continued to sound suspicious. 'Are you going to all the neighbours with a bottle of whisky?'

He eyed the bottle greedily.

Simon introduced us '…and we've bought Cladach cottage down by the seafront,' he finished.

'Yes, yes, I knew it had been sold to people from the mainland,' he said, introducing a note of contempt into the word 'mainland'.

'But we've been coming to the island for years.' I left my answer deliberately vague. The events I'd been party to on Bute hadn't always ended well.

'I suppose you'd better come in,' he said grudgingly, rightly anticipating Simon had no intention of handing over the bottle of whisky on the doorstep. 'My carer will be here soon anyway.'

He shuffled off ahead of us, leaving Simon to close the front door and we followed him into a room which had once been large but was now so crammed with objects it felt claustrophobic.

Every surface was covered: ancient newspapers piled up on several small tables scattered around the room, bookshelves groaning under dusty books and a collection of even dustier ornaments on every available surface.

He noticed me gazing around the room and said in a gruff voice. 'All that stuff was my wife's. Keep meaning to clear it.'

This struck me as a forlorn hope, but I merely smiled as Simon handed over the bottle of whisky.

Phinn took it as though it was no more than his due, though he did say, peering closely at the label, 'Thanks. Though I'm not very keen on this brand.'

He sat down with a thud in a high chair by the window, with a view over the bay, obscured by a drizzle of rain. He parked his zimmer beside him. 'Hope you'll be happy in that cottage.' He chuckled.

I'd a feeling this might be his way of dismissing us, but I was wrong.

Phinn gave a loud laugh as he continued, 'Though you wouldn't catch me living in that place.'

'It certainly needs a lot of work,' Simon agreed. 'But Benny will do a good job, I'm sure. He says he'll be finished by the end of the week.'

Phinn wrinkled his nose as though detecting an unpleasant smell. 'Oh, it'll need more than Benny's skills to sort that place out.'

'What do you mean?' I said, the problem of the stone statue temporarily forgotten.

'Always was an unlucky house. My mother told the story of how it was the cause of two brothers falling out, then one drowned and the other lost his wife.'

'Oh, dear,' I said. 'We bought it as an executor sale – we'd no idea of the past history.' Then, curious about what he'd told us, I said, 'What happened to the wife? Was it an accident?'

Phinn grimaced. 'Accident nothing. She made off with one of the barmen from the Coronet when it was a proper pub.' He clearly didn't approve of the recent changes which had transformed the building into a successful hotel, bringing lots of tourists to the island. 'Being employed at that place out at Ascog – the one that's Strathloch House in the telly programme – gave her a taste for the high life if you ask me.'

Simon looked over at me, his frown signalling he was concerned about how much we should say to Phinn regarding the statue Benny had found.

The decision was made for us. 'She came back, you know when she heard he'd died. Tried to claim the cottage, but by then they'd been long divorced. Stupid woman. Said he'd stolen from her – but what would that be? They were as poor as church mice. That was one of the reasons she left. Well, the story was she searched the whole place and found nothing.'

'What was she looking for?'

He chuckled. 'That was the funny bit of the story – she wouldn't tell anyone. Made finding it kind of difficult if no one knew what she was looking for. Probably something of sentimental value – she was that kind of stupid woman.' He fell silent and rubbed his hands together, lost in thought.

'And she never found whatever it was,' I prompted, but he glared at me before continuing, 'She kept insisting she'd been robbed. No luck.' He chuckled. 'Her husband always was an impulsive man. Wouldn't surprise me if he'd chucked whatever it was into the sea on one of his fishing trips to spite her.'

Simon gave an almost imperceptible shake of his head. I understood what he meant. We exchanged a covert glance. Was it possible she'd been searching for the statue? Nothing else of worth had been found in the cottage. And hiding the statue behind the panelling implied it was of value. But if the circumstances were as Phinn described and they were poor, how come they owned this. Or possibly Phinn was right, and it had some sentimental value. A strange thing to be emotional about, however. Simon and I needed time to discuss this information. If it were true and not merely rumour.

There was a loud knock on the front door and then we heard it open, and a voice say, ‘Hello, Phinn, it’s Deirdre,’ as a young woman wearing a pink overall which almost matched the colour of her hair, came into the room, her oversized hoop earrings dangling.

She stopped as she saw us. ‘Hello, I see you’ve visitors, Phinn.’

‘They were just leaving,’ he growled, putting his hand over the bottle of whisky, claiming ownership.

‘We’re new to the area… we’ve bought the cottage called Cladach on the Shore Road. We thought it would be a good idea to get to know some of the people who’ve lived in the village for a long time.’ Aware I was chattering on, I stopped suddenly.

Deirdre looked disbelieving, but she didn’t comment on our story. ‘I’m Phinn’s carer,’ she said, standing still, waiting for us to leave.

‘I’ve been telling…what were your names again?’ Phinn said.

‘Simon and Alison,’ Simon said in a loud voice.

Phinn made a face. ‘I’m not deaf,’ he said before turning back to Deirdre. ‘They’ve bought that cottage down on the front – you know the one, the unlucky one.’

‘That was a sad story,’ I said. ‘About both brothers I mean.’

‘Yes, well, we don’t speak much about that story in the village. There was such a huge falling out in the family after his wife left. No one blamed her. He was a terrible husband. Some of the family still live in the village.’

‘Ah,’ was my only comment. Family feuds were not unusual, and it sounded as if there was a lot more to this story than Phinn was telling us. Despite my natural curiosity, perhaps I shouldn't ask more questions.

'We should be going,' Simon said, moving towards the door.

But I couldn't resist it. 'What was the story about something going missing?'

Deirdre glared at Phinn. Was she angry that he'd told me the story? Then she sighed. 'My granny knew her well. She always claimed whatever it was it must be valuable, but you'll understand when she left, she was glad to get away. Then again, she wouldn't tell anyone what the valuable item was.'

'Though I'm sure she could have collected it at some point, surely?' Now that I'd started, I wasn't going to let the opportunity to find out more pass.

'She and the barman went to live in Australia,' Deirdre said. 'As far away as they could from Bute. Everyone thought they'd never return to the island. But then her husband died, and she came back. Word was she thought she'd a claim on the cottage, though of course it was rented from the husband's employer. And she must have known that.'

'But no luck in finding what had happened to her…,' I stopped.

'No.' She laughed. 'It was all such a muddle.'

'No reason for her to get the place, being divorced,' Phinn muttered.

Deirdre hesitated as though weighing up what she should say.

'My granny said that's what she wanted everyone to believe but truth was they were still married, had never divorced.'

'Really?' Phinn looked as surprised as we were at this.

'She didn't ever live in the cottage. Turned out it

was owned by the family who lived at Strathloch, and they decided to sell it. She didn't want, or possibly couldn't afford, to buy it. Couldn't get back to Australia quick enough to her barman – now they could marry. And no one in the family wanted to buy it. Too many bad associations. I heard someone from London bought it as a holiday home but didn't use it.'

She stopped. 'Why are you so interested in the story?'

About to say, 'I'm a writer and interested in all kinds of stories,' I suddenly thought that might not be a good answer.

It was Simon who made the next move. 'As you know we bought the cottage – we'd no idea of the history of the place. We're having it renovated, taking down the wooden panelling in the living room.' He paused. 'Behind the panelling was the original fireplace and hidden there we found an old stone statue.' He gave an embarrassed laugh. 'But of what value it could be, I've no idea.'

There was a silence in the room, then Deirdre said, 'That must have been what she was searching for. How strange.'

'From what you've told us, there must have been some reason she was anxious to find it. There would have been no money to buy anything of value.'

'Probably,' Deirdre agreed as Phinn said, 'That's what I told you. She was a sentimental fool. Fancy coming all the way from Australia to look for an old lump of stone.'

I didn't say anything more about the statue. This intricate carving of a knight was no "old lump of stone". Of that I was certain.

And this left us with a dilemma about what to do next. How I wished I'd listened to Simon's first suggestion and gone straight to the police. Now the story of the statue would be all around the village.

TWENTY-FOUR

'We're not going to be able to find the person who might have a claim to the statue.'

'Yes, you're right, Simon.' Yet there was something odd about that story. Too many confusing elements. And Simon had a point. We didn't have the time or the resources to be tracking down the present descendants of the family. But it did confirm one possibility. This stone statue had once been important to someone, even if for no more than sentimental value.

We walked back down onto the seafront in silence, not only because we were thinking about what had happened and what we should do, but because the wind was fierce enough to take your breath away.

We stopped by the brightly painted bus shelter and sat looking out over the water. The waves were being whipped up into a frenzy, crashing in foam onto the pebbly beach. Wracks of seaweed lay piled up against the harbour wall, the briny smell catching at my throat.

The local bus, the number 60 to Ettrick Bay, trundled past on the opposite side of the road, empty of passengers. Surely the weather must change soon. I'd envisaged the time over Christmas and New Year being one of cold, starry nights, long walks in the crispness of a winter's afternoon round the Port Bannatyne Loop or along the Tramway route to enjoy tea and cake at the Ettrick Bay tearoom.

Instead here we were, trying to pass the time on a cold and blustery day, reluctant to return to the hotel.

'Let's go,' Simon said, standing up and stretching. 'It's too cold to sit here for long. We can go along as far as the next bus stop and pick up the bus to Craigmore.'

We walked past the cottage, hearing the reassuring sounds of hammering and banging through the open windows, before continuing along the shore road to wait for the bus.

As the bus reached Guildford Square I said on impulse, 'Drat. I knew there was something I meant to do when I was at the Hall earlier. Contact Wilson. Why don't I get off here and you can go on back to the hotel.'

'I don't think so,' Simon said. 'If you're going to the Hall, I'm coming with you.'

'I don't want to talk to him. I'll leave the folder with the arrangements to date in his office and put a note on top to remind him about Valeria's replacement. I don't like to leave them in the lurch, but he must find someone to take over. You can wait in the entrance hall.'

I didn't say why I preferred not to speak to Wilson. If he'd made no attempt to find a new administrator he'd try to persuade me to stay on.

We jumped off the bus to walk briskly up the High Street and Simon followed me into the Hall. He chose a seat in the corner of the entrance, whispering, 'I can hear the actors are on stage. Hurry up in case they decide to have a break.' He sighed. 'I suppose it's best to sort everything out now.'

I wasn't sure this plan of mine would work, but I gave him what I hoped was a reassuring smile before tiptoeing along to Valeria's office.

I felt a pang of sympathy for the actors. It must be such a difficult way to earn your living in normal times – now, with everything that had gone wrong, it must be well-nigh impossible.

Fortunately scanning the papers I'd been working on before bundling them together and putting them into the folder was the work of a few minutes. Everything seemed in order, and I left the folder in a prominent place on Wilson's desk with a note explaining the details and reminding him of his promise.

Job done and luckily no sign of Wilson I came out of the office about to say to Simon, 'That's it, we can go now.' By the time we reached Rothesay it would be time for coffee, though there remained the problem of how we would pass the afternoon.

Simon wasn't sitting at the entrance where I'd left him, and it took me a few minutes to locate him standing in the shadows at the back of the corridor.

'Is there another way out of the theatre?' he whispered, grasping my arm.

'Why can't we use the main door?' I said.

'I'll tell you outside,' he said. 'Let's get out of here.'

'This way,' I said, quickly leading him to the back exit.

Once outside I stopped. 'I can't wait. Tell me what's happened.'

'I decided to sneak in to the theatre and watch. But they weren't rehearsing. From what I heard there's a problem about that woman who's playing the bad fairy, Somnia. What's her name again? Rona?'

'Rhoda, Rhoda Hunter,' I said. 'Why? What's happened to her?'

‘It seems she’s disappeared. Didn’t come down for breakfast and when they went to look for her she wasn’t in her room. There was a great furore on stage because Wilson was demanding to know where she was, and no one seemed to know.’

This was yet another blow for the company. Could anything else go wrong?

TWENTY-FIVE

With Valeria and Cormac dead and Rhoda missing how was Wilson going to cope? Of course there was every hope that Rhoda would turn up, but in the present circumstances and with the awful weather, where could she possibly be?

'What do we do now about the statue?' I said as soon as we were settled in the local café and had given our order.

To my surprise, Simon seemed to have changed his mind again about taking it to the police station.

'You're probably right, Alison. It might not be worth anything. However,' he grinned, 'though I don't usually agree with your madcap schemes, it might be a way of passing the time. That story about the family in the cottage is certainly intriguing.'

Then he said in a hearty voice, 'Let's go with the option of taking it to the Bute Museum. Someone there might be able to help.'

'Ah, that is a good idea. Let's go now.'

Simon laughed. 'Fine. And how about a trip to the cinema this evening?'

'What? Oh, sorry, I was miles away.' I was becoming more and more excited about his suggestion that the museum could help.

'Indeed you were,' he said. Then a solemn look came over his face. 'I hope you're not worrying about The Mickle. That's nothing to do with us. You've done your best – let Wilson sort it out.'

'Of course, of course,' I said. I took a gulp of coffee, before realising it had gone cold.

'Now what were you suggesting about this evening?' I tried to focus on the present.

'I wondered if we should go to the cinema in the Discovery Centre.'

'What's showing?'

'No idea,' Simon said, 'but it will be warm and comfortable.'

This sounded a good idea – there was nothing else in prospect. In the circumstances whiling away an evening in the cinema would be perfect.

Coffee finished, we walked across to the Discovery Centre. The film showing that evening was one neither of us had seen and although the subject matter seemed more suited to Simon's taste than to mine, I was in no mood to quibble.

'The film doesn't start till 7,' I said. 'Do we go back to the hotel?'

'We can go to the Museum now, then back to the hotel, but we might have an early dinner before the film,' Simon said.

'Should we not have the statue to show at the museum?' I said.

'Better to explain and we can arrange to bring it in at a time that suits them.'

We walked in silence up towards Stuart Street. But when we reached the museum, the heavy oak doors were shut and barred.

'I thought they were open at this time of day,' I said, feeling a surge of disappointment.

Simon turned to the notice board. 'Look,' he said. 'It says here that the museum is closed for redecoration. It won't re-open until next week.'

I put my ear to the door, trying to detect sounds of activity but it was impossible to hear anything through the stout doors.

'I guess that's it, then,' I said. I shouldn't have been surprised – at this time of year many establishments used the quiet winter months to catch up on the various repairs needed to see them through the tourist season.

'Don't be disheartened, Alison,' Simon said. 'This might be a sign we should take it to the police.'

I wasn't going to give in so easily. 'You said you were happy for us to find out more about it before we handed it over.'

Simon shook his head, but I knew I'd won.

We'd no option but to go back to the hotel for a while and book one of the restaurants in town for dinner.

Fortunately, Ambience had a table free and we were able to have a seat at the window, overlooking the gardens. I gazed out as we waited for our order to be delivered. Despite the weather, there were many people out and about. So near to Christmas, the shops were increasingly busy.

About to turn away as the food arrived, by the light streaming out from the restaurant I caught a glimpse of someone hurrying past the window, head down.

'Look, I think that's Rhoda,' I said.

'Where?' Simon peered out of the window, but by then Rhoda, if indeed it was Rhoda, had disappeared around the corner towards Guildford Square.

I stood up. 'Should I go after her? Check if it's her?'

'No, sit down, Alison. You're probably imagining it…it's someone who looks like her. But if it is Rhoda she must have a good reason for being absent from rehearsals. Probably had enough of Wilson's changes.'

Even so, I was disturbed by this sighting. Was Simon right and it was someone who resembled Rhoda? It had been the merest glimpse after all.

But several questions remained. She knew what kind of trouble they were in, how perilous the situation. The Arran trip had been rearranged, but Wilson was hoping to make up some of the money they'd lose by putting on extra performances while they remained on Bute. Rhoda must surely know how important it was for everyone to pull together in these difficult times.

I tried to dismiss the sighting, persuading myself I'd been thinking about her and imagined the woman I saw was Rhoda. That was all. I certainly wasn't going to tell Wilson. There were enough rumours already.

TWENTY-SIX

Once in the cosiness of the cinema I felt myself beginning to nod off and had to make a great effort to keep awake.

There was a reason this was a film we hadn't heard of. It was only mildly entertaining, one of those where the angst of the main characters occupies large stretches of time. Other people must have read the reviews because apart from a young couple more interested in each other than in the film, we were the only people in the cinema.

In between dozing, I kept thinking about the statue, wondering if we'd made a mistake in leaving it in our room at the hotel. But then again the only people who knew about it, apart from Benny and Gus, were Phinn and Deirdre. I didn't see either of them breaking into The Four Winds Hotel to steal the statue.

'Did you enjoy the film?' Simon asked, as we came out into the cold night air.

'Mmm, it did pass the time,' I replied, hoping he wouldn't expect me to be able to discuss the film in detail.

He laughed. 'That's about all it did. Never mind. One day nearer reclaiming the cottage.'

The hotel was quiet as we came in. I was surprised there'd been no word from Wilson, no acknowledgement of the information I'd left on his desk, but he had lots to think about.

We were up bright and early the next morning. The rain had stopped, but the wind had swung around, and the Wemyss Bay ferries were still off, though there was word that the Rhubodach to Colintraive ferry might operate later in the afternoon.

'Not that it's of much help to us,' Wilson said glumly. He'd joined us for breakfast, but there was no sign of any of the rest of the cast.

'Has Rhoda returned?' I ventured, hoping he might have news. If all was well, I could pester him about Valeria's replacement.

He shook his head. 'No, I did go to the police to report her missing, but she has to be gone for forty-eight hours before they'll take action. I can't understand it. She gave no sign she was unhappy, or that she had troubles of any kind. Why would she leave us in the lurch like that? Just as well there's no performance tonight.'

That was it. I'd have to wait a little longer for a response about a new administrator. Tempted to mention my possible sighting of her in town, instead I said, 'What will you do now?' Surely they wouldn't be able to continue with Cormac dead and Rhoda missing.

'We'll have to try to find a replacement if she doesn't return soon. No one can double up with her part, that's for sure. She's one of the major characters in the play.' He took off his glasses and began to polish them on the hem of his jumper. 'But she must be on the island. There's no way she could have left with the weather being so disruptive to the ferry service.'

'Perhaps you could advertise locally? I'm sure there are people with acting experience on the island. There's a thriving theatre group.'

Wilson shook his head. 'No time. I could ask Felicity to step in if I could find a replacement for her. But if we don't find someone right away, we'll have to call off the production.' He sighed. 'And goodness knows how we'll repay the money then. We'd need someone who knows the production, who can step in easily, who…'

He stopped and gazed fixedly at me. 'You've had a lot to do with the pantomime, Alison. You've seen it a couple of times, been around for rehearsals.'

'Sorry, absolutely not,' I said. It was bad enough being involved in making the arrangements for the company without taking on one of the roles in the play.

A look of disappointment crossed his face, but he acknowledged how determined I was not to agree to his suggestion with a shrug. 'We'll have to hope that Rhoda returns…and soon.'

For a moment I considered again whether I should tell him I might have spotted Rhoda in town, then decided against it. It had only been the briefest of glimpses and I may well have been mistaken. There was no point in getting his hopes up.

He looked so despondent that 'Is the weather forecast for tomorrow any more promising?' I said, attempting to change the subject.

'Another day of high winds although the rain should slacken off some time this afternoon. The ferries should be running again on Friday. Now the Arran ferry is rebooked let's hope the accommodation is still available – else we might have to invest in some tents.'

'I'm sure it won't come to that,' I said before realising he was joking.

Simon drank the last of his coffee and stood up.

'We'd better be going, Alison.' And with a nod to Wilson, 'I hope Rhoda turns up soon.'

We left him staring glumly at his bowl of cereal as though hoping to find a solution to his problem there and went back to our bedroom.

'Let's have a look at that statue again,' Simon said as we got ready to brave the elements. He bent down to reach under the bed for his suitcase and unzipped it to bring out the statue. He switched on the bedside light, dispersing the gloom of the morning, and held it up to examine it more closely.

The more I stared at it the clearer the details of the carving of the knight in full armour became. His embossed shield and the hilt of his sword were visible still, though the statue had suffered some damage. The face of the knight was only just recognisable. His nose was broken, and a bit of his chin was missing.

'It's rather damaged,' I said. 'But there must have been a reason for hiding it.'

'It's been lying behind the panelling for a long time,' Simon said. 'I wonder where it came from. It must have a connection to the island. There must be someone who can tell us more about it.'

'The museum is closed, but I seem to remember Eliza, who works there, lives in Rothesay. She's an expert on island artefacts and might be able to assist. I'm sure the library would be able to give us contact details if we explained the situation.'

'It's worth a try,' Simon said. 'That might help us decide what we should do next.'

'And how we might track down the family who owned the cottage.'

Suddenly there was a purpose to our day, and I felt excited as we rewrapped the knight carefully and prepared to go to the Rothesay library.

But first I wanted to go to Montague Street and buy, among other items, a new umbrella – the previous one having suffered a sad fate in the recent weather.

As we walked slowly along the street, taking time to look in the colourful shop windows, we almost ran into Phil as he came tearing out of the local Bookmakers.

He stopped suddenly when he saw us.

'Why, hello, Phil,' I said.

He muttered something in reply which I didn't catch, then hurried off saying, 'Sorry, I'm late for rehearsal.'

'How rude,' I said, as we stood looking after him.

Simon grinned. 'Perhaps he's lost money on a horse. Come on, let's finish the shopping and go to the library.'

TWENTY-SEVEN

When we phoned her Eliza was helpful, if rather surprised, at our request.

Even better, she arranged to meet us at the museum. 'Yes, it is closed to the public,' she said. 'But we need access and I'm sure it's fine given the circumstances.'

'Mind your feet,' she said as she opened the main door in response to our knock.

We tiptoed our way through the entrance, carefully avoiding the pots of paint and ducking under the ladders. Exactly like the cottage.

'I'm happy to have a look at it for you, but I can only give you a rough guess as to the value. For that you'd need a valuer from one of the big auction houses on the mainland or someone who specialises in artefacts.' She paused. 'That's if it's genuine, of course. There are a lot of fake items about.'

'That's all we want to know at this stage: is it genuine or fake.' Once again Simon went through the story of how Benny had found it, omitting the visit to Phinn and what Deirdre had said. All we were interested in was the provenance of the item.

Eliza frowned. 'A strange story indeed. There must have been a good reason for hiding it there. Or you'd have thought so. Let's go through to the back room and have a look.'

I took the bundle from my bag and passed it to

Eliza. She placed it on the desk and unwrapped it slowly, taking care with it.

Pulling a magnifying glass from a drawer underneath the counter, she switched on the lamp beside her, swivelling it around so that the statue was clearly illuminated.

In this spotlight the details of the carving of the knight, although eroded, were easier to make out. I felt my pulse quicken.

Simon and I exchanged a glance. The time Eliza was taking to examine the object could only be a good sign.

Finally with a sigh she switched off the lamp and straightened up.

'I can tell you that this is not some imitation. To all appearances it's genuine. To put a value on it would take more time and I'd like to send some photos over to a friend of mine.'

She paused, fiddling with the magnifying glass, waiting for our response, before continuing, 'He would want to see the object for himself, but I don't think anything can be done right now. Not with the weather. It's impossible to get off the island till the ferries are back to normal.'

'You're right. But is there an urgency about it?'

'I suppose not,' she said. 'Not after all this time.'

Eliza examined the statue again, more slowly this time. 'I would say nothing about this statue… and be careful where you keep it. My first impression is that it is a genuine artefact of some age and might be of value. Word gets about quickly. My suggestion is that you contact the proper authorities, let them examine it and give you an opinion.'

'Thank you,' Simon said. 'I'll let you know what we decide. And if we hand it over to the police that will be the end of the matter. They can pursue the right course of action. And now we know it's of value, that might be the best thing to do.'

'But what we want to do is track down whoever might legitimately own it,' I persisted. 'Let them decide.' I'd grown rather fond of this knight.

I began to rewrap the statue to put it back in my bag, aware now of the responsibility of guarding the statue. Simon would want to do as Eliza suggested, but I was determined to find the owner.

Eliza said, 'Wait a minute. Let me take some photos. That way I can send them over to my colleague and we can make a start.'

She placed the statue carefully on a table in the far corner, switched on a powerful desk lamp and trained the beam on the knight. A few moments later she said, 'That should do. I've taken the photos from several angles, and I'll send them over at once. Have you a number where I could get in touch with you as soon as I receive a reply?'

'I have this.' I scrabbled in my bag and pulled out an old business card and handed it over.

'You can contact us on that mobile number,' I said.

As we walked out of the museum I said, 'That's one question answered,' while Simon said, 'That settles it. We'll take it to the police as soon as Eliza gets back to us with an answer.'

I muttered under my breath. We stopped and Simon pulled me around to face him. 'Why are you so reluctant to let this go, Alison? We decided that if this was valuable we'd hand it over. There's no way we can hold on to it.'

'I know you have a point. It's only that…'I took a breath. 'We need to find out more about this, about the people who lived in the cottage. If it's handed over, we'll never find out.'

Simon hesitated, then gave a deep sigh. 'Oh, all right. If it's lain there all that time, a few days more won't make a difference. But that's all we have – a few days. Now that Eliza at the museum knows about it, she may well contact the authorities herself. Especially if the expert she's contacting confirms her suspicions.'

'But you heard what she said, that she'd be in touch with us as soon as she had a reply from her colleague.'

Beyond finding the owners I'd no idea what we would do. But that was for later.

The afternoon had brightened. The rain had stopped, the wind had subsided, and it seemed possible the ferries would be on again soon.

'You're very quiet,' Simon said as we made our way back down to Guildford Square.

'Wondering where to start,' I said.

Instead of answering, Simon said, sounding cheerful, 'At least this change in the weather means The Mickle should be able to leave the island. That will be a relief for them.'

As we strolled along he said, 'If the weather holds we could walk out to the cottage. See what progress Benny has made.'

I didn't think Benny would have moved on much further since yesterday, but in the absence of an alternative, I agreed.

We settled on having lunch in The Kettledrum. At this time of the day, the café was busy but we found a table in the far corner, where it was quiet.

'Why so down, Alison? You know we've no option but to take that statue to the police eventually. I'll go along with your idea of waiting for Eliza to contact us if you're really keen, but we're not likely to be able to track down the owners in the next few days.'

'Even so,' I said, 'I'd like to have a try, find out more about it.'

Simon smiled and pulled out his phone. 'In that case we need some help.' He scrolled through, before saying, 'I did have a look on the internet before we went to the museum. I may be wrong, but I have an idea where that statue came from.'

'Really? Why didn't you say?'

'I didn't want to tell you before we had some confirmation it might be genuine.'

He passed the phone to me to show me a photo of the inside of St Mary's Chapel.

'You think it's something to do with St Mary's? That's the medieval chapel beside the High Kirk Hall.' I peered at the screen. 'I didn't pay much attention to the chapel, if I'm being honest.' If this was a church, it was unusually small with a timbered roof and plain glass rather than stained glass windows. 'It doesn't look particularly imposing.'

'This is all that's left of the original church – the Chancel.' He swiped to the next photo and zoomed in. 'What do you see?'

I took the phone from him to have a better view. The interior was dark and at first I couldn't make out much. 'There's a tomb on one of the walls – it looks like a lady, though. From her dress I'd say it was early medieval?' Simon waited as I tried to make sense of something lying beside her. 'Oh, wait, is that a baby beside her? And a dog at her feet?' The more I looked at it the clearer it became.

I looked at Simon, feeling curious. 'But what is that to do with the statue of the knight?'

'Look at the tomb on the next photo. Zoom in on

that… it's a Knight's tomb. You can see he's in full plate armour with his head resting on a helmet. What do you notice?'

At first I wasn't sure what I was looking for. Then it came to me. 'There appear to be some empty little niches, below the tomb. Is that it?'

'Yes,' Simon said. 'And I wonder if the statue we have once stood in one of those niches.'

TWENTY-EIGHT

Before we could investigate further, there was another upset. After a substantial lunch (I blamed it on the fresh air) I wasn't inclined to take up Simon's suggestion of a long walk, though the weather continued to clear.

'I think I'll go back to the hotel, put my feet up and read my book,' I said.

'Are you feeling okay?' Simon looked anxious. 'I think you're too involved with that theatre company. My fault, I guess.'

Shaking my head I said, 'I'm fine, but I'm not in the mood for a walk. You go ahead.'

We parted company at the corner of the High Street beside Guildford Square and Simon set off saying, 'I'll see you later. I'm heading for Loch Fad, but I'll see how far I manage.'

I was doubly glad I hadn't agreed to go with him – a gentle stroll was one thing, but the walk he was proposing was almost five miles.

Indeed, the walk back to the hotel at Craigmore was quite enough for me. I suspected I wouldn't be reading long – I was exhausted. A combination of the sea air, the concerns about the work at the cottage and the issues about the statue worried away at me.

When I entered the hotel Wilson came running down the stairs.

'Any word about Rhoda?' I blurted out before I

could stop myself.

It looked as if he was about to ignore me and continue out of the hotel, but then he hesitated.

'No,' he said. 'I've reported it to the police.' He paused, then said, all in a rush. 'It's awful, awful. The confirmation that Cormac's death was murder affects everyone.'

'Oh, how terrible. I hope you'll still be able to make the Arran venue, so that the pantomime can go ahead. It'll be hard work but will take everyone's mind off those dreadful deaths.'

This, if anything, only made him gloomier. 'There's not much chance of that. Understandably everyone is on edge, wondering what will happen next. And there's the problem of Rhoda and the part of the Wicked Fairy.'

'But the weather has changed at last – the ferries will be back on, and you can rebook.'

Wilson shook his head. 'You don't understand. Arran has cancelled. We're too late. The ferries and the hotels you arranged were fine but the venue we hired has taken on number of other events as they thought we'd decided not to come. Apparently there was no confirmation. All Valeria did was make a provisional booking. I can't understand what Valeria was up to, why she wouldn't have followed through the plans we agreed.'

This was a blow. The audiences on Bute had been good, even for the extra performances, but it was unlikely there would be enough demand to continue on the island for a further week. 'Will you head back to Glasgow or skip Arran and head to Islay?'

'Why would we go back to Glasgow? There's no chance of finding a venue there at this time of year. No, we'll have to try to sort something out for Islay.

We'll stay on Bute for another few days.'

He looked at me hopefully. 'I don't suppose you'd have time to help out again? Sort out the trip to Islay?'

'What about the person from Glasgow you intended to employ in Valeria's place? I left a note reminding you.'

'Yes, yes.' Wilson scuffed his feet, refusing to look at me. 'That's been rather difficult. The woman I had in mind has accepted another job. She won't be able to join us.'

This was the last thing I wanted to hear. And it put me in an awkward position. It wasn't as though I was busy, had a million other things to do. Though I did suspect this replacement for Valeria had been no more than a fantasy of Wilson.

'It all depends,' I stalled. 'We're supposed to move back into the cottage at the end of the week and there will be lots to do, clearing up and then there's the redecoration to arrange and we hope…'

I stopped, aware Wilson was paying no attention to my litany of home responsibilities.

'Most of the schedule is fine, Alison. Thanks to you.' Flattery, I thought and waited for him to continue. 'It's only a matter of taking a day to sort it all out.' He ran his fingers through his hair. 'I'm hopeless with this kind of thing. That's why I had to engage Valeria, though it took a chunk from our budget that we could ill afford.'

'I might be able to help,' I said cautiously, 'but only if there's a clear understanding Islay will be the last place I arrange.'

Wilson grabbed my hand and shook it vigorously. 'I can't tell you how grateful I am, Alison.'

My mind was already turning over the possibilities.

'I know Arran can't accommodate you right away, but it might be possible to find out if they could offer you a couple of days at the end of the tour.'

Wilson looked at me as if I'd said something of great import. 'Oh, do you think so? I wouldn't have thought of that.'

'I'm not promising,' I said. 'But I can ask. That way you wouldn't lose so much money.'

Relief written all over his face, Wilson said, 'You've lifted a weight from my shoulders.'

'I suppose the sooner I start the better,' I said. 'I'll come along to the Hall first thing in the morning. That will give you time to sort out the revised schedule for me.'

I must be mad, I thought as I watched him walk away with a spring in his step, slamming the front door behind him. Why on earth was I involving myself when I'd promised I'd done as much as I could? I reassured myself that this wouldn't take long. It was hardly a difficult task. The only problem was Arran – the company would be on schedule for the other venues.

As I was about to walk over to the stairs to head for my room, looking forward to an hour of solitude with my book, the front door opened, and Rhoda came in.

She stopped as she saw me and we stood still, staring at each other.

Rhoda was the first to speak. But she didn't explain, didn't mention her disappearance. All she said was, 'Why, hello, Alison.'

Even if she'd no intention of telling me where she'd been and what she'd been up to, she'd have a lot of explaining to do to Wilson.

TWENTY-NINE

When I went to the Hall early next morning, another rehearsal was in full swing and I stood watching, waiting for an opportunity to let Wilson know I'd arrived.

There was a lighter atmosphere as Wilson put them through their paces. As he'd said, he'd solved the problem about the part of the King by cutting it out altogether.

'The Queen can pick up any extra lines,' he said when Joel raised the issue. 'In fact given the age we live in, it will be a good thing for the Queen to be seen as the important figure, rather than merely as an adjunct to her husband. Yes, much more modern like this, where she does the toast to the Princess Beauty.' Cormac wouldn't be missed then. We'd heard nothing more about his death, though the police were, I was sure, busy on the case.

No one dared quibble with this arrangement for the Queen's part to be augmented and though she tried to hide it, Felicity was surely happy with a bigger part. Not that there was any disagreement. The storm had passed, the ferries were on again and everyone seemed pleased to be back working with the prospect of leaving the island soon.

And contrary to expectations, Wilson welcomed Rhoda back without a word of criticism, or none that I heard. Whatever her explanation for her absence, it must have been enough to satisfy Wilson because he couldn't stop grinning. He'd also be pleased it was one fewer problem for the police.

There was a pause after the christening scene, and I signalled to Wilson.

He came loping down from the stage, jumping from the platform instead of taking the stairs at the side, saying to the actors, 'Take ten.'

'Great. You're here, Alison. This shouldn't take you long.'

'Have you decided what you want to do?'

'Yes. I've decided we'll go with your suggestion. That involves minimum change. We can finish up on Arran in the last week if possible.'

'So you want me to arrange the new schedule?'

'No, not exactly.' He shook his head. 'I know much depends on the times of the ferries, but I've spoken to The Four Winds hotel, and they can accommodate us. It seems only sensible to stay here. There are a couple of tweaks I still want to make especially with cutting the part of the King. We'll put on extra performances. That will make good use of the time. And bring in some extra income.'

Privately, I wondered how many more changes to the script the actors would put up with, but all I did was murmur in agreement.

I had to find out what he knew. This was the opportunity I'd been waiting for. 'Any word on Cormac?'

He looked uneasy, casting a glance over at the cast who were standing around chatting. Felicity and Joel were sitting on the steps, engrossed in conversation. Even from this distance it was clear Felicity was infatuated. But then I suspected this was no more than Joel would expect.

‘There’s been word back from the police, but I don’t want the others to know yet. I’ve a production to look after and the news would only create a disturbance.’

‘And…’I waited.

Wilson moved closer. ‘It **was** murder,’ he said in a low voice. ‘He was poisoned. The poison was in the goblet.’

This confirmed what I’d already heard. But the important question remained. ‘How could the killer know Cormac would be given that goblet? There were several on the tray – he could have chosen any one of them.’

‘It was someone who knew Cormac well. Knew he always had to have a drink on stage to help him through the performance. An analysis of the goblet revealed dregs of whisky.’

‘Really? A bit of a gamble.’

‘Not if you knew Cormac well. He was lucky to get a part in this pantomime – he had a reputation in the theatre world as unreliable.’ He gazed past me as though recalling the highlights of Cormac’s career. ‘I admired him a lot. But it’s the story of so many actors – two failed marriages, too much alcohol, then a steady decline. He became unpredictable – wouldn’t turn up on time for rehearsals – if he turned up at all.’

‘Did Joel not notice one of the goblets contained whisky instead of blackcurrant juice?’

Wilson raised his eyebrows. ‘Joel was too busy trying to hog the limelight. Did you not notice? If it hadn’t been for Cormac dying like that I intended to speak to him about it.’

I couldn’t resist asking, ‘If Cormac was such a problem, why did you employ him?’

Wilson made a face. ‘Not my choice. He was a friend of Sir Donald …been to school with him or some such story – secured the part that way. I could hardly refuse our backer's request.' He sighed. 'Mind you, heavy drinking is the curse of our profession. He wasn't the only one in the cast who liked to steady their nerves by having a drink to hand. Usually had a hip flask somewhere in his costume and took a sly nip whenever he could.'

'You'll have to tell everyone sooner or later. They're bound to find out.'

Wilson acknowledged the truth of this with a nod. 'Yes, but I'll wait until I hear when the police want to continue the interviews. One good thing that's come out of this storm trapping us on Bute – we should be able to get the police interviews over with before we leave.'

'Of course. I'd better make a start.'

'And I'd better get everyone back to work.' He clapped his hands. 'Right everyone. Break over. Take your positions.'

I left them once more rehearsing the latest changes to the script, though only Joel looked happy. I'd a feeling Wilson had increased his part, even if under duress. But then he was the star of the show.

As I walked down the stairs towards Valeria's office, I reflected on what Wilson had told me. Terrible as it was that Cormac had been killed, it looked like a well-planned murder.

I stopped, my hand on the office doorhandle. What was it Wilson had said. Something about another member of the cast having a liking for alcohol.

And despite Wilson's protestations Joel must have noticed the goblet didn't contain blackcurrant juice.

There was only one explanation. Someone who knew Cormac well had taken the opportunity to kill him. Could that person have been Joel?

THIRTY

Simon's first reaction when I brought him up to date with events (and my suspicions) was to sit down, put his head in his hands and groan.

'Oh, no, Alison, surely you're not involved in another murder. I can't believe it.'

'Not me…we…' I said. 'We were both there at the performance and saw what happened. The police will want to interview everyone.' What a task, I thought, remembering the full house that night.

'Yes, but we should never have accepted that offer to go back stage.' I could tell he was seriously worried.

He was right, but even so we would still have been interviewed by the police as members of the audience, a fact I didn't hesitate to point out to him. 'It will take some time for them to get around to us. It won't be anytime soon.'

He didn't sound convinced, but just then my mobile rang, and I scrabbled in my bag to find it.

'Hello, Tara,' I said, walking towards the window. 'Good to hear from you, all the time thinking guiltily that apart from a couple of phone calls and texts I hadn't been in touch since we'd arrived on the island.

'How are you getting on at the cottage?' she said.

'We're having work done,' I said. 'We're living at The Four Winds Hotel this week while the workmen are in.'

'But it will be lovely when it's finished. And a week isn't such a long time.'

'I suppose not,' I said as she continued, 'I heard the news about the deaths at The Mickle, Alison. They appear to be jinxed.'

Inclined to agree, but not wanting to add to the rumours, I said, 'I'm sure the police will sort it out.'

'But if it wasn't a heart attack, if Cormac was murdered, it must be someone in the company who's responsible surely?'

'Mmm. It does look as if Cormac's death was deliberate. You're right. At first the belief was that he'd had a coronary. He'd the classic signs of a heart attack in waiting.'

Tara sighed. 'I do hope the police find the killer soon. It can't be pleasant for anyone. Did you see any of the performances?'

I wondered if I should tell her I was working, in a limited capacity, for the company. In the end I gave her a brief account. Given the way news travelled on the island, I was surprised she hadn't found out already.

Her reaction was remarkably similar to Simon's. 'Gosh, Alison, how come you always get mixed up in these events.' There was a pause before she said, 'The reason for my call was to invite you and Simon to have supper with us tomorrow night. My cousin and his wife have come up from Surrey and are staying with us over Christmas and New Year. It would be good for them to meet you. They're from the island but went to live in Surrey many years ago.'

'Let me check,' I said, putting my hand over the phone while I relayed Tara's invitation to Simon.

He nodded enthusiastically and I said to Tara, 'Sounds good.'

There was a sigh of relief at the other end of the phone. 'Thanks, Alison. These cousins are much older than Warren and me and conversation can be a bit tricky. It'll be good to have some lively input.' While I wasn't sure this was an accurate description, that we'd be up to "lively input", we agreed a time and said goodbye.

'That's something to look forward to,' Simon said. Tara and her husband, Warren, lived in a converted farmhouse near Straad and the prospect of an evening in a warm house with good company was lure enough in itself. Besides, Tara was an excellent cook.

But we couldn't ignore the subject of the pantomime for long. As I started to put my phone back in my bag, 'What happens now?' Simon said. 'Do you have to go back to the Hall immediately?'

'Yes. I feel sorry for Wilson – though he's more your friend than mine.' A sly dig to remind Simon that he was the cause of my being involved.

But Simon was having none of it. 'I wouldn't call him a friend, Alison. He was a student of mine and one of the crowd who went to the pub on a Friday night. To be honest, apart from the course, we'd nothing in common.'

Better to change the subject. 'I'll let you know what's happening as soon as I hear from Wilson. Anyway, there's not much we can tell them about the incident of Cormac's death. At least no more than any other member of the audience. Probably less so, given we were sitting so far back.'

'Don't be too long. Shall we walk along to the pub when you get back? We could have a meal there.'

That seemed a good idea. Another night with the option of sitting in our bedroom or in the hotel lounge wasn't appealing.

THIRTY-ONE

The next evening I was glad of the opportunity to wear something smarter than usual. By that I mean I put on a dress rather than the jeans, sweater and warm coat that had become my uniform since arriving on Bute.

'Has there been any word from Eliza about the statue?' I said, as I picked up a pair of my favourite earrings.

'What?' Simon looked up from the television news channel he was watching.

'Don't tell me you've forgotten,' I said. 'Eliza said she had a friend who was an expert in that area.'

'No, of course I haven't,' he laughed but I knew it wasn't much occupying his thoughts.

We decided to go to Tara's by taxi. It would be simpler than the 'who drives' discussion.

Of course we should have realised the deaths at the Hall would be the talk of the island as we no sooner settled ourselves in the cab than the driver began, 'Some carry on that with the theatre crowd. Their performance must have been pretty rubbish for someone to want to murder one of them.' He chuckled.

Simon appeared about to speak and I nudged him hard. 'What was that for?' he muttered, looking perplexed as he noticed the frown on my face.

'Don't say anything,' I hissed. There was no point

in adding to the gossip. Whatever Simon had originally intended to say he now said, 'Thank goodness the storm has passed. Are you busy at this time of the year?'

If he was surprised by this turn in the conversation, the driver gave no sign. 'It's been quieter than usual. But we should get a fair number of people coming over to the island for Christmas.'

The rest of the journey passed in idle chat about the weather and the cost of Christmas. 'Kids expect so much these days,' the taxi driver grumbled as we reached Tara's house.

We stepped out and I paused for a moment to gaze at the display of decorations while Simon paid the fare. Out in the country there were no street lights to distract from the myriad fairy lights strung over the trees encircling the house, and a series of illuminated stepping stones marked the entrance to the front door.

'Isn't it pretty?' I said as we stood waiting for our knock on the door to be answered.

'Mmm, suppose so,' Simon said. 'But then they do have two small children. It would be a bit much for our place.'

I was saved from answering as the door was pulled open. 'Great to see you,' Tara said, ushering us along the hall and through to the sitting room. A tempting aroma filled the air. This was promising. We'd had nothing to eat since a sandwich at lunchtime and I was hungry.

The first thing I noticed was the enormous Christmas tree dominating the corner, the branches weighed down with every kind of ornament imaginable.

She must have noticed the look on my face as she laughed, 'You might guess the children decorated the tree – no such thing as too much where they're concerned.'

There was no one else in the room but Tara answered the unspoken question, saying, 'Warren went into Rothesay with Kiernan and Yvette to pick up the case of wine he ordered.'

She looked solemn. 'It's been hard work having guests for this long to be honest. Warren suggested they go with him to give me a bit of time to prepare the meal. Thankfully the children went down early. Yvette and Kiernan were from Bute, but that was many years ago and Yvette has always wanted to make a trip back.'

From the way she spoke, I suspected the prospect of having guests right through Christmas and New Year was proving challenging.

Then recollecting her duty as a hostess, she said, 'Do take off your coats and sit down. I'm so pleased you could come along.'

No sooner were we seated with a drink than there was the sound of the front door opening to much laughter.

Warren came into the room, followed by a man distinguished by his height – particularly noticeable in the low ceilings of this conversion – and a woman no taller than I am, her elegantly styled silver hair surprisingly unruffled considering the weather we'd been having.

'Meet Kiernan and Yvette,' Warren said, introducing us.

Kiernan smiled and came over to shake our hands warmly. 'Great to meet you. Tara has told us so much about you both.'

I glanced over at Tara and raised my eyebrows, but she carefully avoided my gaze. What had she been telling them, I wondered.

It was then I realised everyone except me was casually attired. I'd somehow expected Tara's guests would be smartly dressed. Well, they were, but it was in casual clothes of slacks and warm jumpers, and I felt decidedly overdressed.

Tara disappeared into the kitchen from time to time, assuring us, 'Dinner won't be long. I prepared most of it earlier,' as I tried to avoid the temptation of the bowls of crisps Warren had set out to accompany the drinks.

In the middle of hearing the story of Kiernan and Yvette's journey by car from Surrey to Bute – fraught with one disaster after another because of roadworks and intermittent bad weather – Tara appeared, taking off her apron as she said, 'Dinner's ready if you'd like to go through.'

This was yet another well-designed part of this conversion. Tara certainly had an eye for colour and style evidenced in the pale colour scheme perked up with pops of tartan in the seat covers and the curtains. Somehow it contrived to be cosy and airy at the same time.

'This is lovely,' I said, gazing around. 'You've changed the colour scheme.'

'All Tara's doing,' Warren said proudly as Tara set a tureen of soup on the table, asking us to help ourselves.

The evening continued well, the rest of the meal quite delicious, making me think I'd have to do a bit of practice before inviting them back to ours. Once the cottage was ready, of course. Which might take some time.

'Let's have coffee in the lounge,' Warren said, pushing back his chair and we followed him through.

Trouble was once settled there with coffee and a nightcap I began to feel incredibly sleepy. Partly the effect of eating too much, several glasses of wine and now sitting comfortably in front of the log-burning fire. Though the walls of the building were thick, you could hear that the wind had started up again and the rain was driving against the windows.

Later I thought how much more sensible it would have been if we'd made the decision to go straight back to the hotel after dinner. We'd lingered so long at the dinner table, it was late when we finished.

And if we had left, Simon wouldn't have mentioned the difficulties The Mickle was having. Though in fairness, he was prompted by something Warren said. As we sat back in the comfortable chairs, Warren said, 'Tara tells me you've been working with The Mickle Theatre Company, Alison? How is that?'

Before I could reply, Simon jumped in. 'It's temporary – Alison is helping them out because they are…' he struggled for the right way to say in but in the end came out with… 'having serious problems…'

As his voice tailed away Kiernan said, 'Ah, yes those deaths. Mighty strange, don't you think?'

Simon nodded and Kiernan went on, 'Tara told us about it. Funny thing is, I ran into Phil Aitken a few years ago when he was doing a play at the Surrey Metropole.' He turned to his wife. 'What was the name of that play?'

'A Long Shot Again,' she said. 'We went to see it one night.'

'Oh, yes, he wasn't much of an actor. But he knew how to promote himself. There was a woman somewhere.'

'His wife?'

'No.' Kiernan shook his head, frowning as though

trying to recall. 'Veronica? Verity? No, Valeria… that was her name.'

'Really?' This was interesting.

'They didn't stay for the full run. They left suddenly but no one knew why. It was quite a story for the local paper, but I can't remember the details.'

This was indeed strange. And stranger still that there had been problems before they joined The Mickle.

We said goodbye with promises of meeting up again before Yvette and Kiernan left, though I did stress it might have to be a meal in a local restaurant.

We were both quiet on the journey back to the hotel by taxi and luckily this driver wasn't talkative. I could scarcely keep awake, far less engage in conversation.

In the middle of the night I awakened with a start. All manner of jumbled thoughts went through my mind. Yes, some were to do with the statue and who might own it, but there were more concerns about what had happened at the theatre company. Even if Valeria's death was an accident (now in doubt), there was still the problem of Cormac. Someone had wanted Cormac dead. But what could be the motive? He was no longer famous, he wasn't (as far as I knew) especially well off and while he wasn't the most popular person in the company, there was no indication he was the subject of hate. And though Joel had served him, he hadn't been responsible for setting out the tray with the goblets.

Was the story about Phil and Valeria that Yvette and Kieran had told us of relevance? Something prompted their sudden departure from Surrey. Money troubles? Money had been disappearing from the expenses account with no evidence it had been spent on the pantomime tour.

I couldn't discuss this with Simon. He'd tell me yet

again that it was nothing to do with me – and he was right. Especially with my track record of becoming involved in unfortunate events every time I came to the island. And yet, and yet. I was, I reasoned, part of the company, even if only on a temporary basis. It would surely do no harm to make a few enquiries

Decision made, I fell into a troubled sleep, convinced there was more to the story of the deaths than anyone knew…or perhaps was saying.

THIRTY-TWO

It didn't take long to sort out the arrangements for Islay. Because of the winter sailings timetable, I had to book the company in for a day later than Wilson and I had discussed, but in the circumstances we agreed that would be fine. The accommodation was even easier – there were a couple of places on the island with spare capacity, except for Christmas Eve and Christmas Day. The fashion for having a celebratory meal in a restaurant seems to be on the increase, but that didn't matter to the company. They would be back in Glasgow on the twenty-second, all being well.

Clutching the details I'd printed off, I walked along the corridor to Wilson's office, determined this time to pin him down about a replacement for Valeria. I certainly wouldn't be able to travel with them, though this way of arranging the schedule island by island seemed to me both haphazard and foolish. Then I remembered the story about Valeria. With the company on a tight budget there would be no way to replace the missing money. Perhaps Sir Donald would come up with more funds – I hoped so, else the company might be back in Glasgow sooner than anticipated.

Wilson wasn't in the office, and I left the details for the trip to Islay on his desk. The conversation about a replacement would have to wait till later, but I could add yet another prompt. More strongly worded this time. I looked around for a pad of sticky notes to attach one to the single sheet.

The papers on his desk looked in danger of falling over and I wanted to make sure my note wasn't lost among the pile and lifting a pad from the top of his in tray I quickly scribbled, 'Here's the schedule of ferry times and information on the hotels for Islay. You have to confirm and pay by 5 p.m. tomorrow night. Good luck with the rest of the trip.' Then I added for good measure, 'I'm sure you'll find a replacement for Valeria who'll be able to deal with the rest of the tour. I've done all I can.'

As I put the sheet down in a prominent place on top of the other papers, I couldn't help but glance at the one on top of the pile. It appeared to be a bank statement for The Mickle main account. Was it only the Expenses account Valeria had had access to? And why hadn't he kept a closer eye on how she was spending the money?

But before I could have a proper look, a voice said, 'What are you doing, Alison?' Wilson stood framed in the doorway, his face thunderous. 'Snooping around?'

Alarmed at the change in his usually quiet demeanour I drew myself up, hastily replacing the bank statement and the list together. 'Of course not. As you weren't here I was leaving the information for Islay on top of your pile of papers.' I waved my hand around, almost dislodging the entire pile. 'I wanted to leave it in a prominent place to make sure you found it.'

Wilson said grudgingly, forcing a smile, 'Oh, thanks, that's good of you.'

'And all the payments have to be made by

tomorrow,' I stressed.

'Fine, fine, I'll deal with it.' He seemed preoccupied. He came over and sat down at his desk.

'I'll be off then,' I said and began to edge towards the door.

If I thought I'd manage to slip away out I was wrong.

'Wait, wait,' he said. 'What about the other venues? What are we going to do about those?'

'What are you going to do, you mean.' I was determined to stand my ground.

'According to the new schedule we're staying on Bute for a further three days. Plenty of time to forge ahead with the plans for the rest of the tour.'

Why, oh why, did I hesitate?

THIRTY-THREE

After dinner, this time at the hotel, we went into the lounge. Most of the cast were there, dotted around the room: some watching football on television, others in a huddle in the corner, Joel, Phil, and Lucian playing cards. With only a couple more performances scheduled on Bute, the cast were at a loose end. Wilson seemed to have given up his regular script rewrites. Maybe he'd run out of ideas.

Of Wilson there was no sign, but Rhoda was sitting on her own reading a magazine as though nothing had happened, she had never gone missing.

'Let's go up to our room,' Simon whispered, though it was unlikely any of the actors would try to dissuade us.

Our room, though described as a 'double' wasn't large and the television of the ancient variety with a limited number of channels. But I had a good book and Simon's suggestion was preferable to becoming involved in a conversation with anyone in the lounge.

But as we began to sneak out, there was a commotion in the corner and Joel stood up, pushing back his chair, and flinging down his cards on the table. 'I don't play with cheats.'

At first I thought he was speaking to Lucian and couldn't believe this mild-mannered young man might be cheating at cards. Then Phil leaned back in his chair saying, 'If this was another age, Joel, I'd call you out. How dare you accuse me of cheating.'

It was clear he wasn't troubled by the allegation, no matter how he protested, and he grinned as Joel pushed past us to stomp out of the room, muttering, 'I've lost enough money for one night.'

'That leaves you and me, Lucian,' Phil said, pulling the cards towards him and beginning to shuffle the pack.

Lucian shook his head, then stood up. 'I think I'll call it a night. I'm feeling exhausted with all these changes and rehearsals.' He yawned, but it was obvious he was pretending.

Phil shrugged. 'Suit yourself.' He gazed around the room. 'Anyone else want to play?' he called but there was no response, and he began to put the deck of cards back into the box.

Neville, who'd given every appearance of being engrossed in the football match raised his head and caught Lucian by the arm as he went out. 'You know Phil's a professional gambler,' he said. 'You don't want to get mixed up with him. Steer clear.'

Lucian nodded. 'I know – he's always betting on something or other. I don't think he was cheating. He's very good. Joel doesn't like to be beaten at anything.'

'There you go then,' Neville said. 'Leave playing with Phil to the big boys.'

Lucian's face grew red, and he muttered something I didn't catch as he hurried out.

Neville looked over at me and raised his eyebrows. 'Never become involved with someone who's a regular gambler,' he said.

'Let's go,' Simon whispered, steering me by the elbow. 'We don't want anything to do with these shenanigans.'

Simon was right. This pantomime might have the outward appearance of everyone pulling together and having a jolly time, but in truth there were so many tensions in the cast. Then again, perhaps this was understandable in view of what had happened.

But once back in our room, I found it hard to concentrate. After I'd read the same page several times I said, 'What did you think of that episode with Phil?'

Simon turned from the television where he was watching a programme about wildlife in Africa. 'What? Oh, no more than a spat. I expect when you all live as closely as they do for a long time there are bound to be difficulties.'

'But if he was cheating at cards…'

'Nothing to do with us, Alison. You must have picked up what Joel's like. Can't bear it if he's not top dog. I expect that applies to cards as much as anything else.' And he turned back to the programme.

Even so, the scene that had played out downstairs nagged at me. If Phil had been cheating, Joel was right to be upset. And surely Phil was aware of the impact of this behaviour on the others.

I sighed and went back to reading my book. There was something odd about the incident I'd just witnessed, some dim memory but I couldn't recall what it was. Perhaps I'd remember later.

THIRTY-FOUR

The next day we awakened to a cloudless sky. For a moment I was disorientated as Simon pulled back the curtains saying, 'Look. Another change in the weather. I suspect we're in for a cold snap.'

I struggled to be fully awake after my disturbed night. 'Better than that awful storm,' I yawned.

Simon was already dressed. 'Did you have a bad night? I'll make you a cup of coffee.'

'No, thanks.' I swung my legs out of bed. The coffee on offer on the hospitality tray in the room was of the cheapest kind. A much stronger brew was required.

'I might go along to the library today. I've an idea for an article I could pitch,' I said once we were settled in the dining room for breakfast. I watched Simon over the rim of my cup, to see how he would react.

'I thought you were having a break from work till after New Year?' he said.

'Oh, I'm not intending to write anything, but it's a good opportunity to make some notes,' I said, adding,

'After what you told me about the statue I might try to find out more information about St Mary's. I've been online and it appears there's a lot of interest in what remains of the original building. It'll give me something to do, and the weather looks as if it will hold. You never know when it will turn again.'

A few hours apart might be a good idea. We were still trying to adjust to this new life of being together all the time – not easy after Simon had been working in America for several years and I'd become rather used to doing as I pleased.

'I'll take advantage of the better weather and go out to Scalpsie Bay,' Simon said. 'Sure you don't want to join me?'

I shook my head. 'I'll walk to the library – that will give me plenty of exercise,' I said, and having agreed our separate plans for the day, I set off in a lighter mood. I'd every intention of going to the library to find some background information on St Mary's, but I also intended to call in at the Hall.

Wilson was trying hard to keep everyone motivated, but it wasn't easy and even with his fondness for making changes, there were only so many he could do without turning it into a different pantomime. This morning the members of the cast had already had breakfast and gone over to the Hall.

'Oh, that Wilson Wright keeps them busy,' Gladys Jaxman said as she cleared away the breakfast dishes. 'Doesn't like to see them slacking. Better than having them hanging around here.' As the owner of the hotel she probably preferred not to have them in the hotel all day. They could be hard work.

My time was limited. As we came out of the hotel Simon said, kissing me on the cheek, 'I'll see you back here at one o'clock – we can have lunch together.'

I watched as he drove off. He was right: the temperature had dropped considerably, and I was glad I'd be indoors for the morning. The walk into Rothesay was bracing though and I kept to the prom, watching the seagulls swooping and diving. In the marina those boats overwintering on the island bobbed at anchor, their flags fluttering in the increasing wind, showing the variety of ports these boats had journeyed from.

The library was quiet this early in the morning. I'd been here on many occasions and was well used to the microfiche system. Where to start? My idea was to write a couple of linked articles about St Mary's which might be of interest to one of the magazines specialising in Scottish interest stories.

Of course, while trawling through the microfiches, searching for information, it was difficult not to be distracted. There were so many other stories about the history of Bute, I found it hard to concentrate. And my mind kept drifting back to the strange little statue found behind the wall panelling in the cottage. Could Simon be right? Was our statue one of those originally set in the tomb of the Knight?

A hunt through the archives uncovered a story in an early edition of the local paper The Buteman about the initial renovations of the Chancel. It appeared Simon's information had been correct: the statues located in the niches had disappeared some time before the 1890s. The one found in our cottage must be of some value if it had been hidden like that. But I soon realised what a task I'd set myself. This could take all morning.

I sat back. What did it matter? Simon was right. It was really no concern of mine apart from a nagging curiosity. And then there was the possibility if the owners couldn't be traced we might fall heir to the statue, I thought, then dismissed the idea as unlikely. Of course there would be someone with a better claim to this artefact than us. Much depended on the decision of the expert Eliza had contacted.

Suddenly realising I'd have to go if I wanted to fit in a visit to the Hall before meeting Simon, I closed down the microfiche and gathered my belongings. My plan to research articles on St Mary's would have to wait till later.

I came out into the chilling wind, shivering as I began to walk up to the Hall. I stopped. If it was quick, I'd have time for a coffee.

The Coffee Stop was quiet – only a couple of young women seated at the window table overlooking the street, so I slipped in, opting for a table at the back. The fragrant smell of fresh baking hit me as soon as I entered, making nonsense of my resolution to have no more than a cup of coffee. Then I reasoned it was cold outside and the extra calories essential for my walk up the High Street.

As I enjoyed the treat of a large slice of carrot cake with my cappuccino, I scrolled through my phone. Engrossed in the weather forecast for the next week, I was startled to hear a voice beside me say, 'Hello, Alison. Are you also hiding?'

I looked up to see Rhoda standing beside me. Close up she looked older than I'd first thought and little laughter lines had gathered at the corners of her eyes.

'Mind if I join you?' she said.

'Of course.' I managed a smile of welcome.

She pulled out the chair opposite me and shrugged off her heavy coat. 'I'm glad to be somewhere warm,' she said.

'Shouldn't you be at the Hall with the others?'

'What?' She looked up from examining the menu and leaned forward, putting her elbows on the table. 'I've told them I had to go to the Post Office, to send a Christmas card to my aunt in Australia. I'll have a walk down there after my coffee. Might even buy a few stamps.'

I waited, unsure how to respond.

She chuckled. 'A lie of course, but I had to get away for an hour. It's all become so difficult.'

'In what way?' Perhaps this encounter would be useful – she might have information about Cormac.

'I'm sure I don't need to tell you. There's so much disquiet in the company. Oh, Wilson is trying to do his best, but his way of doing so isn't helpful. I mean how many script rewrites can we deal with?'

'Possibly he's making sure the production is perfect before you go to the next venue.' I knew this was unlikely, but it was a prompt…and it worked. Now that she had started she seemed eager to have someone to confide in.

'It's all because of Joel. From the beginning he's been determined that he would hog the limelight.'

'Well, he is the biggest star…' I ventured, but Rhoda would have none of it.

'You mean because he's in that Soap, The House at Strathloch? Don't believe all you hear. The word is he's about to be written out. Come to a grisly end.' She sniggered, then covered her mouth.

'Sorry, I shouldn't be telling tales out of school. But everyone in the cast knows. Except, it would seem, Wilson. He kowtows to Joel all the time.'

I was finding it hard to make sense of this. 'Surely Joel is a big star? Look at the way he's mobbed wherever he goes.'

Rhoda was dismissive. 'Oh, you mean that gaggle of teenage girls who hang around the Hall? We all know how fickle they can be. Wait and see what happens when he's dropped from the Soap.'

This didn't sound plausible. Joel's part in The House at Strathloch was central to the action.

‘Someone will surely snap him up?’

Rhoda tapped her spoon on the saucer. ‘Don’t you believe it. He’s upset a lot of people in his climb to the top. I’ve a feeling he’ll get his just desserts.’

She couldn’t disguise the glee in her voice as she continued. ‘I heard he went out to the Strathloch House with Benita, expecting a warm welcome, but the owners only let them in with some reluctance. Didn’t recognise him at first.’

This story made me feel sorry for him…almost. But then I’d seen for myself how he treated others in the cast, determined to have most lines, be centre stage.

‘It’s been a difficult time for everyone,’ I said. ‘What with Valeria’s death and then Cormac’s. I don’t suppose there’s been any more word…’ I let my voice trail away, watching for her reaction.

At first it seemed she wouldn’t say anything but suddenly she glanced around before leaning forward and saying in a low voice, ‘Don’t you think it’s suspicious that there have been two deaths?’

‘Well, yes, I do,’ I admitted, ‘but surely Valeria’s was an accident.’

‘We’ll soon find out,’ she said. ‘But Cormac’s death was no accident.’

I waited, but she stood up and grabbed her coat. ‘I must be off. I told Wilson I’d be quick. He’ll be fretting about something or other.’

And might be worried you’d disappeared again, I thought but instead ‘I might see you later,’ I called after her, but she was already out of the door and almost running down the street.

I pondered what Rhoda had said. Then another idea occurred to me. Did Rhoda have proof Cormac’s death was deliberate?

THIRTY-FIVE

After leaving the café I walked quickly to the Hall. I'd still no clear plan of action. Despite my many promises to myself (and to Simon), I couldn't help but speculate on the deaths at The Mickle. Wilson was looking more and more dishevelled each time I saw him, the problems weighing heavily on him.

I made straight for Valeria's office, ignoring the muted sounds of voices from the theatre on the floor above. I'd have to find a way of talking to each of the cast independently. But who to start with?

Felicity perhaps? She'd been noticeably quiet. I could use that as a way of introducing the subject. Say we were worried about her, after the alarming events with Valeria and Cormac. Or Benita? She had lurked in the background, saying little. Though she must be friendly with Joel if he'd agreed to take her on a visit to Strathloch.

In the end the best idea was to take a few of the papers from the pile lying on my desk as a way of making it look as if I was on official business.

But as it turned out the first person I talked to was Neville. I came out of the office to go upstairs to the theatre as Neville came tearing in through the main door and we collided heavily, sending the papers I was carrying flying.

'Look where you're going, why don't you,' he said, making no attempt to apologise, far less help me pick them up.

'I think it was your fault as much as mine,' I said, feeling the anger rise. There was no need for him to be so rude.

He stopped and for a minute I thought he was about to make a snippy remark. To my surprise he said, 'Sorry, sorry. I'm so taken up with this dreadful business.' He didn't have to explain. He bent down to help me retrieve the papers.

'That's okay,' I said slightly appeased. He was right – all this trouble must be difficult for the cast to deal with.

'Is there…is there any more word?' I said. 'About Cormac? Or Valeria?'

'Apart from the news that Cormac was deliberately poisoned…and that Valeria's death is suspicious?' He handed over the papers. 'I dread to think who might be responsible. It has to be someone in the company, that's the worst of it.'

'You have some ideas, then?' I was determined to keep him talking. I might not have this opportunity again.

He stroked his chin. 'If I had, I wouldn't tell anyone. There's enough gossip going the rounds without my adding to it. I'm sure the police are making progress.'

Drat! This was hopeless. I'd have to speak to the others and hope that, despite what he'd said, Neville might have confided in one of them.

'I'd better get back to the theatre,' he said but then he turned around as he left, saying, 'I'm not saying he had anything to do with the deaths, but I don't think bringing Joel into the company has helped. Some monstrous ego that young man has. He's always on a short fuse with anyone who dares to cross him.'

The phrase “people in glass houses” sprang to mind, but I said nothing.

‘Yes,’ he went on, ‘I don’t know why Wilson insisted on bringing him in to the pantomime cast.’

‘He’s a big name. Sometimes a production needs a star name to attract an audience.’

Wrong thing to say. Neville snorted. ‘Really? You think so? I suppose if you mean an audience of screaming teenage girls, that’s true. But this is meant to be a family production. We don’t need that kind of audience.’

I mumbled something about, ‘Guess it takes all sorts,’ but either he didn’t pick up or chose to ignore my comment.

He laughed. ‘Cormac was the one he couldn’t abide. Probably because as an old trooper Cormac recognised how little talent Joel really has. And didn’t hesitate to say so at every opportunity.’

He turned and without a word of goodbye began to walk away briskly upstairs to the theatre, leaving me staring after him. There were so many undercurrents in this company, so much resentment and envy, it could have been any one of them who’d been responsible for the deaths.

The papers were scrambled together anyhow, and I shuffled them to give some semblance of order.

I tried to remember what I’d heard about Valeria. Someone had mentioned a gambling habit, but that was to do with Phil, not Valeria. So what had happened to the money in the expenses account?

But if Neville was right, could Joel have been so angry with Cormac that he killed him? Even if it was true, there was no possible motive to kill Valeria. She had no direct say in the production, at least not in anything that concerned Joel’s role in the pantomime.

Surely it was a long shot. But it might have given the quick-tempered Joel a motive for wanting rid of Cormac.

THIRTY-SIX

Unable to think of a way to question the cast members individually, I decided not to linger at the Hall. I put the papers back on my desk. There was plenty to think about. A reason for the missing funds was becoming clear, but there was no motive for killing Valeria. If it had been deliberate and not an accident.

There was no option but to ask Wilson, but not yet. It was all such a muddle. Motive and opportunity were the watchwords of any major crime, but on this occasion I'd little evidence of either as far as Valeria was concerned.

Simon was right. I'd more than enough to deal with in my home life without becoming embroiled in this. And yet, and yet.

I hurried out of the building, hoping a local bus would come along soon. Else I wouldn't make it back in time to meet Simon as promised.

But I was out of luck, and a glance at the timetable on the bus stop told me I'd missed one a couple of minutes before. With the next one not due for thirty minutes, I'd be better to start walking.

I reached Guildford Square only ten minutes late, which I considered reasonable, but Simon was pacing up and down in front of the parade of shops, impatience written all over his face.

'I'm not very late,' I said, trying to catch my breath.

The frown on his face told me that wasn't what was troubling him.

'No, that's not the problem,' he said. He looked sheepish. 'The walk wasn't such a good idea – not without proper shoes. I called in at the library expecting to find you there, but the librarian said you'd left a couple of hours ago.'

'I couldn't find what I was looking for and I decided to abandon the research on St Mary's.'

'So what did you do instead?'

Ah, this was the question. What was I going to say? Suddenly seized by inspiration, I said, 'I thought I might write an article about Strathloch House. You know, the one in the soap opera starring Joel Bennett.'

'And that proved fruitless?'

'I may have been looking in the wrong place,' I said. 'Then I went for a cup of coffee and suddenly remembered I wanted to speak to Wilson.'

'You went along to the Hall?' He sighed. 'Oh, Alison. Please leave all the investigation to the police. You know how I worry about you. You've surely had too many lessons about how dangerous these situations can be.'

Stung by his words, I said, 'There's no need to worry. I didn't see him.' Which wasn't a lie, more an omission.

The look he gave me made me think he wasn't convinced, but all he said was, 'How about lunch?' and a few minutes later we were snug inside a local café.

'Oh, I almost forgot. There's been a development in the statue affair.'

'Really? So soon?'

He smiled. 'When I decided to opt out of the Loch

Fad walk, I stopped by St Mary's Church. I thought it would be a good idea to check for myself the Knight's tomb with the niches for the statues of the armed knights.'

'I must have missed you,' I said. 'You must have left shortly before I came out of the Hall. What did you discover?'

'I'm convinced now that the statue found in our cottage is one of the missing statues.'

'Really? What makes you so certain?'

Simon reached into his pocket and brought out a couple of sheets of crumpled paper, placing them on the table and smoothing them out. 'I've also been investigating but I didn't want to tell you till I was certain. This is a sketch of how it might have looked when the statues were there.'

'So what do you think happened?'

'My guess is they went missing when the Chancel of the original chapel was being renovated.'

'But how on earth did one of them end up behind the panelling in our cottage?'

Simon sat back and sighed. 'No idea. And there should have been twelve of them. So goodness knows what happened to the others.'

'What do we do now?'

'We wait till Eliza comes back with an update from her colleague. Once we have that confirmation then I think we have to make a choice.'

I looked up from trying to decide between a chicken wrap (the healthy option) and the cheeseburger (not quite so healthy, though it did come with salad). 'But we are going to try to find the owner.'

There was a pause as the waitress came over to take our order and then he said, 'It may be valuable…or it may not. Either way, now I've a good idea what it is, there's nothing we can do till Eliza has some news for me.'

'Perhaps we should try to find out more about it?'

Simon shook his head. 'Leave well alone…or rather leave it to the experts…' Before he could finish, his phone rang and he pulled it out of his pocket.

I could only hear one side of the conversation, but it sounded hopeful whatever it was. It was only when he rang off with, 'Thanks again, Benny,' that I understood there might be good news about progress at the cottage.

'Excellent news, Alison,' Simon said. 'That's Benny getting back to me. I phoned him earlier. He says they're bang on schedule and the work should be finished tomorrow. Thank goodness. I don't want to spend any more time in that hotel.'

'It's fine, surely. Gladys has tried to make our stay as comfortable as possible.'

'No, it's not that. I feel I'm always on tenterhooks, trying to dodge contact with the actors. I'll be glad to be home.'

'So will I,' I said, but I wasn't as enthusiastic, anticipating the amount of work waiting for us to clear up after the workmen. Still, Simon was right. By the weekend we'd be home, the police would be dealing with the problem of the statue and The Mickle would be leaving for Islay.

We came out into a cold wind, but the rain was beginning to clear again, and the arc of a rainbow shimmered over Rothesay Bay. A trio of seagulls swooped over one of the large yachts, stridently calling. Possibly they'd spotted a source of food, though feeding them was actively discouraged.

As we reached Craigmore, pausing once or twice to watch the next ferry creaming into the harbour, my phone buzzed, and we stopped in the nearest shelter to let me answer it. It was a battle against the wind to make out who was calling. The voice was no more than a whisper and twice I had to ask the caller to repeat. It was Rhoda. 'I have to see you, Alison. There's been a development and I can't talk to anyone at The Mickle about it.'

Frustratingly, she would say no more except, 'Can we meet? How about somewhere away from the hotel or the Hall. There's a café out at Ettrick Bay. And it has to be soon.'

'I know it well,' I said and after agreeing a time I switched the phone to silent. Simon was staring at me. 'What was that all about?'

I'd no option but to tell him and he said nothing, merely shook his head.

'It's Rhoda,' I said. 'It sounds as if she wants someone to chat to. She's probably feeling depressed about the delays to the tour.'

'I hope that's all it is.' He stood up. 'Let's walk. It's chilly sitting here.'

But I hadn't told him the full story of the phone call and I was curious about what Rhoda might have to say. And surely Rhoda wasn't the only one who'd come to the realisation that The Mickle was in deep trouble.

THIRTY-SEVEN

Simon declined to come with me to meet Rhoda, which suited me well. I was curious if what she had to say was connected to her disappearance.

'I'd like to pop over to the cottage if you're going to Ettrick Bay,' he said. 'Check on the work so far. You can drop me off.' He was beginning to fret about the progress of the work, despite Benny's reassurances earlier.

'I won't be long,' I said. 'I could text when I'm finished and pick you up to go over to the mainland. We need lamps for the living room, and this would be a good opportunity.'

I can't say Simon is a fan of shopping but a trip to Greenock and the purchase of new lamps would make us feel we were making progress in moving back to the cottage. But I wasn't surprised when he muttered, 'Yes, but not today. It will be too late by the time you come back. Let's arrange a full day out and buy everything we need at the same time. I'll take the bus back to the hotel and see you there.'

When we stopped outside the cottage we were greeted by noises of hammering and banging, accompanied by tuneless whistling. This didn't sound promising, given we'd been told Benny and Gus would be finished in time to allow the painter to complete the job by the end of the week. Yet again I wished we'd left well alone until the Spring.

With these concerns, I wasn't inclined to linger and saying, 'I'll text you as soon as I can,' I drove off through Port Bannatyne to take the left turn towards the bay.

The Port was quiet. An elderly man was walking his dog over by the playpark and a couple stood chatting in the bus shelter, moving restlessly to keep warm. The boatyard was deserted, crowded with boats laid up for the winter, though the buoys still bobbed about in the choppy waters of the bay, marking out the berthing places for summer. Even the school was quiet: at this time in the afternoon the children would be indoors at lessons.

A couple of horses, rugged up, grazed in the field below the farm, pausing to look up as I drove past, but the Tramway walk out to the bay, so popular in summer, was deserted and I didn't meet any other cars on the road. At the old Ettrickdale Smithy, now a private residence, the outside was bedecked with fairy lights, glittering even at this time of day. A wrought iron sculpture of a horse had been added to the front garden as a reminder of the history of this building as a working blacksmith's shop.

My meeting with Rhoda would be a short one – the tearoom closed early in winter, but as I came down to the bay, there were several cars in the car park.

After locking the car I stopped for a few minutes to look over the steel grey water. The wind was fiercer here, whipping up the sand beneath the waves to create an eerie pink light. Seaweed, brought ashore on the last tide, bunched up all along the edge of the beach. The glamping pods in the field beside the tearoom were full, judging by the buckets and spades and the carelessly discarded beach towels on the front decking.

I shivered and pulling my coat tightly around me, opened the door to the tearoom to be greeted by a wave of warmth.

At this time of the afternoon the only other occupants of the café were an elderly couple and three teenagers.

Rhoda was sitting opposite one of the large windows with a view of the bay, but she was busy scrolling through her phone and looked up, startled, as I said, ‘Good to see you, Rhoda. Hope you haven’t been waiting long.’

She slammed her phone down on the table and beckoned the waitress over. ‘They close in half an hour,’ she said.

‘They do work hard all summer,’ I said, ‘and at this time of year there aren’t many tourists.’

My defence fell on deaf ears as she said abruptly to the teenage waitress, ‘Two coffees, no sugar.’

I smiled and said, ‘Thank you,’ attempting to make up for Rhoda’s gruffness. There was nothing I could do about her bad mood and I said, ‘What was so urgent and so secret we had to meet out here?’

She looked around, but none of the customers was within earshot. Even so, she leaned forward and began to speak in a low voice. ‘It’s about the pantomime cast, about the players.’

‘I’d guessed that,’ I said.

There was a moment’s hiatus as the waitress came over with our coffees before Rhoda spoke again. ‘What do you think of Joel?’

Now was not the time to be saying what I really thought about him – that he was arrogant and self-centred. And she’d said as much during our last conversation, so I’d no idea why she should suddenly be asking me. Then I remembered the conversation with Neville and cautiously said, 'I think he plays the part of the Prince well,' I said, watching all the time for her reaction. 'Certainly his teenage fans seem to think so.'

She sat back, fiddling with the spoon, tapping it on the saucer. 'I don't mean his acting ability. I mean about these deaths.'

I'd guessed correctly then but holding my hands up, said, 'Oh, don't ask me about that. I've no idea. I'm sure the police will sort it out.'

Rhoda looked out past me to the view of the bay. 'There is something going on, that's for certain. You might not believe me, but Joel's position in that soap opera isn't as secure as he thinks. He's made a lot of enemies.'

'Oh, really?' I wasn't about to remind her what she'd said before about Joel.

'Yes. He's young of course, has no idea how quickly you can rise to fame…and how quickly fall. Once the public tire of you there's no going back. And television is worst of all for that.'

Perhaps she was talking about herself, but it was Cormac who sprang immediately to mind.

Thinking I could do with another coffee but not wanting to break the flow of Rhoda's story, I waited.

'I know you're only helping Wilson out as a favour, but we need someone with no vested interest in the company, who doesn't know too much about the personalities involved…'

'I've finished the job I promised to do,' I said. 'The rest is down to Wilson. He's going to hire a new administrative assistant to take care of all the paperwork, to sort out the schedule for the rest of the tour.'

Rhoda laughed. 'Do you think so? Where is he

going to get the money for that?'

How much did Rhoda know about the state of the company's finances?

Out of the corner of my eye I could see the kitchen staff were beginning to clear up and the waitress who'd served us was busy wiping down the tables. In a few minutes she'd reach ours. I wanted to put an end to this conversation, and this seemed a good opportunity.

'I think we'd better leave. They'll be closing in a few minutes.'

But Rhoda wasn't to be so easily put off. She grabbed at the sleeve of my coat.

'Wait a minute, Alison. We can't leave it like that. You must know why there are money problems in the company.'

I shrugged. The waitress was coming ever closer, slowing down as she approached.

'I did hear there had been trouble with the account Valeria managed. But surely the main account is safe, and it won't cost much to hire a temporary assistant.'

Realising we had to go, Rhoda gathered her belongings and shrugged on her coat. 'I don't think it's as simple as that, Alison.' She hesitated. 'You know I was away for a couple of days?'

'Yes,' I said, waiting for what she might say next, glad she'd raised the subject before I did.

But now she looked as if she thought she'd made a mistake and I said, 'There must have been a good reason.'

She sighed. 'Yes. I had to check something out on the mainland.'

'But the ferries were off.'

'There was a short weather window when the Rhubodach to Colintraive ferry was on, though it meant I couldn't get back till the storm subsided. I had to stay in the Colintraive Hotel.'

'Really? It must have been important.'

But now the café lights were going out and we stood up, ready to leave.

As I started to speak, Rhoda shook her head. 'I'm waiting on confirmation of something and then I'm going to the police. To be honest, I'm worried there will be another death.' She made a face. 'You must realise it has to be someone in the company who's responsible. Please listen to what I'm saying. You're in a good position to find out more – you're working with us but you're not one of us.'

Her story about Joel could only mean one thing – she suspected he might be the killer.

THIRTY-EIGHT

I left the meeting with Rhoda more confused than ever and stood at the café entrance in the gathering dusk, watching as she roared off in her car, skidding as she took the bend to the Ettrickdale Road too fast.

What had Rhoda been hinting at? And did she expect me to follow up? From what she said I could guess she believed someone in the company was responsible for the deaths of both Valeria and Cormac. Problem was, I couldn't think of a motive for either death. Valeria wasn't an actor and her death only created difficulties for the theatre company. And Joel was the star of the show with nothing to gain by Cormac's death. Joel was quick-tempered, liable to act on the spur of the moment, and it would have required careful planning to put poison in the goblet without being detected.

Surely the deaths had created far too many complications to be the work of a member of the cast.

Rhoda apparently believed that, as an outsider, I'd be in a position to find out the truth. I was less certain. From what Wilson had said, the only money problem was with the expenses account. The main account was solvent. But if Rhoda was correct, there were other financial problems. Unless, unless.

I tried to estimate how much the takings might have been from all the performances already staged on Bute, even after the costs of hiring the Hall were factored in. There was a possibility Wilson was using the money he'd taken in box office receipts as a way of financing the next part of the trip.

Stop it, I said to myself. Leave well alone. But Rhoda had seemed genuinely upset, not only for herself, but on behalf of the others in the company. And she seemed to be concerned that whoever was responsible for the deaths might kill again.

As I started to walk towards my car the lights in the café dimmed and the waitress who'd served us came out, saying goodbye to someone unseen as she turned to walk towards the bus stop.

'Hi,' I called after her. 'Would you like a lift into town?'

She spun around and smiled. 'That would be good. The bus isn't due for another fifteen minutes and it's cold standing waiting.'

I opened the passenger door and she slipped in, saying, 'Usually I get a lift into Rothesay, but the stocktaking had to be done tonight so I said I'd take the bus.'

Darkness began to descend as we drove back and I put my headlights on to full beam, narrowly avoiding a rabbit scurrying out in front of us. As we passed the Ettrickdale Forge and St Colmac's cottages the fairy lights adorning the windows and the doorways twinkled welcomingly.

'I hate it when Christmas is over,' said the waitress who'd introduced herself as Kerry Dawd. 'When everyone takes the decorations down the place looks so sad.'

'I have to agree,' I said. 'Now, where would you like me to drop you?'

'I live at Craigmore, but if you drop me in Port Bannatyne I can catch a bus from there.'

'No, I can take you over to Craigmore. It's on the way to the hotel.'

She looked puzzled. 'I thought you lived in the Port.' And then I had to explain as briefly as possible about the work at the cottage.

Kerry chattered as we drove along but during a lull in the conversation, I said, 'Have you seen The Sleeping Beauty Pantomime?'

She shook her head and grinned. 'I'm rather old for that.'

'I thought you might be a fan of Joel Bennett?'

'Most certainly not. He's made himself unpopular here.'

Now I was intrigued. 'Really? There seem to be any number of teenage girls who are fans.'

'That's as may be. But you know he's in that stupid Soap? Well, of course some of the filming has been done on the island at Cois Na Farraige House. That's the place out at Ascog that's used as Strathloch.'

'Ah, yes, I remember someone mentioning that. But I didn't know that was its real name.'

She laughed. 'Everyone calls it Strathloch now.'

I couldn't resist the next question. 'What makes you think he's unpopular?'

She turned her head, gazed out of the window, although by now darkness had fallen over Kames Bay as we rounded the corner into Port Bannatyne.

'Valeria Dixon is…was…a relative of mine.' Then she said, seeing the look of astonishment on my face, 'Not a close relative. But she was a second or a third cousin on my Mum's side. When she saw her name on the poster credits she was pleased as punch.'

'So she met up with Valeria?' Concentrating on the shore road through Ardbeg where the cars parked all along one side of the road effectively made it single track, I couldn't see her face.

'Oh, yes. 'A deep sigh. 'She was so excited. She'd no contact details, of course…I think they lost touch years ago… but she went along to the Hall, and I believe they had a good chat about the various branches of the family. They planned to meet up again…but then she died in that awful accident.' Then she said, 'Valeria wasn't entirely happy, though she wouldn't say why. We all get fed up with our jobs, I guess.'

'Mmm…her death was very sad.' I'd no intention of saying that there was a suspicion about how she'd died. If everyone believed it had been a tragic accident, that was fine.

'Next house on the right past the junction,' she said and a few minutes later we pulled up in front of a small modern house set between a couple of large traditional Victorian villas.

As though guessing what I was thinking, she said, 'My parents managed to get enough money together to buy this place. It's a bit of a comedown for them, but at least being modern it's warm and cosy.'

'Why? Where did they live before?'

She stepped out of the car, then leaned back into the passenger side. 'My great grandparents worked for the owners of Cois Na Farraige and lived in the rather grand lodge house. When Mr Arris died young they were kept on by the new owners, and my grandparents and then my parents worked for the family who bought it from them. The tenancy of the Lodge House passed down through the family. But eventually the people who owned the house also had to sell.'

'Ah, they decided it would be better to sell such a large house?'

A shadow crossed her face. ‘I think “decided” isn’t the correct word. The owner’s business crashed, and my parents had no choice but to find somewhere else to live. If only the family who bought it from the Arris family had been able to hold out for another couple of years. Look what’s happened to the present owners of Cois Na Farraige. They’ve done rather nicely out of renting it out as the location for the Soap.’ She stood up. ‘Thanks for the lift – that saved me a wait at the bus stop. See you.’

I watched as she ran nimbly up the driveway. At the front door she turned and waved before disappearing inside.

I sat for a few minutes before starting up the car. This was yet another strand to the strange story of what was happening at The Mickle. So many people seemed to be connected. But that was the truth of life on the island. Then I thought, Why was nothing ever simple?

THIRTY-NINE

The hotel was busy. The cast had taken over the lounge, the seats in the entrance lobby and, as I saw when I peeped in, even the dining room. Benita and Neville were seated at one of the tables, a chessboard in front of them, frowning in concentration.

I heard Phil call over to Benita, 'Did you go back to Strathloch…or whatever its real name is?'

Before she could reply, Joel said, 'The owners were delighted to show us around, tell us about the history of the house…'

I didn't wait to hear more of this story, knowing it wasn't true, but my attempt to creep past to reach the stairs to my room failed. The door to the lounge was ajar and Wilson was sitting there.

He stood up and came out into the hallway. 'Not back at your cottage, Alison?'

'No,' I said, poised with one foot on the stair to show I'd no intention of lingering. 'But the cottage should be ready tomorrow if all goes according to schedule.'

He looked so glum I felt I had to ask, 'How are the plans for the rest of the tour going?'

At this he appeared even more despondent. 'Not well, not well at all.'

'What's the problem?' I said.

'It's the weather,' he said. 'As you know the date for travelling to Islay is Monday, but the forecast is for more storms at the weekend.'

Just then Rhoda came in, bringing a gust of fresh air. She stopped when she saw us.

'Something wrong?' she said, but the look she gave me made me think she suspected that, despite my promise, I'd told Wilson about our meeting at Ettrick Bay.

'We were chatting about the problems with the weather,' I said hastily. 'About how difficult it is making arrangements to travel around the islands when it's so unpredictable. Such a nuisance when you have to…'I trailed off as I caught Wilson staring at me, ending up lamely with, 'I'd better go and find out what Simon has planned for this evening.'

When I met up with him a few minutes later, Simon said, before I'd time to take my coat off. 'There's been more news, Alison. About the statue.'

He was so excited about this latest development it saved me explaining why Rhoda had been insistent on meeting me at the Ettrick Bay tearoom.

'Oh, that's good. What's the story?'

'It would appear there's a link with that house, the one that doubles for that soap opera location.'

I laughed. 'Yes, it is tricky to say. I think it's Cois Na Farraige – but in the Soap it's called Strathloch for obvious reasons.'

'Because no one can pronounce the real name?'

'No, because you might not want too many people identifying the location. Though a few minutes ago I heard Joel boasting about how welcoming the owners had been when he and Benita went over. Though that's not what I heard.' I smiled. 'But enough of that. Tell me what's happened. Has Eliza been in touch?'

'Not yet. And I'm really curious about the statue and if it might be one of those from the Knight's tomb at St Mary's.' He bit his lip. 'Your streak of curiosity must be catching.'

I ignored this. 'And?' I said.

Simon looked pleased with himself. 'I managed to contact Calum. You remember him? He's a member of the Bute Antiquarian Society – knows everything about the history of the island – and it struck me he might have useful information.'

I grinned. 'Your golfing partner, you mean.'

'Well, yes, that too. And…' Simon looked as if he'd every intention of spinning the story out. 'Calum told me the original owners of that house had been involved in a restoration project at St Mary's. Not long after the project was completed, it was noticed that the statues in the niches around the Knight's tomb had gone missing. There was a suspicion that the owner of the house had something to do with it…'

'Cois Na Farraige,' I prompted him, not at all certain my attempt at pronunciation was any better.

'Yes, well, that's the story. There was a huge market for artefacts among the gentry at that time so there would have been no problem in finding buyers who were prepared to pay.'

'But what value would there be in the statues. They're not worth much, surely?'

'That's where you're wrong. This kind of antique still has a great value on the market – wealthy collectors who want a piece of history and don't ask too many questions.'

'But that means whoever owned our cottage must have known about it? If the original owner of Cois Na Farraige was involved, how did one of the statues end up behind the panelling in the cottage? It would only be of interest if it could be sold.'

Simon shrugged. 'Too dangerous to sell it on the

island? And perhaps no opportunity to go over to the mainland?'

'That makes no sense. There were far more boats travelling between the mainland and Bute in the past. And sailing directly from Glasgow. When did you say the statues disappeared?'

'Calum confirmed what I found on the internet – the records showed the statues in the niches had disappeared by the 1890s. The restoration was completed about then, so that makes sense.'

'That's a co-incidence,' I said and told him about my meeting with Kerry and how her great grandparents knew the original owners of the property, had worked for them.

'Ah, the Arris family. Yes, Calum knew their story. They were from Glasgow originally. He made his money at the start of the Industrial Revolution. They had a property in Charlotte Street but as the factories began to encroach on the area, he moved his family to Bute and kept a small house on in the West End.'

'They were the original owners?'

'Yes, but it was rather a tragic story. Samuel Arris died suddenly in 1892 without making a will. He was only thirty-five. He left a widow and three young children, and the house had to be sold.'

'Heavens, that was young even for those days. What did he die of?'

'An accident. He was crossing the road at Jamaica Bridge on the way from his office to Central Station to pick up the Rothesay steamer at the Broomielaw when a carter lost control of his horse. He was trampled to death.'

There was yet another puzzle. 'But if the Arris family was involved, why did they not sell them? That money might have helped save the house.'

Simon shrugged. 'It's only a guess, but possibly they were hidden until an opportunity arose to sell them. If Samuel Arris didn't tell the family about the statues they would have no way of knowing about them when he died suddenly.'

'Which means the rest of the statues might still be hidden at Strathloch. And the one in our cottage was either stolen by whoever lived there or was given in payment to keep the workmen quiet.'

'We have to find out who might have worked on those renovations and if there was any connection to our cottage…who lived there at that time.'

Simon chewed at a fingernail. 'I suspect it must have been one of the workmen who renovated St Mary's Chapel.'

None of this helped, except that we had a back story that might or might not be true. 'Unless the story Phinn told us about the woman who came looking for something in our cottage makes sense.'

Then I had an idea. 'Do you think Benny would know about the Arris family? It's a long shot, but his family has been in the building trade a long time, worked all over the island.'

'Mmm. Might be worth asking. Though I doubt if Benny's firm was around in the 1890s.'

'And we can check again on progress, Simon. Benny still says they should be finished by Friday.'

'Yes, and we can have that shopping trip. The ferries are running again to timetable if you still want to go to the mainland tomorrow to look for new lamps.'

'Yes,' I said, 'there are several items we have to buy. We can make a list.'

'Oh, no,' groaned Simon. 'Not a list.'

We drove to the cottage in good spirits but when we

drew up outside, Simon said, ‘That’s strange. The place is in darkness. I thought Benny said he was going to work on to make sure he finished on time.’

‘Perhaps he has finished,’ I said, but Simon didn’t appreciate my joke as he said, ‘I think he’d have phoned me.’

The front door was ajar, and Simon went in first, switching on the lights as he went ahead, calling out, ‘Hi, Benny, are you there?’ Although it was unlikely Benny would be working in the dark.

There was a strong smell of cleaning fluid but thank goodness the musty, damp odour had gone. We pushed open the door to the living room to be met by a scene of devastation. Bits of panelling lay strewn across the floor and there was no sign of the replastering work having started.

‘This will never be finished by tomorrow,’ were my first words but Simon put out an arm to hold me back.

‘Wait, Alison, don’t move.’

I tried to peer around him and when he moved aside I saw what had alarmed him. Amid this scene of chaos lay Benny. My first thought was, Oh, no. Had he been attacked? And could it have been anything to do with the discovery of the statue.

FORTY

I stood there, not daring to move. 'Is he dead?' I croaked, scarcely able to get the words out.

Simon didn't answer but knelt down, checking for a pulse.

Whatever would happen next? It was bad enough to be involved with the deaths at The Mickle but to have this happen in our own house was too much.

Simon stood up, straightening his back. 'No, he's alive. Call for an ambulance, Alison.'

I picked my way over the bits of panelling and squeezed past the furniture in the hallway to make the call before hurrying back into the living room. 'They'll be here as quickly as possible.'

There was a soft groan from Benny, confirming he was indeed alive, and he turned his head a little. 'Don't move,' Simon said, placing his hand on Benny's chest. 'Help will be here soon. In the meantime you have to lie perfectly still.'

'What do you think happened?'

Simon stood up and took off his coat to place over the recumbent figure of Benny. He pointed. to the ladder in the corner, now lying askew on the floor.

'It looks as if that's what happened,' he said. 'He fell off the ladder.'

Of course. In the heat of the moment I hadn't noticed. I checked myself in time from making the comment that that fate might have befallen Simon had he carried on with the renovation work.

'But where's Gus?' I said, looking around as though he might suddenly emerge.

'No idea. But Benny shouldn't have been using the ladder on his own.'

'If you stay with Benny, I'll fetch a blanket,' I said and once Benny was comfortable, I went into the kitchen to put on the kettle, more for something to do rather than any desire for tea. But no sooner had I filled the kettle at the tap than there was the welcome sound of the ambulance arriving and, abandoning my task, I opened the front door.

Quietly and efficiently the ambulance staff organised taking Benny to hospital, one of them saying, 'Can you tell me what happened?'

Simon shook his head, 'We came back to check on the progress of the work and found him like this. I can make a guess he fell off the ladder and banged his head, but I don't know for sure.'

'No matter, the hospital will deal with it,' and then they moved him carefully into the ambulance, no doubt lest there should be broken bones, while he was making more soft moaning noises, much to my relief. He was still alive, that was the important thing.

Amid this confusion, as Simon and I stood debating if one of us should accompany Benny to the hospital, a voice said, 'Hello, what's happened?' It was Gus, carefully balancing a cardboard container with two large cartons. He stopped suddenly, surveying the scene before him, mouth open.

'There's been an accident. Looks as if Benny fell and possibly hit his head.' Simon stopped and frowned. 'Where were you?'

'He sent me out to buy a new saw from Bute Tools and suggested I bring back some soup from the local shop,' Gus said, indicating the cardboard container. 'It was freezing working here and he thought soup would be a good idea while we worked on.'

This was a long speech for Gus, but Simon wasn't satisfied. 'You must have been gone some time,' he said. 'The cottage was in darkness when we arrived.'

Gus shuffled his feet. ' I didn't mean to be so long. But I met someone in town and…' He didn't finish, but we could guess the rest.

Simon shook his head. 'Well, you're here now.'

'They're taking him to the local hospital,' I said, and Gus dumped the carton on the floor, almost spilling the soup in the process. 'I'll go with him…and I'll let his wife know what's happened,' he said, rushing off before we could stop him, leaving us to follow him to the front door, watching the ambulance as it sped off, siren blaring.

'What do we do now?' I was the first to speak.

Simon looked around. 'It's not what I expected, that's for sure. It's clear Benny was nowhere near finished. No wonder he didn't want us to come over to check. I shouldn't have been so trusting.'

'You're right. I don't know how Benny thought this would be finished by tomorrow. It looks nowhere near completed…and look at this muddle.'

Simon walked over to pick up a piece of the panelling. 'Even had he managed to finish, surely he didn't expect us to clear up. And what about the plastering – never mind the promised painting?'

We stood and stared for another couple of minutes until finally Simon said with a sigh, 'Come on, Alison. There's no point waiting here. Watching it isn't going to improve matters. Best go back to the hotel. I'll phone and find out how Benny is in the morning and then have a word with Gus. He must have some idea about why the work is so far behind.'

We closed the living room door over tightly, but I wasn't sure what good that would do. The dust was everywhere…a fine film on the carpet in the hallway and in the kitchen it was the same story. I could only guess upstairs would be no better. Whatever the outcome, there would be no possibility of moving back here without an army of cleaners to deal with the mess.

I felt wretched, annoyed once again that we hadn't decided to live with the old-fashioned décor… and the panelling. If only Simon hadn't precipitated matters by starting on the ceiling. If only, if only…

'Let's go.' Simon broke into my thoughts. This wasn't the time for regrets. In the morning we'd have to make a decision about what to do next. The thought of spending Christmas in the hotel wasn't appealing, but we couldn't come back here meantime, not until the work was finished.

Simon shut the front door behind us with a bang. Perhaps tomorrow would be better. We could only hope.

FORTY-ONE

We were left with a difficult decision. Should we book another week in the hotel, or should we cut our losses and move back into the cottage, clear it up as best we could, close up the living room and use the rest of the house. It wouldn't be ideal, but it might be better than more time in the hotel…and cheaper. And while we waited to hear how serious were Benny's injuries, we'd no idea when the work could be finished.

'We can't go on talking about it for ever,' Simon said as we rehearsed the arguments for and against for the umpteenth time. Then he stopped. 'Sorry, Alison, this situation is depressing me.'

'I know, I know,' I said. If only something would happen to make the choice for us.

Sighing deeply, Simon said, 'Firstly we have to find out about Benny – how he is…'

'We can't go to the hospital,' I interrupted, 'and badger him about finishing the work.' That would be heartless.

Simon chuckled. 'Of course not. But once we know, we can have a word with Gus.' He stopped. 'He might be able to explain why the work is so far behind.'

I understood Simon was annoyed he hadn't paid more attention to the details, checked on the progress, rather than taking Benny's assurances at face value.

Even so, in the absence of a better idea, his suggestion was good and next morning after breakfast we set off for the hospital.

The road to the Cottage Hospital was quiet – too early for the school traffic to the Rothesay Joint Campus – and the car park outside the single storey building was almost deserted.

'What shall we say?' I muttered, trying to keep pace with Simon as he strode rapidly towards the entrance.

'We don't have to see Benny. We only want to enquire if he's okay. Besides, if his injuries are serious he'll be taken to the hospital at Inverclyde.'

Only a little comforted, I followed him in to the Reception Desk.

The news was good. No bones broken and only mild concussion though, 'He'll be here for a couple of days,' according to the nurse on duty.

'Next step to find Gus,' Simon said as we left.

Now that we knew Benny wasn't badly injured, would make a good recovery, Simon was determined to find out what had caused the delay to the work on the cottage.

There was one snag. We didn't have a contact number for Gus, had no idea where he lived.

'Not a problem,' Simon said when I pointed this out to him. 'We know he lives in Port Bannatyne. We can ask in the general store.'

Oh, the benefits of local knowledge, I thought as we drove back to the village.

The store was busy with customers, including an elderly woman at the Post Office Counter, trying to decide whether to send her parcel first or second class.

'It's only going to Yorkshire,' she said several times over. 'Surely it can't cost as much as that for First

Class.'

I admired the patience of the shopkeeper and the way she finally persuaded the woman to part with her package, reassuring her it would be delivered in plenty of time for her granddaughter's birthday.

'Oh, Gus. Yes I know him,' the woman said, Sadie according to the silver badge she sported. Then a pause. 'What do you want with Gus?' A note of suspicion in her voice.

Simon tried to explain, and I could see her eyes light up. 'Poor Benny,' she said, but it was clear that while she genuinely did feel sorry for him, she was interested to know more of the story.

'Of course I understand,' she said. 'Gus lives at the top of Quay Street in the house with the yellow front door and the flamingos in the front garden.'

Seeing my look of surprise, she added, 'Oh, not real birds – wrought iron flamingos he picked up from a house renovation he was doing. If you ask me the owners were glad to be rid of them. Ugly things – they look nothing like flamingos. But he's proud of them. Takes all sorts.'

Interesting as the story was about Gus and the flamingos he'd acquired, we were keen to leave.

The bell over the shop door jangled suddenly and an elderly couple came in, the man rubbing his hands together.

'Any chance of coffee?' he said, and Sadie excused herself to start up the coffee machine in the corner, setting it hissing and bubbling.

'Thanks for the information,' Simon said as we sidled out with a nod to the couple, now making themselves comfortable at the tiny table and chairs at the front window. In the summer, a café operated on the pavement outside and was always crowded. But not at this time of year.

As we walked up the hill to Gus's house, I said, 'How are we going to tackle this without seeming unfeeling about Benny's accident?'

'Let's not worry about that. Gus must know the state of the cottage isn't defensible. That it shouldn't have been in such a mess. Remember we were told that by this stage the painter would be finishing off and we'd be able to move in by the weekend. Maybe he'll start the conversation when he sees us.'

Simon was right. Gus opened the door almost before the sound of the doorbell died away.

The expression on his face could best be described as embarrassed as he shuffled his feet and avoided our gaze.

'Oh, hello, Mr and Mrs Cameron. I expect you're wondering about the work at the cottage,' he said, the words coming out in a rush.

'Exactly,' Simon said and waited.

Gus chewed at a fingernail. 'It all got a bit difficult. You see…' he continued, '…there was this other job and what with the expense of Christmas coming up and that…,' he stuttered.

'You mean you were doing more than one job at the same time.'

Gus looked defiant. 'Well, we thought we'd finish no problem. But then the other job turned out to be more complicated and your cottage, what with that business of the statue and…'

Simon held up his hand. 'Stop! Let's not get hung up on what's past. What we want to know is when it will be finished.'

'My uncle might be able to help but he…'

My heart sank as Simon interrupted yet again, saying angrily, 'And is he qualified to do this kind of work, your uncle?'

'He's been in the building trade for years,' Gus assured us, but Simon wasn't satisfied. What's more I wasn't happy about conducting this business on the doorstep and I was chilled through. Already I'd noticed a twitch of the curtains next door.

I tugged at Simon's jacket. 'Let's go,' I muttered.

Gus must have heard me, because he said, 'I'll do what I can, but Benny arranged all the work. It's not my fault.'

I could sense Simon was beginning to lose patience. 'We understand that, but there's not much possibility of Benny being able to complete the work any time soon, is there?'

'Suppose not.' Gus sniffed. He repeated, 'I'll ask my uncle.'

This was hopeless. I pulled a card from my bag and scribbled the phone number of the hotel on it. 'We're likely to be at The Four Winds for another couple of days. Contact us there.'

Gus seized the card. 'Yes, yes, I'll do that,' a note of relief in his voice.

We turned away, but not before I'd caught sight of the curtain twitcher hastily pulling back. A black cat sat on the windowsill, glaring at us.

As we walked down the path, neither of us in a good mood, I glanced over at the garden, no more than an expanse of rough grass and a couple of empty flowerbeds. The scene was dominated by three rusting artifacts which I could only guess were the flamingos Sadie had told us about.

'The woman in the shop was right,' I said. 'Those flamingos are hideous.'

FORTY-TWO

'There's not much possibility of finding a builder to finish the work on the living room,' Simon said as we walked down to Marine Road. 'It was difficult enough to find Benny.'

'Even so, I don't want to spend Christmas in the hotel.'

Simon laughed. 'You needn't worry. I heard Gladys ask Wilson how much longer they were planning to stay as they close over Christmas and New Year. We'll have to find somewhere else.'

'Isn't the festive period usually a busy time for the hotels?'

'You would've thought so. But Gladys apparently has lots of family who come over for Christmas and New Year. That's why they close. Afterwards they plan to start the refurbishment.'

That settled it. We'd no option but to return to the cottage and it might be better to do so soon.

'We're booked in for another couple of nights at The Four Winds, so why don't we use the time to clear as much as we can. We might not be able to use the room over Christmas, but we have the kitchen and the bedrooms upstairs.'

'Suppose so.' Simon sounded glum at the prospect. Then he brightened. 'Maybe Gus's uncle would help with the clearing up – get rid of all the old panels and the building materials. I'll call around at Gus's house again later and hope this uncle is available.'

Considerably buoyed by this decision, we walked back to the cottage to reassess the damage after making a detour to buy milk and a newspaper from the local shop. A couple of days clearing the worst of the mess would be hard work, but it was preferable to spending our time going from coffee shop to restaurant.

A surprise awaited us as we approached the cottage. A tall, burly man, unseasonably clad in a t-shirt and shorts, was standing in the garden, gazing up at the roof.

As we approached he turned and said without preamble, 'That roof needs fixing. Those missing slates will cause you no end of trouble if you leave them like that.'

My first thought was that he was one of those builders, or so-called builders, who turn up unannounced and try to persuade you to part with hard-earned cash to do unnecessary work. We'd met plenty of them in our time.

'We're not interested, thanks,' Simon said politely. I could tell he was about to ask the builder to leave, but before he could do so, the man said, 'I'm Gus's uncle. He said you might need a bit of help.'

Too astonished to speak we stood waiting for him to continue.

In answer to our unspoken question he said, 'I live in the house at the bottom of Bogany Road.' He grinned, 'I was finishing a job in Castle Street when Gus phoned and thought I'd pop along to see what the problem was.'

'Come in, come in,' Simon said, standing aside. Gus's uncle didn't volunteer his name but as he entered the living room, he let out a long low whistle.

‘Gee. Bit of a mess, this. Who did you say did this work? Or rather, didn’t do the work.’

‘A local builder.’ I could sense Simon was reluctant to say, but Gus’s uncle said again, ‘Oh, what made you choose whoever it was?’

I could sense a cooling of the atmosphere with Simon unwilling to say, but Gus’s uncle was persistent. ‘Who did you employ?’

‘Benny,’ Simon muttered.

Gus’s uncle let out a bellow of laughter. ‘Let me guess. You chose Benny because he was available…and cheap.’

Simon prickled. ‘Mostly because he was able to do the work quickly.’

But Gus’s uncle wasn’t going to let him off the hook so easily. ‘Didn’t it occur to you to ask why he was so readily available? All the trades on the island are always busy. You have to book up months in advance.’

‘I must say…’ Simon began, as Gus’s uncle went on, ‘And didn’t it occur to you there might be a problem when you saw he was employing my dopey nephew?’

This discussion threatened to become acrimonious so I jumped in with, ‘Can you help us? Is it possible to do something with this mess?’

Gus’s uncle stroked his chin. ‘I’ve a full order book.’ He began to walk around the room, prodding here, rapping on the walls, kicking aside some of the old plaster and bits of wood panelling strewn across the floor.

‘The good news is,’ he said thoughtfully, ‘it’s mostly mess. The old panelling has been taken off, though not very well. What’s left is mainly a plastering job. I think the guy who works with me might be persuaded to work the weekend – which he doesn't usually do. But it'll cost you extra.'

By this stage we'd gladly have paid anything to get the room to rights and be back in the cottage.

'That's fine, we understand,' Simon echoed my thoughts. 'If you can help that would be great.'

'Okay. I'll get Gus and a couple of his mates down to clear all this mess. Once that's done it'll be easier to assess the rest of the work.''

I must have looked concerned because he added, 'Don't worry. I'll supervise them. Even Gus can't botch the job of clearing up. I'll phone the plasterer as soon as I leave here and let you know if he can make it this weekend. He owes me a favour or two so I guess it should be fine.'

I felt such relief. Not only because there was the possibility that the room would be finished, and we could move back but that we didn't have to tackle the mess.

'I'll give you a call when I find out,' Gus's uncle said, pulling out his phone. What's your number?'

As Simon gave his mobile number, I wandered over to the window. How one small action can set in train a set of events. If Simon hadn't been so enthusiastic about trying to do this room, hadn't found it was too big a job for him, we'd never have employed Benny and the statue behind the old fireplace would have remained hidden. Too late now. We had to salvage what we could…with the welcome help of Gus's uncle.

I turned back in time to hear Gus's uncle say, 'I'll be off then. I'll be in touch later.'

As he started to walk into the hallway, I went after him.

'Sorry, but what's your name? We can't keep

calling you "Gus's uncle".'

He grinned. 'No. I do have a name. I'm Mervin Dawd, but everyone calls me Tich.'

I couldn't disguise my look of astonishment. Had I misheard him?

'It's a joke,' he said. 'My mate is only five feet two and his nickname is Lofty.'

With a smile and a wave he left, banging the front door behind him.

'Thank goodness for that, Alison. Maybe poor Benny has done us a favour by falling off the ladder. It doesn't look as if he was anywhere near finishing.'

I didn't reply. I was still thinking about what Mervin had said.

'Alison, are you happy with this arrangement? You're looking puzzled.'

'What? Oh, yes, happy to think we might have a decent living room soon. It's just that…'

'Yes?'

'It's Mervin Dawd – the name is familiar, but I can't for the life of me think why.'

'There are several generations of many families on the island,' Simon said as he prowled around the room. 'I hope Gus has plenty of friends – there's so much to shift.'

I turned my mind from the issue of Mervin to the immediate problem. 'Let's worry about that later if Gus and his friends don't manage.'

But as we closed the front door behind us, the feeling that I knew the name of Gus's uncle from somewhere nagged away at me. Best not to think about it. That way the answer might come back to me.

Meanwhile we could only cross our fingers that Gus's uncle would be as good as his word.

FORTY-THREE

As we drove past the Hall, I said, 'Could you stop here for a minute?'

'I thought you were finished with all that?' Simon said, but he slowed down to pull up opposite the front entrance.

'I won't be long. I want to check with Wilson if there's been any news about Cormac or Valeria.'

'Oh, Alison,' Simon sighed. 'You've already done more than could be expected.'

Instead of replying, I opened the passenger door to climb out and hurry across the road. I'd no idea if any of the cast would be around, but I was curious to know what their plans were. Or indeed if there were any plans. Working closely with them recently I'd developed a concern about what would happen. I hadn't promised Rhoda I'd investigate as she'd asked me, but it would do no harm to find out about any recent developments.

Silence greeted me as I pushed open the main door and made me hesitate. The actors must be back at the hotel, and I didn't want to start asking questions there – too many people likely to overhear.

I stood in the entrance hall, undecided what to do next, then moved forward to the bottom of the stairs, the better to listen for signs of activity.

Then I heard a loud cough. Or rather a fit of coughing coming from upstairs. Someone was in the theatre.

Good. It must be Wilson.

I ran upstairs but at first could make out little in the gloom. None of the lights were on, not even the emergency lights which every theatre had to have by law and walking slowly down the aisle, I tried to accustom my eyes to the darkness. That was strange. There was no one here. I must have imagined that fit of coughing.

About to turn away, re-join Simon, I heard a cough again. It was coming from the wings. Someone was lurking behind the side curtain.

Curious as to why Wilson would be sitting in the dark, I climbed the side stairs on to the stage, calling out, 'Hi, Wilson, is that you? I wondered how things were…'

No reply. I tried speaking louder, saying, 'We were passing on our way back to the hotel and I thought I'd call in to find out how you were coping, if there was any news.'

Still no reply. Moving forward, I pulled aside the curtain to see a shadowy figure with his back to me, fiddling with something at the corner of the curtain mechanism in the dim light. 'Wilson?' I said.

But it wasn't Wilson there in the semi-darkness. When he turned around I saw it was Phil and it was obvious he wasn't pleased to see me.

'Yes?' he growled. 'What is it?' Then he realised it was me. 'Alison. What a fright you gave me.'

He moved away, catching me by the elbow to steer me back down the stairs and into the auditorium, switching on the lights as we walked up to the top of the aisle.

I didn't ask, but for some reason he thought he had to explain what he was doing. 'I was checking the curtain mechanism,' he said. 'Every performance we've had the wretched thing has stuck and someone has had to yank it to make it work.'

'I didn't realise that was part of your job,' I said.

'We all have to turn our hand to whatever's needed. There's no money to employ a regular technician.' He laughed. 'The jobs I've had to do since I joined this company.'

'I can guess,' I said. Another sign money was tight.

'Were you looking for Wilson?' he said, rubbing his hands together.

'Yes, I did intend to have a quick word with him. But if he's not here, I can catch up later.'

'I can give him a message,' he said.

I shook my head. 'It's nothing important.'

'You can trust me to convey it accurately.' Now he sounded almost jovial after that shaky start to our conversation.

But I'd no intention of confiding in Phil. There was something about him I didn't trust.

'Simon is waiting outside,' I said. 'I'd better go.'

'If you're sure, and…'

But I was already quickening my pace to the exit.

Simon was engrossed in his phone as I came up to the car and at first he didn't notice me.

'Guess what?' he said as I slid into the passenger seat.

'No idea,' I replied, still thinking about my encounter with Phil. What a strange person he was.

'While I was waiting for you, I thought I'd look up the house that doubles as Strathloch. There's lots of information about it on the internet. Quite a history. And the story of the Arris family and the Chancel at Mary's.'

'I suppose most of the big houses on the island have

a story to tell,' I said absentmindedly, my thoughts on the encounter with Phil.

'There's a lot about St Mary's Chapel. From the description, I would say that the statues originally in the niches in the Knight's tomb match up with the statue Benny found behind the fireplace wall in the cottage.'

Now Simon had my complete attention. 'Ah, that explains it,' I said. 'There **is** a connection between the family who owned Strathloch and the people who lived in our cottage.'

But of all the strange things that had happened since we'd arrived on Bute this time, this seemed the least likely.

'Interesting, isn't it,' Simon said. 'I've managed to track down someone who might know more.'

'And you're telling me not to get involved?'

'Yes, but I'm beginning to understand why you can't abide a mystery.'

Still concerned with what was happening at the theatre company, I paid scant attention. That was a mistake.

FORTY-FOUR

There was no immediate possibility of investigating a connection between our cottage, Cladach, and Cois Na Farraige.

Gus's uncle (I couldn't get used to calling him Titch) had assured us that the work would be completed by the end of the weekend. This time Simon refused to extend our stay at The Four Winds.

'I've booked a hotel in Glasgow,' he said in a tone of voice that brooked no argument. 'It's near enough should we have to come over at short notice.' He sighed. 'Pity we gave up the flat.'

It wasn't that being in the same hotel as the cast of the Sleeping Beauty was unpleasant, but I'd a feeling Simon was on edge in case further problems about the tour might involve me. I'd come to realise how much Valeria had been responsible for organising the affairs of the company. Wilson was disorganised in the extreme. It didn't appear that he'd benefitted from Simon's Management course at all.

We caught the morning ferry with a sigh of relief, after checking with Gus's uncle that there was nothing else he needed.

'Don't worry about a thing,' he said, momentarily lifting his head from sawing a plank of wood.

Over in the corner a small slight man whose thick-framed glasses covered most of his thin face was busy plastering the far wall. I could only assume this was Lofty. He raised his hand in greeting before returning to his task.

Simon looked the most cheerful I'd seen him in days as we drove away. 'Great to have someone with everything under control,' he said.

I murmured a non-committal response. That's what Benny had said and look what had happened there. Best not to be too hopeful.

The ferry was busy – Saturday crowds heading to the mainland to shop or to have a weekend away and we squeezed into a couple of seats in the passenger lounge in front of a family with three boisterous children.

'Coffee, Alison?' Simon stood up and without waiting for a reply hurried off to join the queue at the onboard café.

I settled back, gazing out of the large window as the town of Rothesay receded, and the ferry swung round out of the harbour into the Firth of Clyde. The prospect of a weekend in a comfortable hotel was exactly what we needed. And we'd come back on Monday morning to the work on the cottage completed. If all went according to plan.

A voice beside me said, 'Why, if it isn't Mrs Cameron,' and I looked up to see Kerry standing there.

'Hello. Having a day out?'

'A shopping trip. Mind if I join you?'

'Good to see you again,' I said. 'We've had a delay with the cottage, and it isn't ready yet,' I went on.

'Everything takes longer on an island,' Kerry laughed.

'Exactly,' I said and told her the story of the problems we'd had with workmen.

'Oh, you might have guessed Mervin Dawd is my uncle.'

'Of course. That's why the name is familiar,' I said.

'Generations of workmen in the family,' she said. 'They've worked on all the big houses on the island.'

'Including Cois Na Farraige?'

'Yes, among others.'

'And going back generations?'

She looked puzzled. 'Yes,' she said.

A glimmer of an idea was beginning to form.

'Do you know the cottage in Port Bannatyne – the one we've bought. Cladach?'

'Yes, I seem to remember one of my relatives lived there, but a long time ago.'

'Why, hello,' Simon said, approaching with two carefully balanced cups of coffee and putting an end to our conversation. As I introduced them, he gestured towards the café. 'Can I get you a coffee,' he said, but Kerry shook her head, holding up a can of coke and saying, 'I prefer this.'

'Oh, that wasn't what caused the delay…' I said, resuming the conversation, but a warning glance from Simon and stopped me.

Fortunately Kerry didn't notice as at that moment there was a shout from one of the other passengers, 'Look, a dolphin,' and everyone rushed over to the other side of the ferry, though Kerry stayed put.

'Is that an unusual sight, then?' I said.

Kerry smiled, but she made no comment.

We chatted for the rest of the journey. Kerry was entertaining company and had a fund of stories about the people she met through her job at the Ettrick Bay tearoom. I suspected she found life on the island challenging. 'I finish college next year,' she said, 'and then I'll be off.'

The ferry began to slow as we came towards Wemyss Bay and I said, 'We'll be docking in a few minutes. Good luck with the shopping.'

Kerry raised her eyebrows. 'I hope so.'

On impulse I said, 'Let me give you one of my cards. My phone number's on it.'

'Thanks. I'm staying with a friend in Glasgow for four days – there's so much to see and do there. She's managed to book us tickets for the Theatre Royal.' A frown crossed her face. 'Though I'm not sure the Opera she's chosen is my kind of thing.'

'I know there are a couple in here somewhere,' I said, pulling out my purse, my diary, a couple of bunches of keys, a packet of tissues and several old receipts and putting them on the table in front of me.

'At last,' I said triumphantly, laying a somewhat crumpled flyer for The Sleeping Beauty Pantomime on the pile before handing a card over to Kerry.

'What's this?' Kerry said, lifting the flyer and laying it on the table to smooth it out.

'Oh, that's The Mickle Theatre Company. They are touring some of the islands with the panto. Simon and I went along to see it and…' I broke off, aware she wasn't listening.

'Something wrong?' I said intrigued by the look on her face.

'Mmm. My mum went to meet Valeria – I think I told you.' She looked up at me and then pointed to the small photo of the cast. 'I knew about the panto, but I hadn't seen the flyer.'

'You know some of the others?'

'I recognise that person,' she said, pointing to Benita. 'At least I think I do.'

'You've met her somewhere?'

Kelly frowned. 'She looks like someone I once knew. But she's much younger than I'd have expected.'

‘These photos are often retouched,’ I said.

‘No, no, it’s not that.’

‘That’s Benita Grove,’ I said. ‘She’s playing the part of the Fairy Godmother in the panto. She certainly does well in the role.’

Kelly didn’t appear to be listening. ‘That’s not the name I recognise either. Oh, well, no matter. She must have a passing resemblance to someone.’ She handed the flyer back to me. ‘Amazing how your memory can play tricks.’

But now I was intrigued. ‘Yes, sometimes that can happen. Perhaps she’s also related to someone you know.’

It was as though my comment had sparked a lightbulb moment. ‘Ah, that’s a possibility.’ She grinned. ‘If only I could remember who that might be.’

Our discussion was interrupted by the announcement over the loudspeaker that we were arriving at Wemyss Bay, and we said our farewells as we made our way down to the car deck while Kerry joined the foot passengers preparing to disembark.

Kerry refused the offer of a lift to Glasgow. ‘My friend is meeting me at Central Station,’ she said. ‘It’s so easy by train.’

But as I watched Kerry take her place in the queue I couldn’t help but wonder what was the story behind what she had told me. Was it no more than Benita resembled someone she knew? Or did she realise who Benita was, but was unwilling to tell me?

FORTY-FIVE

The weekend was a great success. At least it was from my point of view, though I suspect Simon was less than enthralled by the expedition to Braehead Shopping Centre. Even so, he appeared pleased with our purchases. Or he was when it was over, and we were sitting having a late lunch in the one of the restaurants.

'Message from Deborah,' he said. 'She's inviting us over for a meal tonight.'

I stopped with a forkful of spaghetti half-way to my mouth. 'Tonight?'

Simon looked puzzled. 'Yes. Is there a problem with that? There's nothing else planned, is there?' A wary look crossed his face. 'You've nothing else on your list?'

'No, nothing like that. It's just…' I gestured to the plate of pasta in front of me. 'You might remember Deborah's idea of inviting people to dinner is to order a takeaway pizza.'

In the end I did my daughter a disservice, because she served up a delicious vegetable stew she'd made from scratch. Sometimes when she's in a vegetarian phase, I've been treated to rather odd concoctions, but on this occasion she excelled herself and it was good to catch up with her news.

It was only later when we were on the ferry back to Bute, after a busy weekend, that I said, 'Do you remember that comment Kerry made?'

'What was that?' Simon had clearly forgotten.

'About recognising Benita.' Under cover of sipping my coffee, I watched for his reaction.

'Really? Do you think so?' He laughed. 'All too often your imagination runs away with you. Benita is a well-known actress – I think she was in that TV play recently about a missing teenager. Most likely Kerry saw her in that.'

I wasn't convinced. There had been something about the way Kerry had said it. I stared out of the window as we approached the harbour at Rothesay, the lights of the town glittering in the darkness. Simon was right. I was seeing conspiracies everywhere.

Once off the ferry we drove in silence to the cottage at Port Bannatyne, both of us probably wondering if Gus's uncle would have fulfilled his promise and finished the work on the living room. There had been no word from him over the weekend and despite a couple of times when we'd considered phoning him, we managed to resist the temptation. Why spoil a lovely weekend.

As we drew up outside the cottage there was no sign of the van, and my heart sank.

Simon leapt out of the car and marched ahead, not stopping to lock up, showing he was every bit as anxious as I was about what we might find.

We needn't have worried. As we opened the door the smell of fresh plaster greeted us and to our delight and great relief, the living room had been completely stripped and replastered. What's more, they'd cleared up every piece of debris.

'First things first,' I said, going into the kitchen to switch on the kettle. The knot in my stomach, worrying about what we'd find back at the cottage had affected me more than I'd realised.

'They've done a great job,' Simon called from the living room. 'The walls are as smooth as silk. Now all we need is a painter. I'll give Gus's uncle a call later – he must know someone who can help.'

I could see Gus's uncle would be receiving regular phone calls from us over the next while, given the amount of work needed in our new home. Even so, I was more optimistic we'd soon be back to normal. And we could certainly live in the cottage once more.

Simon came through to join me in the kitchen.

'Oh, here's the bill,' he said, lifting a piece of paper from the kitchen table. He stopped. 'Wait a minute. It isn't a bill.'

He frowned in concentration. 'I'm not sure I understand this message. It's to do with the statue.'

He passed the note to me. 'Gus says we should contact him about it.'

Simon shrugged. 'No harm I suppose. Though I'm not sure what more he can tell us.'

'It's impossible to keep anything secret,' I laughed. 'Someone must have told him about the statue.'

As we stood there, wondering what Gus's uncle might have to say, my phone rang. It was Kerry.

'Hi, Alison,' she said. 'Hope you had a good weekend. I remembered where I saw that woman in The Mickle flyer. Or at least not her, but someone who looked like her. It was some time ago…'

I mouthed, 'It's Kerry,' as I gestured to Simon to make me a cup of coffee and he smiled, switching on the kettle again.

'…and you might not believe this, but she looks exactly like the portrait of Garia Arris, the wife of the original owner of Strathloch House. I was just a child, but I remember one time I was ill, off school with some minor ailment, and my mother took me with her rather than not turn up for work. It was the hair, you know – that mass of curls. Made quite an impression on me. My hair was long and straight and I'd always wanted curly hair.' She paused for breath, giving me enough time to interject, 'But I thought that when Samuel Arris died the house was put up for sale?'

'Oh, what? Yes, that was the plan according to the story I heard. But many people had fallen on hard times. The Arris family had an army of cleaners and other staff: gardeners, a cook, a couple of maids. Even a chauffeur for a while.' She laughed. 'But then suddenly it was taken off the market and their money problems seemed to be over. Garia Arris married again, and the family and their descendants lived there in great comfort from what I can gather.'

'But they sold eventually?'

'Yes. They were unlucky in not having anyone to carry on the line. The Arris family who owned the house in the 40s had one son, but he was killed in action in the last year of the war. The family who bought it got it for a song we heard, with all the contents, including the portrait of Garia. My grandparents worked on for the new owners but when they decided to sell up because their house was too big, too expensive to keep up, the new owners allowed my grandparents to stay on in the lodge in exchange for some general help. Then my parents took over – housekeeping and general handyman duties. Oh, it wasn't as grand as it had been in the Arris's day, but they did keep on several workmen. My mother got to know the new owners well. Of course then it was sold again, and the most recent owners struck lucky.' There was a note of bitterness in her voice – I could guess the current owners were the subject of envy given the way they had turned around the fortunes of the house.

I sensed Simon's impatience as he moved restlessly, waiting for me to finish the conversation. But I couldn't stop her now. Not without finding out the end of the story.

'And there was more?'

'Oh, yes, it was all to do with the disappearance of the statues from St Mary's. Rumours abounded that Samuel Arris had something to do with it, though he denied it, and no one could prove otherwise. That's how, when I thought I recognised Benita Grove, it brought it all back. And there was a story about your cottage.'

'But I don't understand. Are you saying that your relative who lived here stole the statue and hid it in the cottage?'

She sounded embarrassed. 'I think you have to find out more about who lived in the cottage back then. The workmen who carried out the renovations must have known what was going on. Perhaps the gift of a statue was a bribe in exchange for silence.' She gave a laugh. 'Well, that's the story. Make of it what you will.'

We exchanged a few pleasantries, but I wanted to end the call as soon as possible and think over what Kerry had said.

'What was that about?' Simon said, topping up my coffee which by now had gone cold.

'A strange tale.' Briefly I explained what Kerry had said, ending with, '…and it may well have been one of those employed at Strathloch who found out about the statues.'

Simon's reaction was the same as mine. 'And

there's some connection with the people who lived at our cottage. Why would anyone steal the statue if not to sell it?'

'Yes, and there's the business of her thinking she recognised Benita and then realising it was only because she bore a resemblance to the woman who lived at Strathloch. All very odd.'

'Look, Alison, enough of rumours and stories. Let's concentrate on getting the cottage sorted.'

He stood up. 'I'll go up to Castle Street, see if Gus's uncle is about and ask him to find a painter.'

'And you can also ask him what he meant about the statue.'

Simon shrugged. 'I'm not sure I want to know more. You might have been content to be involved in questionable events on the island over the years. I'm happy going with what the museum has to say.'

And with that he was off, leaving me sitting in the kitchen, mulling over the tale Kerry had told me, wondering if there was any connection between Benita and the woman who had once owned Strathloch. There were too many loose ends.

Simon was right, of course, it was none of my business. But even so, I couldn't help but wonder what was the truth of the story. Another visit to the library in Rothesay was called for – and soon.

FORTY-SIX

My plan to go to the library had to be put on hold. There was a further complication to do with The Mickle just when I thought my time with them had come to an end. I was hoping the next communication would be a postcard from Islay to say they'd arrived safely, and all was well. I should have known better.

When Wilson's name came up on my phone, my first inclination was to ignore it, let the call go to voicemail. But somehow I couldn't do that.

'Hello, Wilson,' I said, trying to inject a cheerful note into my voice. 'Are you making progress?'

'No, Alison. It's awful. We've another problem, but I don't know how we're going to get over this one.' He sounded on the verge of tears and against my better judgement I heard myself say, 'What's happened now?'

'You'll never believe it. I can't imagine why it's come to this. They must be wrong, have made a mistake…'

'Yes, but what is it?' I interrupted him, trying not to sound impatient.

'They've taken Joel in for questioning about Cormac's murder.' He broke off, trying to control the sob in his voice.

'Joel? Why would he want to kill Cormac? What possible motive could he have?'

'They were heard having an almighty row and Joel

was threatening Cormac about something Cormac had said. And Joel did serve up the poisoned goblet to him during the christening scene.' He paused. 'The only fingerprints found on the goblets were those belonging to Rhoda, who filled them with blackcurrant juice as usual and Cormac's. And Joel's.'

'What could Cormac have said to Joel to provoke such a reaction – surely that's no more than gossip. With no substance.' Unless the police had information Wilson didn't know about.

Wilson sounded slightly calmer as he went on, 'Felicity overheard them. She couldn't make out the details only that it sounded serious.'

Odder and odder. How likely was it that the police would take Joel in for questioning on the say-so of Felicity? Although I remembered the story of how Cormac was continually goading Joel, belittling his acting ability, how I'd had suspicions.

There was a deep sigh on the other end of the phone. 'I expect you're right, Alison. It's stupid of me to get into a panic like this. But everything is falling apart and there's no denying Joel had the opportunity to put poison in Cormac's drink. When the police questioned me, what could I do but tell them the truth? How we're ever going to get this show on the road again I've no idea.'

'What is Joel saying?'

'Nothing.' Another deep sigh. 'He's refusing to speak to anyone. Won't deny or confirm any of the details.'

'Take heart, Wilson. It may all be a terrible mistake. Wait and see. I'm sure Joel will be released.' Of course I'd no idea if this was the case. But I was concerned for Wilson.

‘I suppose you’re right. I don’t think they’ve charged him. Only taken him in for questioning.’

‘And you’ve tried asking Felicity if she remembers anything else?’

‘She claims she doesn’t – only that she heard the row and Joel threatening Cormac before stomping off.’ But he sounded doubtful.

I don’t know what made me say it, but a memory came back to me. ‘Didn’t you start out as an actor? If you could take one of the parts that might save the day.’

‘I don’t think so,’ he said, sounding angry. ‘That was a long time ago.’

He rang off and I sat staring at my phone for a while, musing over this conversation. Whatever Cormac had said to Joel, it had upset the younger man very much. But enough to kill him in such a public way? And it didn’t explain Valeria’s death.

None of this made sense. Joel was a well-known actor on the up, while Cormac’s career was very much on the slide. He struck me as a confident young man, or rather over-confident. He was unlikely to let anything Cormac might say cause him the slightest anxiety.

It was none of my business, but when has that ever been a problem? And I felt sorry for Wilson. Now they would have to remain on Bute while waiting for word about what was to happen to Joel.

I considered discussing this latest piece of news with Simon, but as quickly dismissed the idea. Although my association with the company had started because Wilson had once been one of his students, Simon wanted me to back off. No, that would not do at all.

What about Felicity? She might be willing to talk to

me in a way she might not be happy to chat to Wilson.

Before I could change my mind, I grabbed my car keys from the hall table and set off for the Hall. Simon might return at any minute. I didn't want to have to give him a long explanation. Far better to have a word with Felicity first. And as I drove towards town, I rehearsed a variety of questions I might ask her. Whether she would answer them was another matter.

FORTY-SEVEN

While my first thought was to go to the Hall, there was the chance the cast might be in the hotel. But my guess was correct. Wilson had decided it was best to keep everyone busy. The absence of Joel…as well as Cormac… made this difficult clearly and as I walked down the aisle in the theatre, I could hear murmurs of dissatisfaction from the cast.

Wilson was standing centre stage, moving restlessly.

Rhoda faced him, hands on hips. 'There's no way we can continue till we know what's happening with Joel,' she was saying. 'Without the Prince there's no story.'

Phil came over to stand beside Wilson. 'Oh, I don't know about that. A new take on the story might go down well – Somnia might repent, and she could be the one to awaken Beauty. Might be an interesting relationship there.'

Rhoda giggled, then changed it to a cough when Wilson glared at her.

I couldn't eavesdrop any longer, not because I was reluctant, but because Wilson spotted me in the auditorium.

'Who's there?' he said shading his eyes against the glare of the stage lights.

'It's me, Alison,' I said, hurrying forward.

This interruption appeared to be welcomed by several of the actors as Phil said, 'Let's have a break.

That okay, Wilson.' A statement rather than a question.

Wilson waved his hand absentmindedly and the others took this as a sign of agreement, scurrying off into the wings before he could change his mind.

'I wondered if I could be of help,' I said, sitting down in a seat in the front row.

He sat down beside me, staring at the stage. 'Thanks, Alison, but I don't see how. It gets worse and worse. I keep wondering who'll be next.'

'Do you really think Joel is responsible? That he killed Cormac?'

Wilson sighed. 'I've no idea, that's for sure.'

'What reason would Joel have to murder Cormac? I know they didn't get on, but surely it wasn't so bad that Joel would kill him?'

'That's what I keep asking myself. And no matter how many scenarios I come up with I can't think of one that makes sense. I felt so guilty having to tell the police about Joel.'

'What steps have you taken? Have you questioned the rest of the cast?'

He turned to look at me, frowning. 'The police have been doing that. How could I start asking everyone?'

'Because,' I said, 'if you can find out the truth you might be able to continue with the tour.'

He laughed. 'That's very unlikely. Once word gets out about what's happened, I doubt if any of the remaining venues will want to honour our booking. I mean, Valeria you could believe was an accident and, while enquiries continued, that Cormac's death was due to natural causes. But now we know he was poisoned, and Joel has been taken in for questioning, there's no chance.'

'Maybe I could have a word with some of the

actors, see if they might be willing to talk to me, an independent listener.'

This suggestion didn't meet with the enthusiastic response I'd hoped for. 'Really? I'm not sure there's anything to tell. And now it looks as if Joel is in the frame, the others will be more concerned with what happens to them, whether they have a job.'

He had a point. Joel wasn't popular but if he was charged with Cormac's murder the company might not be able to salvage the show.

'But what if Joel isn't guilty? What if he's released. Do you understand what that means?'

Wilson took a moment to reply, as though weighing up his response.

'Oh, I understand only too well, Alison. If Joel can come up with an alibi, prove he didn't do it, it means someone else in the company is responsible. But I don't think that's likely, do you? The police seem fairly convinced of Joel's guilt. We'll have to abandon the tour.'

Wilson might be unwilling to consider the option. But if Joel didn't do it, didn't kill Cormac, there was a murderer still lurking in The Mickle. And where might he – or she – strike next?

FORTY-EIGHT

My first attempts to gather evidence weren't successful. Though Wilson finally agreed my remaining with the company would be a good way to find out what had happened, other members of the cast were suspicious.

Wilson clapped his hands as I followed him up on to the stage. As he began, 'Listen up, everyone,' my heart sank. Surely he wasn't going to tell everyone I was about to question them about Cormac's murder?

But to my relief he said, 'Alison will be around for a few days. There's still work to be done.'

I heard Benita say in an aside to Phil, 'Why is she really here? I thought she was only with us to help with the tour arrangements.'

But she at least had the grace to lower her eyes as I stared at her.

Understandably Wilson was being as vague as possible. Seized suddenly by inspiration, I said, 'It's important the tour continues in some form. I'll be negotiating with the venues about a reduced format of the pantomime and the associated publicity while Wilson rewrites the script.'

There was a collective groan from the cast as Lucian said, 'Oh, not more changes.'

'It's only a precautionary measure,' I tried to reassure everyone. 'Nothing will happen until we hear about Joel. But we must make plans. Wilson has asked me to carry out a consultation exercise. Find out how each of you feels about continuing the tour and what suggestions you might have to rescue the situation.'

I wasn't certain this was what they wanted to hear, and it was a reminder that Joel might be the killer. On the other hand, I was pleased with myself for coming up with this idea. It would be a good cover for talking to each of them individually and in that guise I could hopefully glean relevant information.

Amid grumbles and mutterings, Wilson dismissed them with a 'I'll see you back here tomorrow morning, but don't stray too far. As she said, Alison will be checking with everyone how each of you thinks we can best proceed. I expect no less than full co-operation. The very future of The Mickle depends on how we work during the next few weeks.' He stopped. 'Or if we work.'

The note of menace in his voice seemed to dispel any resentment. The actors knew that unless the tour could be rescued, they would be out of work, with no income. Not a situation any of them wanted, particularly at this time of year. I anticipated co-operation from everyone, though Felicity stood sullenly at the corner of the stage.

As the actors drifted away in little groups, Wilson turned to me, rubbing his hands. 'I think that went well, Alison. Bit of a good wheeze for you to have that idea about a consultation.' He stopped. 'But I'm assuming it's no more than a cover for what you really intend to do. We don't want too much input. If everyone comes up with different ideas, that could make it very awkward, very awkward indeed. And I believe we'll have to cancel in the end.'

'Don't worry,' I said. 'I'll be discreet,' though in

truth I wasn't as confident as he sounded.

But now he thought there was a plan to help move everything forward, Wilson was on a roll. 'So, Alison, how do you want to start? Who are you going to tackle first?'

'I thought I'd make a list tonight and start first thing in the morning,' I said, improvising.

'Fine, fine. There's no word yet if Joel is to be formally charged with Cormac's murder. And if we have to call off, so be it. At least we tried.'

'I thought you'd a couple of performances left?'

'Yes, but they're extra performances and I don't expect big audiences. I'll make sure everyone is here promptly tomorrow,' he said. 'It'll be an all-nighter for me, rewriting. But that means we can start the new rehearsals tomorrow, while you question them.'

This made no sense for various reasons. One minute Wilson was anxious to continue no matter what, the next he was talking about calling off the tour.

And far from putting people off, the notoriety of the company might encourage a bigger audience. 'But what if Joel is innocent? Is freed?' I said.

Wilson looked surprised at the suggestion, and I suddenly had the idea that Wilson was glad Joel was out of the way. He'd been a nuisance to the Director from the start from what I knew – always interfering, making sure everyone knew his status as a television star was what gave the production its popularity with audiences, trying to suggest alterations to the script that would increase the size of his part. But the idea that he had killed Cormac I found impossible to believe. Cormac was no threat to him.

Despite Wilson's promises to rewrite the script, it was a huge undertaking, with no guarantee the company could make the new version successful in the limited time available before the departure for Islay.

Unless someone had a good reason for wanting Joel out of the way.

FORTY-NINE

Taking on the role of consultant wasn't as easy as I'd imagined. Especially as it was no more than a cover for trying to find out more about the circumstances in which Cormac had died.

And I hadn't reckoned the difficulties there would be interviewing actors. Apart from their ability to dissemble while appearing to answer the questions, I'd a strong feeling Neville and Felicity were increasingly suspicious.

'What I don't understand,' Neville said, 'is why Wilson asked you to do this. Surely this is something he should have done himself?'

'It's because he wanted an independent viewpoint,' I said, the same story I'd told the others.

'Bloody silly if you ask me.' Neville leaned so far back in his chair I thought he was about to tip over. 'Okay, Alison, fire away with your questions.' He sat forward with a bump and leaned in close. 'Though I'm not guaranteeing I'll give you the answers you expect.'

I drew back, taking refuge in pretending to consult my notebook. The questions I'd hurriedly prepared now began to look decidedly sparse. It would take a lot more than these to encourage Neville to talk.

But what I hadn't reckoned with was the actor's delight in hearing the sound of his own voice and all I had to do was ask a question and off he went, giving me his opinion on anything and everything, most of it not relevant to what I'd asked.

I had to make a great effort to concentrate on what he was saying. My mind began to wander. This exercise was a waste of time. I was learning nothing new.

I was brought back with a start as I heard Neville say, '…and as for Joel Bennett, what a bad decision that was. How Wilson could ever have thought it was worthwhile employing him, I've no idea.'

'But surely it was because Joel was a well-known actor, a sure-fire hit with the youngsters because of his role in the TV series,' I said, watching for his reaction. 'And besides,' I went on before he could reply, 'you must have had a say in it. Someone with your experience.'

His face became red as he tried to control his anger. 'You'd think so, wouldn't you. But Wilson always overrode any suggestion I made. I told him Joel would be a liability. Everyone in the business knows his reputation as an interfering know-all. His quick temper.'

'Surely that's a bit strong,' I pretended to protest, at which Neville laughed. 'Have you heard he's about to be written out of The Family at Strathloch? Fell out with the producer once too often.'

'Really?' I said. I wasn't going to let Neville know that I'd heard this story from another source. I fiddled with my pen, hoping he'd continue. And I wasn't disappointed.

'Yes. Kept wanting his part to be made bigger, turned up late on set, argued with Maria Asti who's the leading actress. Everyone was fed up with his antics.'

'It'll be difficult to write him out?'

Neville chuckled. 'I've heard he's going to come to a grisly end. Drowned off Rothesay Pier or trampled to death by a herd of cows. Or perhaps stabbed through the heart by a love rival…'

'Yes, yes,' I said. 'I get the drift, but this isn't taking us further forward in finding out how best the fortunes of The Mickle can be improved.'

'What? Oh, yes.' The fanatical look in Neville's eyes disappeared. Now he looked sly. 'I could give you a list of possibilities, Alison, but I think you should interview some of the others. My perspective is quite different.'

He stood up, making it clear he considered the interview at an end. 'I should get back and find out what Wilson is up to now. I reckon he needs all the support he can get.'

As he reached the door, he turned to look at me, saying, 'Good luck with this mad idea of Wilson. Not that I'd expect any less of him, given the way he's been behaving recently. I'm sure you'll come up with a great answer for us that will save the company.' He winked, slowly and deliberately, leaving me staring after him as he closed the door behind him. This strategy was a ridiculous idea and Neville knew it.

But I'd no time to brood. Almost immediately the door was flung open, and Felicity came striding in.

Anger was written all over her face. 'What nonsense has Wilson got us involved in now? As if it isn't bad enough with all that's happened, with all the changes of script…'

She sat down with a thump in the chair opposite me and regarded me sullenly.

I was beginning to think yet again that this was a bad idea, but I had to make the best of it.

Taking a deep breath, I said, 'Wilson is doing no

more than trying to rescue a dire situation. Everyone has a contribution to make to the success of this tour. With so few people, everyone's opinion counts.'

'And getting fewer by the day,' Felicity muttered, but she looked less annoyed.

'Let's not waste time then,' I said, adopting a brisk manner. Whatever the outcome, I had to appear professional, and I began to go through my checklist of questions.

As we continued, Felicity became more animated, engaged in the process, and I sighed with relief. If I could manage to get through the interviews with Neville and with Felicity, the others should be easier. Or so I hoped.

'Sorry I was so abrupt,' she said as we came to the end of the prepared questions. 'It's all been so terrible. You've no idea how delighted I was to get the role of the Queen. I mean it was such a coup for someone straight out of drama school. It will be awful for me if the tour is cancelled.'

'I expect you were chosen because you were right for the part,' I said, yet again aware how self-absorbed these actors were.

She didn't look the least bit abashed or modest but instead said, 'Yes, of course. If I hadn't been talented there's no way Wilson would have hired me.' Now that she had what she considered due praise, she was more amenable, and I seized my chance.

'How well did you know Cormac?' I said. 'Did you know him before the start of Sleeping Beauty?'

At first I thought she wasn't going to reply, but she shrugged, saying, 'I knew of him, but I hadn't met him. He was well-known in acting circles…and not always because of his talent. He had problems.' She stopped. 'But I suppose you know that. Oh, he was in demand at one time, but to be honest he was so old it was surprising he was still in employment.'

As Cormac wasn't much older than I am, this was a harsh estimation, but then Felicity was young.

There was nothing else to be learned from Felicity and I was about to thank her and wish her luck when she said suddenly, 'Cormac may have been old, had a drink problem, but there are plenty of actors like that in the profession. Drink or drugs – one of the hazards. But not me,' she added hastily. 'It's the surest way to ruin your talent.'

'And…' I prompted her.

She frowned. 'There were plans to remove Cormac. But of course Wilson wouldn't hear of it. And he was right. Chopping and changing the cast in the middle of the tour is not a good idea. It's bad enough when you have so many changes to the script.'

'But Wilson will have to adapt now, won't he?' If it goes ahead, I added silently.

'Yes, of course. But how would it have looked if poor old Cormac had been fired?' She examined her fingernails. 'Not that it really matters. Having the Queen on her own works perfectly well.' A little smile flickered across her face, and she put her hand to her mouth, but not before I noticed it.

'So if Wilson didn't want to fire Cormac, who was it who thought the pantomime would be better without him?'

She gazed directly at me, widening her eyes to appear innocent and once again I had to remind myself I was dealing with a group of actors.

'I've honestly no idea. It must have been a rumour I heard somewhere.'

She might be trying all the tricks of her trade to convince me, but I knew she was lying. And if she wouldn’t tell me, I could only hope someone else in the cast would be more forthcoming.

FIFTY

This process of interviewing the cast of Sleeping Beauty was more difficult – and more tiring – than I'd anticipated. What had I expected? That one of them would know the truth about what had happened to Cormac and would blurt it out to me?

There was an edgy atmosphere, and I began to suspect they'd closed ranks.

And there were few ideas about how to improve matters though Esme, secure in her position as the star of the show, did remark, 'If you ask me the best thing Wilson can do is move on. He can recast Lucian to the role of The Prince.' She grinned. 'He's a lot more attractive than Joel in many ways. Joel has a big conceit of himself.'

She was right, but I didn't say so. This was a pantomime and there had been so many versions over the years, that as long as the central theme involving the Princess, the Prince and the Good and the Bad Fairies was delivered that was all that mattered to the audience.

Attempting to move matters on, I said, 'Joel has only been taken in for questioning. He may have been released by now, and everything will go back to the way it was before.'

She made a face. 'Maybe.'

With this lack of progress, by the time I reached the cottage I was ready to put my feet up with a glass of wine. It was not to be.

Simon was fizzing with excitement as I came in. 'Guess what, Alison,' he said.

Too weary to speculate I said, 'Tell me. But let me sit down first.'

A few moments later I was sitting at the kitchen table with a glass of wine as he said, 'It's about the statue. Eliza was as good as her word and contacted someone she knows well. It's been examined by the Department of Archaeology at the university, and they're convinced it's one of the original statues from the Knight's tomb. I've been in touch with Calum to tell him the news, given he was such a help. And now Eliza will advise me what to do next.'

'I'm not sure I'll have time to come to the museum with you,' I said, taking a sip of wine. 'I've yet to interview several of the cast.'

'I'm happy to go along on my own,' he said. 'Although I expect you'll want to come with me when I hand the statue over to the police.'

That left me with a problem. Of course I was interested, but it might be better if Simon dealt with this. 'I'm sure you'll do better if I don't tag along. You can tell me all about it.'

He shrugged. 'Suit yourself.' But it was clear he was puzzled by my decision.

Changing the subject, I said, 'Any luck with finding a painter for the cottage?'

Simon brightened. 'Yes, Gus's uncle has been a real help. His mate is coming over tomorrow to give us an estimate.'

'Brilliant. Remember to be nice to him. We need the room decorated as soon as possible.'

And there were several items still to be ordered…new curtains for a start. But I didn't want to mention another shopping trip to Simon yet.

Simon jumped to his feet. 'I think I'll phone Eliza now. She said to call at any time.'

I wasn't sure she meant as late as this, but Simon went into the hallway, and I poured another glass of wine.

He returned a few minutes later, flushed with excitement. 'There's a chance the museum may be able to have the statue as one of its exhibits – once it's been through the proper channels, of course. Eliza is delighted.'

'Great news,' I said, but my mind was still on the problem of interviewing the remaining members of the theatre company.

FIFTY-ONE

At first I thought I was dreaming. The sound of the music seemed to be coming from a long distance away. It was only when Simon nudged me, muttering, 'Did you forget to switch your phone off last night?' that I realised it was a phone call.

I grabbed my phone from the side table, searching for my slippers as I slipped out of bed before answering the call as I made my way groggily downstairs.

It was Rhoda. She sounded distraught. 'Calm down, calm down,' I said trying to make sense of her garbled story. 'Start again and tell me what has happened.'

It took several attempts before I understood. 'You were almost knocked out by part of the stage curtain falling down on you? Are you certain?'

'Of course I am,' she said in a stronger voice. 'Someone was trying to kill me.'

'Why should anyone want to kill you?' I said.

'Because I have a suspicion about who is behind the deaths of Valeria and Cormac,' she said.

I could feel a frisson of fear. 'And who do you suspect?' I hesitated, almost unwilling to hear her answer.

'I need more proof,' she said, 'but as you're undertaking the task of consulting everyone, I thought you might be able to help.'

This sounded risky. 'Far better you go to the police,' I said firmly, remembering previous occasions when I'd been involved in events which led to danger.

Again I said, in a way I hoped brooked no argument, 'You must go to the police. Apart from anything else if you're right and the curtain malfunction was no accident, your life may be in danger.'

Silence for a moment at the other end of the phone, then, 'Okay, Alison. But what can I say to them?'

'After two mysterious deaths, one most certainly a murder even if there's doubt about Valeria, they must believe you.'

'Come and meet me,' she urged, 'I need support.'

Simon appeared beside me. 'What's that all about?' he said.

A swift decision not to tell him the full story. 'It was Rhoda,' I said. 'There's been a development, and she wants me to help.'

Simon said nothing, merely shook his head as though in sorrow.

'I'll have a quick shower and go over now,' I said. 'That will leave the rest of the day free.'

Before he could reply, I hurried upstairs and by the time I came down to leave, Simon was sitting at the kitchen table, engrossed in his newspaper propped up against the milk jug, eating a bowl of cereal.

'I'll be quick,' I said, and he mumbled something in reply, something I didn't quite catch.

As I drove along by the shore through Ardbeg, dawn came up in a riot of fiery red, the crimson clouds mirrored in the stillness of the water. My mind was a jumble of thoughts. Rhoda was a strange person and I didn't trust her, though I couldn't say why. If she genuinely had a suspect, why would she hesitate to tell the police? It didn't make sense. Was she trying to make trouble for someone?

A car came shooting down the side road and I had to slam on the brakes to avoid an accident. I stopped the car, shaken by this encounter, before driving off slowly. Pay attention, Alison, I told myself firmly and I reached the High Street without further incident.

The Hall was quiet, with no sign of the caretaker who was usually on duty. Yet the side door was unlocked. Probably he'd opened up for the theatre company, then nipped off to collect breakfast from the Electric Bakery.

My footsteps echoed in the quiet as I hurried along the corridor to the stairs leading to the theatre.

'Rhoda,' I called loudly, but there was no reply. I stopped and took a deep breath. Simon was right as usual. What was I doing here? And what did I know about Rhoda? Could I trust her?

I strode across to the theatre but then, my bravado deserting me, I opened the door cautiously and peeped around before going in.

Rhoda was sitting on the apron stage. One of the curtain supports appeared to have come loose and the curtain was lying in a tangle beside her.

As I approached her, a look of alarm crossed her face, then she relaxed. 'Oh, thank goodness you came, Alison.'

I looked at the curtain. The support was lying twisted and broken beside Rhoda.

'Have you told anyone about this? Contacted Wilson?'

She shook her head. 'I was waiting for you. I wanted you to see what had happened.'

It did appear at first glance that the curtain support had come down suddenly, but that could have been no more than a mishap.

As though she read my thoughts, Rhoda said, 'This was no accident.' She gestured to the curtain support. 'If you look closely you can see a couple of the pivotal screws affixing it to the wall have been taken out.'

She stood up, grabbing onto a chair beside her for support. I moved forward to catch her but she waved me away. 'I'm fine, I'm fine,' she said. 'A bit shaken, that's all.'

'You have to tell Wilson,' I said. 'Apart from any other concerns you can't leave the curtain like that. And,' I added in a firm voice, 'you must let the police know.'

'What good would that do? With no proof, they would think it was an accident.'

'Nonsense. With two deaths already in the company, I'm sure they would take it seriously. You must go to Wilson first, then to the police if he won't take action.'

The sceptical look on her face was beginning to annoy me. 'Rhoda, you must…' I began again but she interrupted me.

'You know I went off the island?'

I nodded, waiting to hear what she'd say next.

A sigh. 'I overheard Valeria and Phil having an argument. It was clear they were up to something. I know someone who worked with Valeria and went to see her, to find out if there was a story of some kind.'

'And did you?'

'Only that Valeria had worked in several different companies, but she was a general dogsbody, nothing to do with the finances.'

'But Wilson said she was an expert in finance, that was why he employed her.'

Rhoda shrugged. 'Who do you believe?'

I lifted her phone from the floor. 'Phone Wilson now, Rhoda.'

This time she complied and as I moved away to give her a bit of privacy I couldn't but help overhear the beginning of the call. I didn't think it was good that she was making light of it. This wasn't the way to find out the truth.

I sat down in the front row of the auditorium. Wilson would have to continue without my help. I could take a step back. I'd no inclination to be further involved in this web of deceit and lies. But as I sat there, waiting for Rhoda to finish her call an image sprang to mind of Phil adjusting the curtains. What was it he'd said? Something about "…everyone having to muck in and help." At the time I'd thought nothing of it, but now? Why would Phil have a responsibility for the curtains? A shiver ran through me. If Rhoda told Phil she'd heard him arguing with Valeria she might also be in danger.

FIFTY-TWO

When I got back to the cottage, leaving Rhoda waiting for Wilson, Simon was out. He'd left a note on the kitchen table with a vague "back soon" message and I made a sandwich while I pondered what to do next.

Part of me was intrigued by Rhoda's story. I could only hope Rhoda would be honest with Wilson, tell him of her suspicions. If they didn't act soon, her life was in danger. If Phil was responsible it could only mean one thing. He was the killer.

But Rhoda was right. Proof was needed. In spite of all my promises to step back, I persuaded myself a little more investigation would help find the proof Rhoda needed.

The answer had to lie with Valeria's accounts. If I approached Wilson, perhaps I could have a look at them. But I'd have to be careful. Think of a good reason.

After deliberating several options, I came up with the idea of double checking what might be available for the rest of the tour and suggestions about how Wilson might make up any shortfall. I'd no notion of how he might manage it, but that was a worry for later.

Buoyed up by the feeling I might be close to helping solve the mystery, I decided to approach Wilson and gulping down the last of my tea, grabbed my coat and my bag before going back to the car. Wilson would have made his way to the Hall as soon as Rhoda contacted him.

I was in luck. As I hurried into the theatre, I could hear the murmur of voices. Wilson was standing at the front of the stage while a couple of men were busy sorting the fallen curtain.

'Ah, Alison.' Wilson turned to me, frowning. 'Rhoda said she'd told you the story about the curtain. What do you think? Was it deliberate?'

Now that asked a direct question, I was lost for words. 'It… it... would appear so…' Then in a flash of inspiration, 'What do the Hall staff think?'

Wilson hesitated. 'They say it could have been an accident.' He made a face. 'It was such a close thing. If I hadn't asked Rhoda to bring the copy of the master script I left behind last night she wouldn't have been here. How would I have felt if the curtain had fallen on her, killed her?'

There was no point in dithering. I had to tell Wilson about Phil, about having seen him working with the curtain.

His eyes widened. 'So you think it's Phil who's behind all of this? I can hardly believe it. But it would explain so much. He and Valeria were as thick as thieves – and you know what they say when thieves fall out.'

'You think Valeria was stealing money from the company and giving it to Phil?'

Wilson's laugh was harsh. 'What other explanation could there be? We all know about Phil's gambling habit.'

Of course. Wilson was right. 'And Valeria refused to continue stealing money on his behalf. Cormac must have found out about it – so he had to go as well.' Suddenly I felt very afraid. 'Where is Phil? This means Rhoda is still in danger. What do we do now?'

'Leave it to me,' Wilson said. 'She left a few minutes ago saying she was going for a walk to clear her head. Up towards the Tramway. Phil was still at the hotel when I left. If I'm quick I'll catch up with Rhoda.'

'And make sure she goes to the police.' I felt a surge of relief. 'Thank goodness.'

'What?' Wilson looked preoccupied. 'Oh, yes, of course. I'll make sure she goes to the police.'

He turned away. 'I'll have to go now.'

'Do you want me to contact the police? Alert them?'

'No, no, better that Rhoda tells them. She knows what's been going on.'

At last everything would be resolved. As long as Phil didn't suspect that Wilson was on to him, the police could arrest him at the hotel.

'Are you sure you don't want me to come with you?' I said.

Wilson shook his head. 'Positive. Better that Rhoda doesn't feel she's being harassed. You know what actors can be like – very volatile.'

Rhoda didn't seem to be the volatile type to me, but Wilson knew her better.

'Keep me informed, won't you?'

'Of course, Alison. Once the police have been told I'll be in touch.'

He hurried out of the theatre, leaving me hoping he'd be in time to avoid another death.

FIFTY-THREE

Now I was at a loss. It was early afternoon and Simon might not return before evening. He'd been vague about where he was going and why, but I'd find out soon enough.

The day was crisp and clear, the sky that bright blue you only have in winter. Rhoda's idea of going for a walk strongly appealed to me. It was ages since I'd walked the Tramway route from Port Bannatyne to the tearoom at Ettrick Bay.

As I drove along, I thought of all that had happened since we'd bought the cottage on Bute. Hopefully once this terrible event was over, we could settle down to a more peaceful existence.

The easiest place to park to start the Tramway walk was beside the old church of St Colmac at Cnoc-An - Raer and I slipped onto the verge at the widest part of the road, leaving plenty of room for any tractor that might come lumbering along from one of the surrounding farms.

As I locked the car I suddenly thought it might be a mistake to arrive so quickly. I hadn't allowed much time for Wilson to come along and collect Rhoda. I looked around. There were several cars parked outside the little group of houses to the right of the church, but I'd no idea what kind of car Wilson drove – or Rhoda for that matter. It might be better to delay for a while, go into the churchyard and have a look, wander among the graves, before beginning my walk.

The churchyard was quiet. There were two parts – the lower graveyard was the modern one, well-tended. This older graveyard was neat but many of the headstones had fallen over, or were hard to read, and there was an air of unintentional neglect. So many of the names were familiar – generations of the same family.

Behind me, the ancient church of St Colmac stood roofless, open to the sky. At what had been the main entrance there was wire netting covering what would have been the front door and a notice said in large red letters 'KEEP OUT Dangerous building'.

Through the archway at the bottom of the bell tower, where once there had been church pews there was now thick vegetation, the area long enough disused for rogue sapling trees to have grown to full height.

I peeped in, but nothing remained to show this had once been a vibrant parish church, serving the parishioners of North Bute.

A glance at my watch confirmed I'd been here almost twenty minutes – time surely to be able to move across to the Tramway and begin my walk.

About to turn away, I heard a sound. I stopped. Then as I listened, it seemed like an animal in pain – a soft moaning noise. I stood still, trying to judge where the sound was coming from. I waited in the silence. Was it my imagination? No, there it was again, slightly louder this time.

I shivered. What could I do? It might be a fox, or perhaps a sheep that had strayed in from one of the neighbouring farms. I crept close to the church entrance. Yes, whatever it was, it was somewhere inside. My instinct was to phone the local vet, but first I had to find out what was making the noise.

I moved closer to the entrance, peering through the wire netting. All I could see was the dense undergrowth but as my eyes adjusted to the gloom, suddenly I caught sight of a movement at the far wall, as if of a shadow passing.

Then I heard the sound again and this time the moaning grew louder. If it was an injured animal there was no way I could leave it to suffer. Wilson would have caught up with Rhoda by now. I hadn't noticed any cars going past so they might still be walking back from the Tramway. Perhaps I could catch up with them, ask for help.

Don't be such a coward, Alison, I reproached myself. The graveyard might be spooky, but there was nothing here to harm me.

Taking a deep breath, I pulled aside the net fencing which yielded surprisingly easily to my touch and began to pick my way carefully through the tangle of brambles and waist-high bracken, hoping nothing would jump out at me.

Yes, there was something lying on the grass up against the back wall. My heart began to thud as I came closer. There was a familiar look about whatever was lying there. I recognised the splash of colour. To my horror I realised this was no animal. It was Rhoda.

Pushing aside the thick undergrowth, I came up beside her. She was still breathing, but she was lying at an awkward angle and there was no hope of moving her. A quick look around reassured me there was no sign of her attacker, and it was possible she'd been there for some time.

I took out my phone to dial an ambulance, hoping there would be a signal in this part of the island, and I was in luck. While waiting for help to arrive, I tried to think what to do next. On a cold day like this hypothermia might well have set in and though Rhoda was wearing a coat, I took off my own coat to give her extra warmth.

I seemed to remember an instruction from a First Aid course I'd enrolled on several years ago that you should keep talking to the injured person and I began to speak softly to her, saying the first thing that came into my head.

She didn't reply, but she groaned softly again and moved slightly as I heard the sound of the ambulance arriving.

I stood up and pushed my way through the brushwood, waving to attract their attention.

I remembered the fleeting glimpse I'd had of someone. It could only have been Phil. But what had happened to Wilson?

I shook my head when the ambulance driver said, carefully lifting Rhoda on to the stretcher, 'Are you coming with us to the hospital?'

'I'll come over later. There's something I have to do.'

The ambulance driver smiled saying, 'Don't worry, she'll be fine with us.'

As the ambulance pulled away into the darkening afternoon I stood trying to decide what to do next. Phone the police and say I thought Wilson might also have been attacked?

It was possible Wilson had abandoned his plan to catch up with Rhoda, thinking it better to stay at the Hall. But he must have mentioned Rhoda to Phil, else how would Phil know where she was? I couldn't help but feel whatever the truth, my guess was wrong.

FIFTY-FOUR

In the end I decided I was panicking about nothing. If Wilson had been anywhere nearby I'd have found him. But it wouldn't hurt to have a cursory look before I went over to the hospital to see Rhoda. I shrugged on my coat again, suddenly aware of how cold it was.

I ran through the graveyard and crossed the road to the beginning of the Tramway walk, only pausing to make sure the gate at the entrance was securely fastened. The rough gravel path was deserted and although I walked almost half a mile along the track I didn't encounter anyone. There was certainly no sign of Wilson.

Abandoning my search as dusk turned to night, I hurried back to my car to drive to the cottage hospital in the High Street. I'd no idea the extent of Rhoda's injuries: if they were serious she'd be helicoptered off the island to the Queen Elizabeth hospital in Glasgow. I hoped I'd be in time to see her before that happened, though she might not be able to tell me anything.

As it turned out, her leg wasn't broken as I'd thought and, after a lot of persuading, I was allowed in to see her. 'But only for a minute,' I was warned by the stern nurse in charge. She might not have agreed, but as I'd been the person to find her, that carried some weight.

Rhoda looked fragile, lying in the hospital bed, hooked up to a drip and an array of instruments. She seemed to be slipping in and out of consciousness, but I'd have to try to find out about Wilson and confirm Phil had been her attacker before going to the police.

I leaned over the bed. 'Rhoda, Rhoda, can you hear me? Tell me what happened?' Then realising this wasn't going to be possible, I said, 'Just answer yes or no to the questions,' all the time aware the nurse might come in at any moment and tell me to leave.

I began with the crucial question. 'It was Phil who attacked you, wasn't it?'

She whispered a reply and I leaned closer, thinking I must be mistaken, so I repeated the question. 'Phil tried to kill you?' Now I realised the shadow I'd seen was Phil and thankfully I'd disturbed him in time.

'No,' Rhoda murmured. 'Not Phil.'

Then she said again, a little louder this time, 'Not Phil. Wilson.'

She must be mistaken. About to question her again, I was interrupted by the appearance of the nurse. 'You'll have to go now. You can phone in, and we'll let you know when she's fit for a longer visit.'

'But the police will want to question her.'

'Yes, indeed,' the nurse replied. 'But not yet.'

I came out of the hospital and stood looking over at the Rothesay Leisure Centre opposite where a gaggle of teenagers were larking about before disappearing inside.

It was hard to believe what Rhoda had said. She must be confused, mistaken about her attacker.

There was only one way to find out. I had to find Wilson and ask if he'd abandoned his plan to catch up with Rhoda. I could think of plenty of reasons why

Phil might be the culprit. But Wilson? It was impossible. I couldn't think of a motive.

FIFTY-FIVE

A stop at the cottage before going back to the Hall took only a few minutes. Simon had returned and he was sitting in the kitchen drinking a large mug of tea and looking extremely pleased with himself.

'Guess what?' he beamed.

With my mind still on what had happened to Rhoda I couldn't think what he meant unless he'd heard the news. But why would he be smiling?

'I don't think it's funny,' I said.

'No, but it's so exciting.'

'I think we're talking at cross purposes,' I said, realisation dawning.

'I'm talking about the statue – I may have a real lead at last.'

'Oh, of course.' In all the excitement of finding Rhoda, I'd forgotten about the statue. 'Can we talk about it later? I have to go over to the Hall urgently.' There was no time to go into a long explanation about Rhoda.

Simon gave a heavy sigh. 'I thought you'd finished with all that.'

'I can't explain,' I said. 'I'll tell you everything when I get back.' Then I said, 'What was it you wanted to say to me?'

'You'll never guess. Benita called to ask if we could meet. She says she'd heard about our statue. She has one that's been in the family for a long time.'

‘Good gracious. That’s a coincidence.’

‘Yes,’ he went on. ‘She’s going to call me back and arrange to meet at St Mary’s to compare hers and ours and find out if they fit into the niches on the Knight’s tomb.’

‘Drat. I have to go back to the Hall,’ I said.

‘Oh, don’t worry. She didn’t say when she’d call.’

Right now I had to check what Rhoda had told me and as I drove to the Hall, I tried to think of a way of tackling Wilson. I still found it hard to believe that he could be responsible for what had happened to Rhoda, but she had seemed so certain.

But when I arrived I realised I’d no clear idea what to do next. Best to find Wilson and hope he’d have an explanation.

However I did take the precaution of speaking to the caretaker as I went in.

‘I’ve come to see a member of The Mickle,’ I said. ‘I don’t want to say why, but if I’m not back in twenty minutes could you come and find me.’

I will say this, he didn’t look surprised by this odd request, merely nodded, saying, ‘Aye, twenty minutes,’ and went back to reading his paper. Perhaps he was used to strange demands from the people who used this building. I could only hope he would remember.

I took the stairs two at a time, to end up standing breathless outside the entrance to the theatre. I could hear voices. Good. I wouldn’t be alone when I tackled Wilson. If Rhoda was correct and Wilson was responsible, he couldn’t harm me with other people there.

I pushed open the door. Phil, Lucian and Neville were on stage and turned to look as I came striding in.

‘I’m looking for Wilson,’ I said.

'Aren't we all,' Phil answered. 'No one has seen him today.'

'He might be back at the hotel.'

'We've checked. His stuff has gone.' Neville stood clenching and unclenching his hands.

Lucian stepped forward. 'Why are you looking for him, Alison? Does he owe you money as well?'

'Sorry?' I was beginning to lose the thread of this conversation. 'I need…'

But I didn't have the chance to finish as Lucian said, 'You must be the only person he doesn't owe money to.'

'You haven't been paid this week?' Was that what they were angry about?

'This week or any week.' Neville gritted his teeth. 'He promised we'd be paid today.'

'But how did you live if you had no money?'

Lucian laughed. 'Wilson told us he'd take care of all the expenses and then we'd have our payment with expenses deducted at the end of the month.'

This seemed an odd way of running the company. 'You were happy with that?'

'No, we bloody well weren't, but he persuaded us this would be the best way to help with the cashflow,' Neville said.

'And?' There must be more to this story.

'And he didn't pay any of the bills – not to The Four Winds, nor to any of the other traders. The Hall is seriously out of pocket as are the restaurants we used. He set up accounts everywhere and told them all the same story. There had been a delay in the grant coming through.'

'But surely that was true?'

Neville gave a hollow laugh. 'That was just it. He applied for a business grant, but he was refused. He thought if he could use the money Sir Donald had donated for the tour expenses he could be successful looking for grant money elsewhere. But he didn't manage to get a penny.'

'Was Valeria in on his plan?'

Phil said, 'He persuaded her to withdraw money from the expenses account on the promise of repaying it. Then she discovered he'd be unable to do that. She came to me and I told her to go to the police.'

'Oh. That's what you and she were arguing about.'

Phil grimaced. 'I wanted to give him the benefit of the doubt. More fool me. He was desperate to keep his dream of owning the company alive.'

'And Valeria's death…' I left the question hanging.

Phil shrugged. 'Who knows if it was an accident or if Wilson engineered it. A push on those steep stairs?'

'And even worse.' I gave them a brief account of what had happened to Rhoda. 'I thought it was you, Phil, that you'd run up so many gambling debts and…' I stopped, miserable that I had got it all so wrong.

Phil replied in a flat voice, 'I may be a gambler, Alison, but I'm not a thief…nor a killer.'

We stood in silence, staring at one another till Neville said, 'What do we do now?'

'Go to the police,' I said. 'The only possible answer is that Wilson has left on the ferry. They should be able to alert the police on the mainland to pick him up.'

'Then there's not a moment to lose.' Lucian pulled is phone from his pocket, then stopped, frowning. 'What's the number for the Rothesay Police?'

FIFTY-SIX

The police responded quickly. Or rather, quickly once they had made sense of our story. Everyone wanted to chip in with information and it was only when the Sergeant in charge insisted one person relate events that the police were able to piece the narrative together.

There would be further questions, more meetings, but now it was up to the police to catch Wilson and for the moment all I could think about was a hot bath and a glass of wine. And telling Simon that Wilson wasn't the person he thought.

'I can't believe that Wilson would be a killer.' Simon kept shaking his head as I gave him a brief account of what had happened. 'He seemed so…so…'

'Feeble?' I ventured.

'But why would he do that?'

'It seems he appropriated the tour money from Sir Donald.'

Simon looked more incredulous. 'How could he do that?'

'He persuaded Valeria the money for the expenses should be used until the grant came through. He expected the ticket sales would cover his theft – he'd put in money as they went along in the hope it would work out. You remember how he told us it was his dream of a lifetime to set up his own theatre company.'

'And Valeria agreed to this?'

'Initially, yes. Possibly he pressured her. Do you remember the story about how she left the Surrey Metropole under a cloud? I don't know what happened, but Wilson must have known and seen it as a way to threaten her with exposure if she didn't do as he asked. But then she realised it wasn't going to work. The Bute stay cost more than they'd bargained for and the advance sales for Arran weren't as good as expected. He could only stall for so long and Valeria warned him she was going to the police.'

'And Cormac found out? '

'Yes. He tried to blackmail Wilson. But he'd confided in Rhoda, which put her in danger.'

Simon appeared dazed by this story, saying over and over, 'I find it hard to accept, Alison.'

'So do I,' I said. 'It's all much worse than we thought. But at least the police are now in pursuit of Wilson. They think he won't get far. His description's been circulated on the mainland. The police might catch him as he gets off the ferry.'

Simon opened his mouth to speak, then closed it again, frowning.

'I feel sorry for the rest of the cast,' I said. 'Goodness knows what they'll do now. Cancel everything, I guess.'

'I can't see there's any other possibility,' Simon said. 'They must all be…' He broke off as his phone rang.

He glanced at the screen, then looked away. 'I'd better take this,' he said, getting to his feet and moving out into the hallway.

'Who is it?' I said, but he didn't reply before closing the door behind him.

That was unusual. What could be happening that he didn't want me to know about? Then I thought – perhaps he's organising my Christmas present. That idea didn't last long. It was far too early for Simon to be Christmas shopping.

I couldn't contain my curiosity. I moved over to the door and opened it a fraction. I could hear the excitement in his voice. 'Are you sure, Benita?' Then a pause while Benita replied before he said, 'At St Mary's Chapel?' Another pause. 'Oh, of course, that's the original location. Yes, four o'clock tomorrow is fine.'

I pulled back as he signed off and I sat down on the nearest chair pretending to be engrossed in a magazine.

'Anything interesting? 'I said in what I hoped was a casual tone of voice.

'Yes, that was Benita to make the arrangement to meet.'

'And if Benita also has a statue, there may be others.'

'Will you come along with me.'

A moment's hesitation. 'I'd love to, but Rhoda is coming out of hospital, and I said I'd collect her.'

'That's fine. If Benita does have a statue there will be lots happening as a result. Plenty of time.'

We chatted about The Mickle, about the likelihood of being able to continue, but I could tell his mind was elsewhere.

But the more I thought about it, the stranger this arrangement Benita had suggested seemed. By four o' clock darkness would be falling. I considered saying this, then decided a better plan would be to follow him, find out what was going on. I could phone the hospital and say I'd collect Rhoda later. St Mary's was no more than a few minutes from the hospital.

Simon might be trusting. I wasn't.

FIFTY-SEVEN

Following Simon the next day wasn't as easy as I imagined. For a start, the weather was bright and sunny again for most of the day where I'd hoped for a smirr of rain to give me some cover. But by four o'clock darkness would be beginning to fall.

Late in the afternoon I began to rifle through my wardrobe for something to wear. The weather was cold, so I could justify a coat with a hood. Finally I found a long brown coat lurking at the back of the wardrobe. I couldn't recall when I'd last worn it and had some vague notion I'd saved it for gardening duties. Not that gardening was a possibility with the ground frozen and impossible to dig.

About to pull it out and give it a closer examination, I was startled by Simon coming into the room. Hastily I pushed the coat to the back of the wardrobe as he said, 'Having a clear out, Alison,' in a cheerful tone of voice. Should I tell him I'd be happier if I changed my plans and went along with him? No, he'd only say I was making a fuss and there was no need.

'Yes,' I said, 'thought it was time to make some space in the wardrobe.'

He made no further comment but lifted his coat from the peg on the back of the door. 'I'm off. This is the warmest coat I have – make sure you're well wrapped up if you go out.'

I waited, but he said no more and as he went

downstairs and I heard the front door slam I went over to the window to watch him. He set off smartly down the path carrying a small holdall.

I'd have to be quick. I pulled the old brown coat from the wardrobe, dislodging several other items in the process, but I didn't stop to pick them up. I didn't have to follow Simon quickly. Waiting a few minutes after he'd left should put sufficient distance between us.

As I drove slowly up the High Street I kept a lookout for his car, until the driver behind me tooted at my lack of speed. Ah, there it was, in the car park at the Leisure Centre. He must have parked here and walked the rest of the way.

I slid into a space at the back of the building though I'd be well away by the time Simon returned. Yes, there he was a little ahead of me. He must be going to the St Mary's. I kept well back, my hood up, trying to think of a reason for my being here should I by some mischance bump into Simon or Benita, but nothing came to mind and in the end I had to hope this wouldn't happen.

All that remained of the original church was the Chancel and I tiptoed through the more modern part of the graveyard, though I did notice one gravestone dating back to 1705 as I came up to the semi-circular path of oblong stones leading to the doorway of the building. So many gravestones recorded children who had died young, and I shivered, though whether from cold or from the spookiness of the site, I didn't know. It was certainly eerie here as darkness began to fall and the sun slipped down behind the horizon.

How stupid not to bring a torch. Too late now. I'd have to hope whatever the outcome of this meeting it would be over soon.

The Chancel was as Simon had described it. The bottom half retained the original stonework with a modern timber roof above. The original stained glass in the arched windows had at some time in the past been replaced by plain glass.

I went around to the far side of the building and, standing at the edge of the window, peeped in. At first it was difficult to make anything out in the gloom then I could see the tomb of the Knight on the far side, the niches underneath empty, exactly as we'd been told. It was becoming more and more difficult to see anything inside as the light faded, but suddenly I heard voices and ducked down. I couldn't make out what was being said, but I was certain one of the voices was Simon's.

What to do now? This had been a waste of time. It was perfectly innocent. Better to leave before they came out, collect Rhoda from the hospital and hear the story from Simon later.

As I was about to walk away, the voices were raised as though they were arguing, and I stopped. Why would there be a dispute? I doubled back as quietly as I could, this time looking in at the window, making no attempt to hide.

The full moon had risen and peeped out from behind a cloud, bright enough for me to see Simon standing in the far corner.

There was a woman with him. It was Benita. And she was holding a gun.

FIFTY-EIGHT

Frozen to the spot, I could only watch helplessly as Benita waved the gun around in a threatening manner. I thought briefly about phoning for help, calling the police station, but that might take too long. Time was of the essence. I'd no idea how serious Benita was, but she looked menacing.

Simon was backed up against the wall, clutching something to his chest, the object he had left the house with. With a start I realised what it must be – the statue from the tomb of the Knight.

All these thoughts flashed through my head in a millisecond. More important was to think of a way to help Simon.

As I watched, he put the statue on the ground, apparently at Benita's instruction. Could I dash in while she lifted it, surprise her? It would be a dangerous manoeuvre. If she was startled she might fire the gun.

Taking a deep breath, I decided I had to risk going in. Perhaps I could reason with her. Even if she wanted the statue, didn't want Simon left alive to tell what she was up to, surely she wouldn't kill both of us? Though I didn't relish the idea that I might be the one to be killed, much as I loved my husband.

Whatever the outcome, I had to take action. I crept away from the window and keeping down below the level of the lintels came to the doorway giving entry to the building. I could hear them still arguing. Good. If they were still talking that meant Benita hadn't done anything stupid.

But as I reached the door, I heard a deafening bang.

Oh, no. Was I too late?

I lifted the door latch, then heard loud shouts. Probably she was only trying to frighten Simon. Yes, that was it.

Or what if the gun had gone off by accident. That could only mean Benita was unstable and even more dangerous than I'd thought.

In the end, my determination to do what I could to save Simon overcame any fear I might have of Benita and her madness, and I tugged hard at the door. But to my horror, it stayed firmly shut.

I heard Benita yell out, 'Who's there?' and I stayed stock-still. I heard footsteps as she came over to lift the latch and peer out of the window but crouched down as I now was, I was sure she couldn't see me in the darkness.

Now she had left the window open I could hear what they were saying.

'This is madness, Benita. How can this statue be of such interest to you?'

'Because it is mine, belongs to my family. I have a right to it.'

Simon sounded amazingly calm as he replied, 'No, Benita, while all the statues in the niches disappeared, any that are found belong to the nation. Not to one individual.'

'You don't understand. It's my family's inheritance. I found out I'm related to the Arris family…'

Ah, now I understood. Simon's ploy was to keep her talking and suddenly I had an idea. I crept back to the other window, now knowing Benita had her back to me from this angle. If I could make Simon aware I was here, he could distract her long enough for me to creep in the back entrance. If it was unlocked.

I searched around for something to hit her with. Fragments of broken tombstones lay scattered around, but I didn't think any of these would be suitable, even had I been able to lift one. Then I spied a branch from the ancient tree next to the wall of the old church and pausing only to grab it I went back to stand on tiptoe and peer in. I hoped Simon would spot me, realise what I was up to and keep Benita preoccupied.

Fortunately my ruse worked, and he began to speak louder and louder, urging her not to continue with her absurd scheme.

'It's not possible for you to get away with this, Benita. This statue doesn't belong to you.'

'Of course it does,' she screamed, waving the gun.

I pushed at the back door. If this didn't work, I was out of ideas. But it did and as I rushed in, brandishing the large stick, Benita whirled around. 'You,' she shouted, 'what are you doing here. You're nothing but an interfering busybody.'

I didn't have the opportunity to hit her, though I would dearly have liked to, because now that she was distracted, Simon was able to lunge forward and grab her. The gun clattered to the ground, and I swiftly kicked it out of reach.

Benita struggled but she was no match for Simon, and she slumped to the ground, sobbing loudly.

'I turned up in the nick of time,' I said, holding the stick tightly to control my trembling.

'She wouldn't have shot me,' Simon said, but I wasn't so sure.

In the circumstances there was no way I was about to disagree.

EPILOGUE

'I didn't think I'd ever see the day when you had to rescue me,' Simon said. 'Though,' he added, 'as it was a prop gun, there was no real danger.'

'Yes,' I protested, 'but we didn't know that at the time.'

'There was no other statue. That was Benita's attempt to claim the one found in the panelling.'

It was no longer our concern. The statue was now at the university where it would be the subject of a long investigation, though I hoped it would eventually return to the Bute Museum.

'Wilson wasn't smart enough in the end. But then it was his bad luck the ferry he hoped to catch was cancelled. That gave the police time to act. Some excitement for the passengers on the Wemyss Bay to Glasgow train.'

We were sitting in the cottage in front of a log fire, cosy and at peace with the world, sipping a glass of wine.

Gus's uncle had been as good as his word: the living room and the hall were now decorated and snug. A Christmas tree stood in the corner of the room, its lights twinkling. The tree wasn't as big as I'd have liked, but then again it was a small room.

I felt smug about what had happened, though the result was as much down to the element of surprise as any action on my part.

‘I can scarcely believe what was going on at The Mickle,’ I said. ‘The islanders will be glad to have the Bute Theatre Company back next year.’

‘Mmm. Though it’s amazing that Joel managed to pull everything and everyone together to take a version of Sleeping Beauty to the other islands.’

‘I wouldn’t have believed it possible – one of those things in life that surprises you. Though it’s a curtailed show with a much smaller cast.’

We sat and watched the flickering flames, each of us lost in our own thoughts till at last Simon said, ‘This is fine as a summer home, but perhaps we should think about looking for a more permanent place in the new year?’

‘Sounds like a good idea,’ I said.

HISTORICAL NOTE

The medieval chapel of St Mary stands next to the United Church of Bute (the High Kirk) built in 1795. All that remains of the original church is the Chancel.

The interior of St Mary's is dominated by two tombs, one in the north wall, (the lady's tomb) the other in the south (the Knight's tomb).

The Knight's tomb was built into the existing wall of the Chancel about the end of the 1300s.

The knight is shown in full plate armour with his head resting on a helmet. The details of the coats of arms are now eroded, and a number of armed statuettes that filled the niches between the panels at the base of the tomb have disappeared.

While the overall historical details are correct, for purposes of the plot there have been a number of embellishments. There is no Arris family and no record of when the statues in the niches disappeared, though records suggest they had disappeared by 1890.

ACKNOWLEDGEMENTS

Thanks to everyone who helped with this novel: Joan Fleming, Bill Daly and Joan Weeple for comments, proof reading and support.

And special thanks to Paul Duffy for technical help and general advice.

Printed in Great Britain
by Amazon

85151773R00173